Cloud Nine

When Pigs Fly

Book Nine in the Val Fremden Midlife Mystery Series

Margaret Lashley

Copyright 2018 Margaret Lashley

What Readers are Saying about Cloud Nine & The Val Fremden Midlife Mysteries

"When I read the first book in this series I loved it. I never expected the rest of the series was going to introduce me to the wackiest, weirdest, most wonderful cast of characters I've ever come across."

"A hilarious take on life, love and.....pigs. A story line fit to tickle your funny bone."

"This series is a breath of fresh air. Hilarious, exceedingly well crafted, with amazingly quirky, lovable characters."

"I've loved each book in this wild ride! I hate to see it end."

"Hooked like a fish. OMG Margaret Lashley is the best! Val could be Stephanie Plum's double!! Phenomenal writing."

"Margaret Lashley is my favorite cozy book writer. She always gives the reader their money's worth."

"Plan your day around just enjoying every minute. Her characters are so vivid."

"I find the characters all extremely unique and entertaining. The author is very humorous and has a great imagination for storyline."

"If you want to kick back and laugh and maybe come away with a simple life lesson I highly recommend you take the journey with Val and her Pals."

More Val Fremden Midlife Mysteries

by Margaret Lashley
Absolute Zero
Glad One
Two Crazy
Three Dumb
What Four
Five Oh
Six Tricks
Seven Daze
Figure Eight
Cloud Nine

"WHY IS IT WHENEVER Lady Luck chooses to shine on me, she uses a blowtorch?" Val Fremden

Chapter One

The scrap of paper in my hand was sticky to the touch. No bigger than the kind of note tucked inside a fortune cookie, it could've meant nothing at all. Yet, as I studied it, I couldn't help but think that the fate of a good friend might depend on the single, enigmatic word written upon it.

PObbLE

What in the world could that *mean?*

An exasperated breath forced its way from my lungs. I read the word again.

PObbLE

This has *to be a clue. Otherwise, I have pretty much* nothing *to go on.*

Nearly three weeks had passed since Goober'd rescued me from a mob of enraged campers during a writer's retreat that had gone horribly wrong.

No one had heard from him since.

I'd been the last one to see him alive. According to the law, that may've made me a suspect. But, like it or not, I answered to an even higher authority—the *Southern Guilt Guidebook*. According to *it*, I was definitely responsible.

Somehow. Someway.

I tapped a finger on my desk in the hope that knocking on fake wood laminate would change my luck, or loosen some forgotten detail lodged in the recesses of my addled brain.

I've got to be missing something.

Eighteen days ago, I'd waved goodbye to my tall, lanky friend in the parking lot of the Polk County Police Station in Lake Wales, Florida, about eighty miles east of St. Pete Beach. As a parting gesture, Goober'd waved back, and, in his uniquely goofy way, waggled his bushy eyebrows at me like a billiard ball infested with brown caterpillars.

Geez. It seems like three years have gone by since then.

As in days past, I wracked my brain again, trying to recall anything suspicious about our last moments together. But try as I might, as far as I could tell, Goober'd given no indication anything weird had been going on. But then again, he'd always been such an odd duck. There was no way for me to be absolutely sure....

The last thing Goober'd said to me before he'd taken off had actually been a question. He'd asked me if I'd known my way home. He'd offered to let me follow him. In hindsight, I wished I'd taken him up on the offer.

But I didn't. Mainly because my access out of the parking lot had been blocked by an old hillbilly woman on a "shopper chopper."

Those were the words Charlene had used to describe the strange, customized bike she'd ridden around on. It was a tricycle, actually. Soldered onto the frame where the front wheel used to be was a full-sized grocery-shopping cart. During my stay at that RV park in Lake Wales, I'd seen Charlene use the handy front basket for toting everything from groceries to grannies.

I could still recall the earnestness on Charlene's face when she'd pulled that shopper chopper up behind my car and blocked me from backing up. The toilet-tube curlers pinned in her hair had jiggled around her jawline as she'd proffered her heartfelt apology for chasing me around the RV park with a pitchfork.

In her defense, she *had* thought I'd killed her sister's 94-year-old boyfriend, Woggles with a Tupperware container full of Laverne's snickerdoodles. It was a fair assumption, given Laverne's history with baked goods.

At any rate, Charlene's apology had delayed my leaving, and had put me about ten minutes behind Goober. In theory, I should've caught up with him before he reached the on-ramp for I-4. But I never saw him again. He'd simply vanished somewhere along State Road 60.

The thing was, he should've been easy to spot.

Goober'd been behind the wheel of a 1966 Minnie Winnie. The old RV used to belong to Glad, my biological mom. It was a hard target to miss. Still, compared to today's huge RVs, the thing wasn't much bigger than a tin can. I guess that made the fact that Goober'd left his strange clue inside another tin can kind of fitting.

I looked at it again.

PObbLE

I set the slip of paper on my desk and leaned back in my chair. My eyes shifted up toward the dreamcatcher hanging in the window of my home office. It'd been a parting gift from Goober.

Looking at the hideous thing *now*, I wondered if maybe it'd been more of a parting *shot*.

The crude, makeshift contraption was nothing more than a cheap, wire clothes hanger that'd been hand-bent into a warped circle. A pair of hot-pink thong panties stretched across the width of the circle like a frilly Mercedes logo. If *that* weren't low-rent enough, the folk artist/deviant who'd concocted it had used fishing line to tie three aluminum cans to the bottom half. Two Pabst Blue Ribbon cans and a Skoal tobacco tin dangled from the dreamcatcher like garbage snagged in a spider's web.

Definitely not the classiest gift I've ever gotten.

If the dreamcatcher had come from anyone else, I'd have thrown it in the trash. But it was from Goober. And now, it was all I had left of him.

Five days ago, when I'd first attempted to hang it in my office window, it had fallen out of my hands and crashed onto the terrazzo floor. The impact had dented the beer cans, and caused the Skoal tin to burst open. That's how I'd found the puzzling message within. It'd been duct-taped to the inside of the tobacco lid.

I took one last look at the sticky scrap of paper.

PObbLE

I sighed and placed it back inside my desk drawer.

Goober had called the hideous window decoration a "redneck dreamcatcher."

Now, all I had to do was catch a redneck with it.

Chapter Two

My world had changed significantly since I'd found that cryptic note inside the Skoal tin.

For one, Tom, my boyfriend, had instigated a "healthy eating plan" that seemed to be based mainly on broccoli and its nasty cruciferous cousins. As a result, I'd been forced to stuff my face with tortilla chips and ice cream while he was away at work. As a result of *that*, I'd gained three pounds. As a result of *that*, I'd pummeled two figurines to smithereens with my "Hammer of Justice."

The other major change going on was more furry than frustrating. My life as I'd known it had been taken over by one small, fuzzy, four-legged canine named Sir Albert Snoggles, III.

Tom had named the little Pomeranian mix after a favorite dog from his childhood. I hadn't been too keen on the moniker myself. Not only was the name gross, it was actually longer than the poor little dog it was meant for!

Still, I'd had no choice in the matter. I'd lost a wager with Tom that had cost me a great deal. Though, in hindsight, most of that was just hard-headed pride.

Tom had bet me I couldn't go a month without using my Hammer of Justice to pulverize tacky figurines. If I'd managed to control my addiction, Tom had pledged to get rid of his horrid, plaid Barcalounger. And when I said horrid, I meant horrid with a capital "H." Never in the history of upholstery had a chair so ugly been manufactured and allowed to live. The eyesore was so disgusting that it'd not only destroyed my living room décor—I'd have bet money that in another week it would've caused my eyes to begin to bleed.

Well, long story short, as I said before, I'd lost the bet. But then I found out I'd been hoodwinked by Tom and our friends. It hadn't been a fair wager. So to even the score, I'd taken out my hammer and exacted my own brand of justice on his Barcalounger.

That hadn't been a fair fight either. When I was done with it, that poor chair hadn't had a leg left to stand on.

So, as a consolation prize, I'd consented to allowing Tom to name the puppy Sir Albert Snoggles, III.

Looking back on it now, it was a pretty fair trade.

Unlike Tom's hideous chair, the puppy's name had begun to grow on me. In fact, the fluffy white ball with a grey patch on one foot and the tips of both ears had quickly become my constant companion. Snoggles seemed quite content to lay in the cozy dog bed by my desk as I pecked away at my keyboard for hours on end. To my surprise, I, in return, was quite content to have his company.

"I THINK OLD LANGSBURY will like this one," I said as I typed "The End" on my latest short story. I saved the file and snapped my laptop closed. "It's time for a treat."

As I reached for a jellybean to reward myself, I realized someone else in the room had misinterpreted my meaning.

Snoggles perked up, dashed from his bed, and yipped and danced beside my right shin, twirling around on his tiny back legs like a furry ballerina.

"Uh-oh. I've gone and said the "T" word. I guess I'd better get *you* a treat, too, or you'll think I never keep my promises."

Snoggles yipped again. I tousled his fuzzy head.

"Come on, then. Off to the kitchen."

I padded over to the cabinets and opened the cupboard above the refrigerator. In the meantime, Snoggles bided his time impatiently by tearing up a sheet of newspaper on the floor and running around with it like a deranged squirrel.

"Snoggs! You're supposed to be pee-peeing on that. Not tearing it to shreds!"

At the mention of his name, the pup changed directions and headed right for me, dragging the newspaper with him like a hobo security blanket.

I bent over and put Snoggles' treat on the floor.

"Here you go."

The pup dropped the soggy patch of newsprint in his mouth and dove for the little, bone-shaped treat.

As he slurped it up, I grabbed the chewed section of *The St. Petersburg Times* he'd been dragging around. I was about to throw it in the trash when a photo caught my eye. It was the slightly damp image of a greasy-looking, ham-fisted man puffing on a cigar. He was shaking hands with the mayor.

"Just what we need. Another stupid land developer," I said to Snoggles.

As I tossed the paper in the bin, the words Sunset Beach caught my eye. My gut flopped. I grabbed the crumpled scrap of newsprint out of the trash, spread it out on the kitchen counter and smoothed it with my hands.

I read the article word for word.

It was bad news all around.

According to the article, the guy holding the cigar was one Timothy "Tim" Amsel from Chicago. He was working with the city, trying to gain permission for new construction on Sunset Beach. Next to his chummy photo with the mayor was a rendering of the project being proposed by his company, Progress, Inc.

My eyes nearly fell out of my skull.

It was another ugly, boxy, high-rise condo tower. Worse still, Progress, Inc. was proposing to build it right on the spot where Caddy's now stood. If approved, the project, Randy Towers, would spell the end of my favorite beach bar, as well as the donut shack run by my good friends Winky and Winnie.

I grabbed a pen and drew a Snidely Whiplash moustache on the pig-faced jerk from Chicago.

To me, so-called "progress" could be a downright scoundrel.

It might as well look like one, too.

Chapter Three

The whitewall tires of my 1963 Ford Falcon convertible made a peanut-brittle crunch as they rolled across the crushed-shell parking lot next to Caddy's beach bar on Sunset Beach. It was mid-morning, late August, and already hot as blue blazes. But I, for one, found the heat comforting. Unlike hideous condo towers, the sauna-like weather *belonged* in Florida.

I shifted Maggie into park, hauled my butt out of her red vinyl bucket seat, and looked past half an acre of sand to the sparkling Gulf of Mexico beyond. I took a long, calming breath and tried to savor the sights, sounds and smells of the little slice of heaven surrounding me.

The gentle Gulf breeze in my hair. The warm, soft sand beneath my feet. The reedy whisper of the sea oats. The clean freshness of the salt air....

Sunset Beach meant more to me than to most. It had been my port in the storm when I'd washed ashore five years ago, broke, friendless, and shattered by another failed attempt at love. Sunset Beach had been, in a word, my *haven*. Its unspoiled beauty had been a salve to my mind and heart, and had slowly helped heal the wounds inflicted by a more complicated world.

A walk along its gently lapping shoreline never ceased to calm my frayed nerves. It had been unfailing at delivering solace when I'd felt out of sorts.

And now it was slated for demolition.

Like so many beaches on Florida's west coast, Sunset Beach offered a wide, flat strip of sand as fine and white as cane sugar. At its edge, the wide expanse of the Gulf of Mexico beckoned, glimmering in the sun like liquid turquoise.

When I'd first arrived back in St. Petersburg, I'd sought the sanctuary of the beach *because it was free.* Unlike man, Mother Nature wasn't motivated by profit. Left to her own devices, she'd never charged an entrance fee. As far as I could tell, she'd always seemed content with gratitude as her sole reward.

I took another deep breath of salt air and closed my eyes, letting the breeze twirl my hair into curls that tickled my face.

Of all the places I'd ever been in the world, Sunset Beach was where I'd felt most at home. It had provided the therapy I'd needed to find my feet again. It was also where I'd found the new friends who'd slowly morphed into my makeshift family.

Glad. Winky. Jorge. Goober. Tom....

The buzz of a plane overhead made me open my eyes. I used my hand as a visor and looked up. A small, red-and-white biplane passed directly overhead, blotting out the sun. The shadow flashed across my face for a blink of an eye.

As it banked and headed eastward, back toward Albert Whitted airport in downtown St. Petersburg, a sudden realization caused my temper to flare.

If Randy Towers gets built, those ugly condos will blot out this gorgeous view not just for a blink of an eye, but forever!

And they call that *progress?*

I picked up a freckled cockle shell and flung it angrily toward the water. Nowadays, keeping Florida *Florida* seemed more and more like an uphill, losing battle.

The problem was, most people would probably cheer at the prospect of a shiny new condo replacing ratty old Caddy's beach bar. I'd have been the first to admit the run-down bar wasn't much to look at. But to me, it was hallowed ground. It'd been the launching pad for my fourth life do-over.

Geez. I've already lost so much. Will I have to let go of Caddy's, too?

I picked up another shell and studied it as I chewed my lip.

Sure, Caddy's was nothing fancy. But that's why I liked it. It never claimed to be anything more than it was—a simple, wooden shack for people to get together and have a good time.

A few years back, Greg, the owner, had scabbed a rooftop deck on-to the back of the little building. Even so, Caddy's still looked more like a run-down old beach house than a restaurant. It had a porch that faced the water. And Greg had plopped a few picnic tables in the sandy beach by the porch, to serve customers who came clad in nothing but wet-bottomed bathing suits.

Other than those modest improvements, Caddy's had remained as unchanged as the Gulf of Mexico itself. With no air conditioning or bothersome doors to lock, the place dealt with Florida's tourists and tropical weather like the rest of the natives—it took them as they came.

It had no other choice.

Except to sell out.

I thought about that blasted newspaper article. That Amsel guy wouldn't be making the news unless he'd already negotiated a deal with Greg.

My gut dropped four inches.

Oh, Greg! Say it isn't so!

CADDY'S WAS A PART of the old Florida I'd grown up with and loved. The thought of Sunset Beach becoming just another soulless stack of condos made my heart ache and my temper flare.

I can't let that happen!

I blew out an angry breath and marched across the sand toward Caddy's porch. As my sandals twisted their way across the little sugar-like dunes of sand, I caught sight of Norma, the grumpy head waitress.

Like Caddy's itself, Norma was an institution. She'd been working there since whoever founded the place had nailed the first two boards together and cracked open a beer to celebrate.

"Norma!" I called out.

She looked up and squinted. Norma was no longer a spring chicken. But Florida weather dictated that she still wear the obligatory beach-waitress uniform of short-shorts, a skin-tight t-shirt, and a sun visor.

When I'd spotted her, the tough old bird was standing next to one of the picnic tables, taking a customer's order. One of her big, sandal-clad feet was propped up on the bench, and she employed her raised knee to hold her order pad. She scribbled intently on a pad with a pen, aided by a pink triangle of tongue that wriggled in and out of one corner of her mouth.

I smiled. I'd come to know that Norma had been blessed with a heart of gold—a fact she kept well-hidden behind a mannish face and a voice that could peel the paint off powder-coated metal. Four summers ago, she'd been a godsend to me. Norma'd helped me scrape up enough money to get Glad properly cremated. And she'd cried like a baby at the seaside service.

I gave Norma a nod and a smile, then waited patiently as she finished taking the food and drink order of the half-toasted, half-roasted couple that was huddled under the shade of the picnic table's beach umbrella.

She finished scribbling on the pad, swung her leg off the bench, and looked my way.

"Hey, Val," she growled as I grinned at her. "What's up?"

"A lot. Is Greg around?"

Norma's eyes shifted to the left, then she blew out a breath. "Nope. Should be back around three."

Normally laid back and talkative, Norma seemed out of sorts.

"You okay?" I asked.

"Sure."

"I wanted to talk to you about—"

"Listen, I gotta get this order in," she said, cutting me off. "I don't want the boss to get his panties in a wad."

"Okay."

I sighed and watched as she scurried off toward the kitchen. My crusade against progress had been thwarted for the moment. So, I turned and headed toward my next destination—a little concrete bunker wedged in the sand between Caddy's and the main road.

The tiny, ramshackle establishment was called Winnie and Winky's Bait & Donut Shop. And if Progress, Inc. had its way, it would soon be just another forgotten piece of Florida history as well.

"YEP. I SEEN IT," WINKY said, and slapped a swatter at a fly that was creeping toward a plate of assorted, gooey-looking donuts half-melted by the heat. He poured a cup of coffee into a paper cup and handed it to me through the service window.

"Aren't you worried?" I asked, and jabbed a finger at the newspaper article I'd laid on the counter in front of him. "If this goes forward, your donut shop will be slated for imminent demolition."

Winky shrugged a shoulder at me through the window as he employed the flyswatter as a backscratcher.

"Greg says it ain't nothin' to worry about right now, Val. It's just a propulsion."

"Proposal."

Winky's pale eyebrows nearly met his ginger buzz-cut.

"Proposal?" he asked.

He leaned his freckled head back and sideways, toward the inner workings of the donut shop.

"You hear that, Winnie? Tom finally proposed!"

A muffled sound came from somewhere in the concrete shack. Winky shot me a grin.

"What'd you do, Val? Get Tom drunk? Hold his feet to the fire?"

"Ha ha," I sneered. "He didn't—"

"I know! Let's make us a double weddin'!"

"Argh! Let's not!"

I couldn't decide if I was more annoyed at the idea of getting married, or at Winky's happy-go-lucky attitude. I possessed the talent required for neither.

"I'm serious, Winky. Your shop is in danger!"

I picked up the newspaper article and held it up like show-and-tell prop.

"This proposal is already in the planning stage, see? It needs city approval, of course. But the way things go nowadays...."

"Val, you worry too much."

Like a toddler with ADHD, Winky's eyes were busy following the aeronautic acrobatics of another fly. He took a step toward it. I reached in the window and grabbed him by the frayed neck of his ratty t-shirt. The collar had long-since been removed, though it appeared it hadn't gone willingly.

"Look!" I said, and turned Winky's head toward the ugly structure that stood a hundred yards to his left. It was an orange, angular, three-story house that looked as out of place on Sunset Beach as a wooly mammoth in a raincoat.

"Just look at J.D.'s ugly house. The city planners will approve *anything* for someone with enough money."

Winky stuck his head out the service window like a red-headed tortoise. His upper lip hooked skyward.

"How long you think we got, Val?"

"What do you mean?"

"Till they tear this place down," he said, suddenly looking crestfallen.

I felt like the Grinch that stole Sunset Beach.

"Maybe never." I tried to sound a little more hopeful. "But if these plans get approved, work could start anytime. In a matter of weeks. Maybe even days."

"Then I got me an idea," Winky said.

"What? A protest?"

"Naw. Let's make hay while the sun's shining."

"What?"

"A party. Let's have one here!"

I glanced around at the crude concrete bunker and blanched. It wasn't exactly the Ritz. It wasn't even the Cheez Whiz *on top* of a Ritz.

"Here? At the donut shack?" I asked.

"Yep. Right 'cheer. Well, Sunset Beach and Caddy's, I mean. One last blowout. What a ya say to that?"

"Sounds good to me," Winnie said, coming up behind Winky. The cute, pudgy woman winked at me through her red-framed glasses, then took her place next to Winky like the mate to a redneck salt-and-pepper set.

"You realize that you two could lose your business here, right? Doesn't that bother you?"

"Val, you forget," Winky said. "I come from a long line a people with nothin'. And when you got nothin', you got nothin' to lose. We'uns always find a way to make do."

"That's right," Winnie agreed. "We're in it together, come heck or high water."

A buzzer went off somewhere in the shack. Winnie glanced behind her, then back at me.

"Nice to see you Val, but I've got to get back to the fryer. Donuts wait for no man."

"Or woman," Winky said, then laughed like Woody Woodpecker on crack.

I took a sip of coffee and waited for the staccato sound of Winky's chortle to stop ricocheting off the concrete blocks. I got tired of waiting and reached for a donut.

Winky slapped my hand with the flyswatter.

"Them's for payin' customers," he said.

I jerked my hand back and rubbed where he'd swatted it. Winky looked horrified.

"I didn't hurt you, did I?" he asked. He shoved the plate stacked with donuts at me. "Here. Take all you want."

"I'm fine," I said. "But I will take a chocolate glazed."

"My personal favorite," Winky said, and handed me a napkin.

"Thanks. You know, Winky, I think I found a clue to where Goober might be."

Winky looked around, as if the clue might be dangling from a hook in the air. Or maybe he'd just spotted another fly.

"Where?" he asked.

"Inside a tobacco tin."

Winky shook his head and laughed.

"Uh huh. You mean like them prank calls we used to pull when we was kids? 'Lady, you got Prince Albert in a can? Well, you better done go let him out.'"

"No, Winky. Not like that."

"Well, come on, Val. Goober can't fit in a tin can."

"Not *Goober*. A *clue*, Winky. You remember that redneck dream-catcher Goober left me?"

"Shore do. Quite a work of art, as I recall."

"Well, I found *this* inside the Skoal can."

I pulled the tiny slip of paper from my pocket and handed it to Winky.

"What's it say?" he asked.

"PObbLE."

"Well I'll be." Winky's left eyebrow raised up half an inch. He stared at me intently. "It's 'pobbley' some kind a clue all right," he said, then laughed at his own joke again.

When he finally noticed I wasn't laughing along, Winky shored up his face and handed the tiny slip of paper back to me.

"Don't take this stuff so seriously," he said.

"Geez, Winky. Aren't you worried about Goober at all?"

"Naw. Worryin' just ain't in my vocabulary. Besides, he'll turn up directly. Like I was tryin' to tell you, Val. Us fellers what come from nothin', like me and Goober? Well, we got the advantage."

"The *advantage?*"

Winky tapped a stubby finger to his freckled noggin and nodded slowly.

"We know how to survive by our wits."

Great. Now I'm really *worried.*

Chapter Four

On my way home from Sunset Beach, a thought went through my mind like a bullet through baloney.

Everything changes. And now, I'm no longer footloose and fancy-free.

My life had become complicated.

Again.

For the fourth time in my life, I found myself ensnarled in the tangle of compromises and responsibilities that came lumbering along, hand-in-hand, with romantic relationships.

When Tom had moved in a few months ago, my beloved sweatpants, house moo-moos, and dinners with Ben & Jerry had been obliterated, replaced by daily makeup routines, non-elastic-waist clothing, and Tom's "sensible meals."

The way I saw it, cohabitation had turned out to have all the disadvantages of marriage, and none of the perks. I had to put up with lack of privacy and all of Tom's quirks. Yet, I wasn't entitled to his pension or his life insurance payout when he croaked.

Maybe Winky was right. Maybe marrying Tom *was* the right thing to do. But then again....

Should I really be thinking about marrying Tom just so I get his stuff when he dies?

The mercenary nature of my thoughts shocked my Southern sensibilities enough that I argued back with myself.

I don't want Tom to die. I love him! I just want all the sacrifices to be worth it. Is that too much to ask?

I shook my head to clear my mind and stomped on the gas pedal. Maggie's twin-glasspack muffler roared to life, blowing away my lingering thoughts about matrimony. The void was filled by thoughts about my *other* housemate.

Snoggles.

A wry grin crept across my face.

Why am I so worried about Tom? The compromises I make for him are nothing *compared to taking care of Snogs...and that pup doesn't even bring home a paycheck!*

Sir Albert Snoggles, III's constant demand for attention had spelled the end to my lazy afternoons sprawled out in bed, binge-watching *Forensic Files* "for research" while Tom was at work.

Snoggles' walnut-sized bladder had a two-hour wee window. That meant my ability to skitter off someplace willy-nilly, whenever I wanted, was also out the window.

For a four-pound ball of fur, Snogs had turned out to be a pretty heavy ball and chain. Even so, I didn't mind that much. The frequent potty walks gave me a break from sitting at my computer all day writing. And, secretly, I hoped the exercise would keep my butt from growing wider with every passing hour....

However, what I *did* mind was all the work it now took simply to leave the house. I'd never had children of my own, so I hadn't been prepared for *all the preparation!* I also hadn't been expecting that a tiny puppy could be so darn smart.

I was pretty sure he had ESPP: extra-sensory puppy perception. What else would explain why Snogs would begin whining as soon as I reached for my shoes?

Nope. There were no more quick getaways in *my* future. First I had to cuddle Snogs for reassurance. Next came the obligatory doggy treats to keep him calm. Then, while he was busy licking peanut butter out of the center of a toy bone, I'd get busy scrounging up enough newspapers to line his cage. A walnut's worth of liquid required a surprising amount of newsprint to soak it all up.

But the worst part about having a puppy was something I couldn't blame on Snogs. It seemed that no matter what I did, I always felt *guilty* for leaving him alone.

Guilt sucked.

And for me, guilt had a face. It looked exactly like my adoptive mother, Lucille Jolly Short. Ironically, taking care of Snogs had actually given me a bit more empathy for what Lucille must have sacrificed when she allowed her husband Justas to take me in and raise me.

Still, it hadn't been enough empathy to brave a phone call to her.

Not today, anyway.

I PULLED INTO MY DRIVEWAY and set Maggie's gearshift to park. Then I sucked in a big breath and tried to shift my mindset, as well.

I will not feel guilty about caging Snogs.

Leaving Snogs cooped up in a cage while I was gone hadn't been my first choice. But the little rascal had proven he couldn't be trusted out loose on his own. Only once had I caved in to his whining and left him out while I ran a short errand. When I'd returned twenty minutes later, the little deviant had chewed his way through my tennis shoe, one of Tom's socks, and the plastic handle on the kitchen dust pan.

I climbed out of Maggie's bucket seat and fumbled in my purse for my house keys. As I turned the lock to the front door, I could hear Snogs begin to yip and whine.

How could so much noise come from a blob of white fluff the size of a bag of chips?

"I'm home Snogs!" I called out as I stepped inside.

I kicked off my sandals by the door, so as not to track in any beach sand still clinging to their soles. Then I padded barefoot over to the corner of the living room. When I looked down, Snogs was yapping and bouncing off the sides of his cage like a mop head in a tumble dryer.

"You crazy nutcase!"

I squatted down and slid the lock on the cage door. Snogs sprung through it and licked me in the chops before I could even figure out which end of him was which.

"Yuck! Stop!" I scolded.

Snogs rewarded me with another lick across the face.

"Ugh!"

The fluffy white pup jumped and danced and darted between my feet as I walked over to the sliding glass door that led to the backyard. Despite the messy kisses, the sound of his tiny nails ticking on the terrazzo floor made me smile.

I was a proud puppy mama.

I slid the door open. Snogs shot out into the backyard like a skein of wool fired from a grenade launcher. He bounded across the grass and disappeared behind the fire pit Tom had built for my birthday.

So much energy for such a teensy ball of nothing!

I shook my head and followed the sound of Snogs' tiny yips and grunts.

Grunts? Wait a minute. That's a new one.

I peeked around the fire pit and found Snogs busy christening the patio pavers with a poop deposit. He yipped again, and then I heard another grunt. But it wasn't coming from him. It was coming from my next-door neighbor, Laverne.

Weird. I didn't think Laverne was the grunting kind.

Since meeting the former Vegas showgirl three years ago, I'd come to know that Laverne Cowens valued glitz and glamour over pedestrian practicality any day. Always persnickety with her appearance, she preferred sequins to khakis, and wore makeup and high heels just to take out the trash.

Grunting just didn't seem to fit her normal repertoire.

Another grunt sent my eyes scanning her backyard. I spotted the skinny septuagenarian behind one of her many prize rose bushes. She was standing next to a newly built section of fence she'd had erected to house a compost pile. At six-feet-something in silver high heels, Laverne towered over the four-foot tall, six-by-six square of wooden fence like the Jolly Green Giant's albino grandma.

I watched as she scraped a plate of food over the fence into the pit. Laverne took care not to get any on her outfit, which happened to be a full-skirted, red-polka-dot dress that could have been torn from a 1956 Sears catalogue. I half-expected an animated bluebird to twitter by and land on her shoulder.

I laughed to myself. Laverne was a notoriously bad cook. At the rate her indigestible comestibles would be ending up in that compost bin, I figured it wouldn't be long before she'd be needing to expand her facilities.

"Now you be good, you hear?" she said to the food scraps as they tumbled off into the bin.

If I hadn't known Laverne so well, I might've thought it odd for her to be talking to compost.

"Hey, Laverne," I called out. "What 'cha doing?"

The sound of my voice made Laverne jump as if she'd been stuck in the posterior with a pitchfork. She froze in place, shushed the compost pile with a quick, "Shhh!" then turned and beamed her perfect, pearly dentures at me.

"Hi! Uh...Val. Yes, it's just little old me. All by myself, here. Alone, you know."

I'd heard better adlibbed lies from a first-grader.

"Okaaay," I said, and looked over toward the compost bin. Laverne shifted her body to block my view.

"I'm not up to anything," she volunteered. "Nice day, huh?"

"Sure."

Laverne spotted the puppy bounding at my feet. Her huge, doe eyes and lit up.

"Oh! It's little Sir Albert Snoggles! Isn't he just a handful of precious?"

"He's a handful, all right," I smirked.

Laverne bent over the picket fence to pet Snogs, who danced at the opportunity to have his head petted.

"You're such a good boy!" Laverne gushed.

A sudden creaking sound made me look up. The gate to Laverne's compost bin flew open. A pinkish blur streaked across the yard. It headed straight for Laverne, who was still bent over the fence, petting Snogs.

Before I could utter a word of warning, it rammed into her. Laverne shot straight up and let out a squeal something akin to the sound a rubber chicken might make if it was being squeezed by a talkative harbor seal.

"What in the world is going on?" I asked.

"Nothing!" Laverne squealed.

She grabbed the edges of her hoop skirt and squatted down in the lawn. Her flouncy skirt parachuted around her, making it appear as if Laverne were an ancient, strawberry-blonde fairy who'd just popped halfway through the middle of a red, polka-dotted mushroom.

"What are you doing?" I asked.

Before she could answer, something began to move underneath Laverne's skirt. It poked the fabric upward here, then a moment later, over there. Laverne forced a smile at me, and tried valiantly to chase the poked-up spots with her hands, as if she were participating in a covert game of Whack-a-Mole.

But it was no use. Despite her best efforts, eventually, a little face peeked out from under the skirt's round blanket of polka dots.

The face was pink. And it had a snout.

It was a pig the size of a Boston terrier.

"What in the world...?" I gasped.

Laverne winced. She eyed me sheepishly, and said, "I think you already know Randolph."

Chapter Five

"*Randolph?*" I gasped as I stared at Laverne over the white picket fence.

She was kneeling in her yard, encircled by a red, polka-dotted skirt that was harboring a fugitive pig underneath.

"How did you end up with a *pig*, of all things?"

Laverne shot me an apologetic look and let out a huge sigh. She stroked the pig's cheek, then confessed her clandestine operation to me as if I were the pope.

"Randolph's the pig from the yard sale, Val. You know. The one I got to kiss because I won the bake-off."

I felt the strain of my eyes doubling.

"What? You've got to be kidding!"

Laverne shrugged sheepishly. "No. I adopted him from Arnie, the Boy Scout. Right, Randolph?"

At the mention of his name, the pig grunted and rubbed its snout against the back of Laverne's liver-spotted hand.

"Good grief! What were you *thinking?*" I asked, before I remembered that thinking wasn't one of Laverne's major talents.

Laverne looked up at me. Tears brimmed her huge eyes.

"Val, Arnie told me that if someone didn't do something, Randolph was going to be..."

Laverne put her hands over the young pig's ears.

"...turned into bacon and pork chops!"

My heart pinged. "But Laverne, you can't keep *a pig* in the city limits."

"I know. I was going to take him out to the country. But then I didn't have the heart to let him go. Val, I've been lonely since J.D. and I broke up. Randolph's been good company."

Laverne looked endearingly at the pig. "And you just *love* my cooking, don't you, little Randolph?"

Randolph grunted. It sounded as much like 'yes' in pig language as I could give him credit for. But then again, maybe sentimentality had begun to swamp what was left of my good sense.

"So the compost pile was just a ruse," I said.

Laverne nodded guiltily. "He got too big for the laundry basket. And I had to keep him hidden from my nosy neighbors."

The bridge of my nose crinkled defensively. "I wouldn't have said anything."

"Not *you*, Val. *Nancy Meyers.*"

"Oh. Right."

I visualized the blonde battleaxe who lived across the street. Nancy Meyers took the "ho ho ho" right out of HOA.

Even though my neighborhood, Bahia Shores, didn't have an official home owners' association, Nancy had made it her mission in life to sterilize the streets of any semblance of human activity, including garbage cans in driveways, bicycles on sidewalks, and grass blades longer than 5.25 inches.

I bit my lip and shrugged at Laverne. "If it helps, I can give you the pet rulebook Nancy handed me when she heard Snogs was moving in. But I'm pretty sure it doesn't cover pigs."

Laverne glanced in the direction of Nancy's house, even though it wasn't visible from her backyard. I thought I saw a flash of panic in her eyes.

"Val, promise me you won't tell Nancy!"

I blanched. "Of course I won't!"

"Don't tell Tom, either, okay?"

Laverne's pleading doe eyes were hard to resist.

"Okay," I agreed. "But you've got to do something Laverne. And I mean *quick*. Randolph's hardly a little piglet anymore. He must have doubled in size in less than a month. By next week, he could be as big as a Great Dane!"

Laverne hugged Randolph to her and looked into his eyes as she spoke.

"I know. But what can I do? My big boy is always hungry, aren't you?"

She looked up at me with those big, irresistible eyes again.

"Will you help me find a place for him, Val? Somewhere out in the country, where he can run free?"

"You mean like a farm?" I asked.

Laverne smiled brightly. "Yes! That's it. A farm!"

Geez. Just say no, Val. Say no! For crying out loud, say NO!

"Okay," I said. "In the meantime, keep Randolph in his pen...and whatever you do, keep him from getting loose again!"

"I will," Laverne said. "I promise. Come along, little Randolph."

Laverne stood up and pulled a treat from a pocket in her skirt. She waved it in front of Randolph's snout. The pig grunted enthusiastically and followed her as she coaxed him back to the fenced "compost" area that was actually his covert pen. Laverne tossed the treat inside. Randolph strolled in, and she slid the lock on the gate.

Snogs' little paws thumped against my shin as he danced at my feet. I picked him up and waited as Laverne tottered back over to the picket fence between our properties.

"Thanks, Val. I feel better now that we've got a plan."

"I didn't realize that you had Randolph so well trained. I'm impressed."

"Huh?" Laverne cocked her horsey head at me. "Oh. You mean these? He'd do anything for one of these."

Laverne pulled something from the pocket of her skirt. It was a brown-and-yellow-striped, bacon-flavored treat. Apparently, the irony of it went over Laverne's head like a whole squadron of flying pigs.

"You don't say," I said as Snogs squirmed in my arms, trying to reach the treat. "Are you still up for riding along to the college tonight for your baking class?"

"Shh! Yes," Laverne whispered. She glanced behind her for a second, then leaned in toward me. Boney fingers covered in rings went up to her mouth, as if she were trying to form a screen against prying eyes.

"I want to surprise Randolph with a new recipe," she whispered.

I glanced toward the pen, then let out a sigh that could probably be heard in the next county.

"All right, then. Come over around five-thirty."

"Can we make it five? I need to stop somewhere on the way."

"Sure."

Randolph let out a loud grunt. Laverne winced and locked eyes with me. A line of worry trailed across her forehead.

"Val, do you think the college has classes on how to train pigs?"

"I dunno, Laverne. But I guess it wouldn't hurt to ask."

I sighed again, and tried to shrug away the niggling feeling that had suddenly taken root in the back of my mind. I'd felt it before. I knew its name well. Or, perhaps it would have been more accurate to say that it knew mine.

It was the feeling of impending calamity.

Chapter Six

"So, what's this detour you want to make on the way to class?" I asked Laverne as she angled her long, stork-like legs into Maggie and plopped down on the passenger seat like a geriatric grasshopper in a strawberry-blonde wig.

"I need to get some pig chow for Randolph. Animal Attic is having a going-out-of-business sale."

Laverne snatched a coupon from her purse and waved her trophy at me like the proud bargain hunter she was. "See? I can save fifty percent!"

"I wonder why they're going out of business," I said dryly. "I guess there aren't enough pot-bellied pigs in Pinellas County to make a go of it."

Laverne's red lips wilted into a pout. "That's not very nice, Val. Randolph doesn't have a pot belly."

"Sorry, Laverne. You're right. He's...uh...*pleasantly plump*. And juicy."

Laverne smiled. "That's right."

"So, where we headed?"

"Over off Thirty-Fourth and First Avenue South."

I shifted into reverse. The address sounded familiar, but I couldn't place it. I backed Maggie out onto the road, shifted gears again, and tooled down Bimini Circle toward Gulf Boulevard.

"So, how did you come up with the name Randolph?" I asked, try-ing to distract myself from the trickle of sweat crawling down my back. With the top down, even the forty-mile-an-hour breeze wasn't enough to wick away the heat of an August evening in St. Pete.

Laverne looked up at the sky wistfully. "I called him Randolph be-cause he reminds me of an old boyfriend I had back in Vegas."

"Let me guess. Was he a pig, too?"

"Sort of," Laverne grinned. "He was a cop."

"A *policeman?* Really?"

I swung Maggie right onto Gulf Boulevard and rumbled past the familiar rows of tacky tourist shops and 1950's-era mom-and-pop beach motels that lined both sides of the road. As I headed north, peek-ing out from behind the buildings I caught glimpses of the Gulf of Mexico on my left, and the Intracoastal Waterway on the right.

It was a subtle reminder of our rather precarious geography.

Gulf Boulevard was the main road that straddled a chain of narrow strip islands that outlined the mainland of Florida's west coast like a crumbly, broken-off pie crust.

Not much more than an overgrown sandbar, the long strip of sand ran north all the way to Clearwater, where its remnants formed Calade-si and Honeymoon islands. The fingers of land stretched south along the coast past Treasure Island and Sunset Beach, before coming to an abrupt end just past St. Pete Beach at a place called Pass-a-Grille. There, it dangled precariously into the open mouth of Tampa Bay. Just to its south was Fort Desoto, a state park boasting a semi-wild stretch of coastline that consistently ranked as one of the most beautiful beaches in the world.

"Yes, Randolph was a policeman," Laverne said, and stretched her knobby knees. They were so sharp I feared they might cut through her Spandex yoga pants. "Not as handsome as your Tom, of course."

I would hope not. Especially if he looked like a pig!

"You said Randolph is good company, Laverne. How so?"

"Well, he's polite, and he never argues."

"I hear that. But he doesn't have much of a vocabulary."

"No, he doesn't." Laverne turned and showed me a pout. "As much as I hate to admit it, Val, I got used to having a man about the place. You know, I'd been fine on my own until I met J.D. He kind of filled a hole in me I didn't realize was empty. You know what I mean?"

My heart pinged with a strange, somewhat unwelcome familiarity.

"Yeah," I answered. "If you don't mind me asking, Laverne, why'd you and J.D. break up?"

Laverne sighed. "I don't mind, honey."

I waited a beat and rolled my eyes. "So, why'd you break up?"

"Same reason most people do. Irreconcilable differences."

Laverne sighed and shook her head. "But we all know that's just a made-up term for plain old, everyday hard-headed stubbornness."

I glanced over at the idiot savant sitting beside me. Disguised in a sequin-splattered shirt, purple yoga pants and gold high heels, she looked as if she might have escaped from a geriatric mental ward. But I knew better. I smiled and waited for her next words of wisdom.

"Turn here," she said.

I hooked a sharp right onto scruffy Thirty-Fourth Street. A block later, I took a left onto First Avenue South. The ugly, run-down buildings blighting the roadside jarred my memory.

That's it! Ferrol Finkerman's office is around here somewhere....

Finkerman was the lousy, ambulance-chasing dirtbag attorney who'd plagued me like a starving mosquito with his hair-brained libel suits and thinly-veiled extortion plots. The last thing I needed was to get back on that jerk's radar screen.

"Do we *have* to go this way?" I asked.

But by the time the words had left my mouth, it was already a moot question. The dingy strip mall that housed the lout's office came into view on the right.

As I drove past it, I caught sight of a sign on Finkerman's door. It read, "We've Moved." A banner above Sultry Sam's Sex Shoppe next door read, "Going Out of Business." As we cruised a little further along the strip mall, I spotted a sign posted amongst the litter and weeds between the sidewalk and the asphalt parking lot. It read, "Coming Soon: The Shops of Heron's Walk."

It appeared as if the whole strip center was going to be demolished. I guess that was one bit of progress I wasn't going to complain about.

"There it is, on the left," Laverne said, and pointed a finger across the street. "Animal Attic."

I pulled in, parked, and in a self-preservation tactic, waited in the car while Laverne ran in. I was afraid if I went inside, I'd buy another tchotchke for Snogs. He already had a three-foot-tall mountain of toys. But for some reason, he ignored them all in favor of chewing up my shoes.

Go figure.

As I sat in the parking lot, a red tow truck flew by, hauling an obnoxiously yellow Hummer. Ferrol Finkerman drove just such a vehicle. I sat up and tried to get a glimpse of the license plate as it passed. But I was too slow.

Still, I was pretty sure the Hummer belonged to Finkerman. I hoped so, because the thought that there might have been fleets of the blasted things burning up the roads made my nose crinkle in disgust. I tapped a finger on the steering wheel.

Had Finkerman's Hummer broken down? Or, better yet, had he not made his car payment?

The thought of Finkerman's Hummer being repo'ed gave me the best smile I'd had in a week.

It was still on my face when the door to Animal Attic flew open, and Laverne emerged with a hairy ape-man behind her. The bag of pig chow he was toting over his shoulder was almost as big as he was.

"Hi, Jake," I said. The swarthy guy from New Jersey was my neighbor and a doppelganger for the illusive Missing Link. "I didn't know you worked here."

"It fills in the gaps between appointments," Jake wheezed. "Where you want this?"

"Oh! Hold on." I jumped out of Maggie and opened the trunk.

Jake dropped the huge sack of chow in. It landed with a thud like a dead body, making Maggie squeak and bounce like a carnival ride.

"You could use some new shocks," Jake said.

"Speaking of shocks," I joked, "how's the dog psychology biz?"

"Slow," Jake said. "Thus the necessity of this lovely gig."

"Jake, do you train pigs?" Laverne asked.

"I haven't," Jake confessed. "But you know, pigs are pretty smart. Smarter than dogs, for sure. In fact, the only animals smarter are chimps, dolphins and elephants."

"Well, that explains my ex-husbands," I quipped.

Jake shot me some side eye, then directed his conversation at Laverne.

"Pigs are trainable, for sure, Laverne. You thinking of getting one?"

"Uh...I..." Laverne stuttered.

"No, Jake," I said. "That enormous bag of pig chow is for her baking class tonight."

"I'll ignore that remark," Jake said. "So, you've got a pig. Indoor or out?"

"Uh...a bit of both?" Laverne said weakly.

"Huh. Good idea. You know, pigs make excellent indoor pets. They don't have sweat glands like dogs and cats. And they don't shed. All in all, a pig's a pretty good choice for a pet."

Laverne beamed. Then, suddenly, she winced in what appeared to be horror. "Jake, don't tell Nancy Meyers. She'll—"

"No need to explain," Jake said, shaking his head. "Mum's the word."

"Who's Mum?" Laverne asked.

Jake locked eyes with me for a second, then looked back at Laverne. "Uh...nice shirt," he said.

Laverne giggled and shifted her shoulders, causing the sequined words on her shirt to glitter in the late-afternoon sun.

"Virginia is for Lovers," Jake read out loud. "Huh. I always thought Virginia was for smoked ham."

ON THE WAY TO CLASS, I thought about telling Laverne about the clue I'd found in the Skoal tin. But from the worried look on the poor woman's face, I figured she had enough on her plate dealing with Randolph.

I pulled into the parking lot at St. Pete Community College and killed the ignition. Laverne and I climbed out of the car. I waited for a moment and watched her absently toddle off down the sidewalk toward the scene of her next baking fiasco.

The sun was just beginning to set. The sky was pinkish gray, like the dying ashes of a crushed-out cigarette. The air was almost as hot. The dog days of summer were nearly over, but they were getting in their last humid hassles. In a few days, September would arrive and give us hope (though mostly false) that a cool breeze was just around the corner.

As I walked toward my classroom, I swiped at a trail of sweat tickling the back of my neck.

"Hot one, tonight," said a guy wheeling a janitor's cart.

"Sure is."

I reached for the doorknob to my classroom and spotted a hastily-scrawled note taped to the door. It read, "*Mystery Writing for Fun & Profit* has been cancelled until further notice."

What?

I called after the janitor guy.

"Hey! Sir! Do you know anything about this?"

The guy turned his head. "What's that?"

"My writing class is cancelled. Do you know why?"

"Uh...yeah. But I'm not allowed to say."

The know-it-all grin on his face sent my imagination spinning. I *had* to know what he knew.

"I'll give you five bucks," I said.

The guy's grin broadened. "Twenty."

I dug through my wallet. "I've got thirteen bucks."

"Deal."

I handed over the cash. He stuffed it in the shirt pocket of his blue janitor uniform.

"So, what do you want to know?" he asked.

"Well...for starters, is Angela Langsbury okay?"

"You mean the old lady who teaches the class?"

"Yes."

An image of the scrawny old woman flashed in my mind. Her stiff, brown helmet of lacquered, dandruff-raining hair. Translucent skin the color of skim milk. A wrinkly face permanently stuck in sarcastic mode.

"That lady's one tough old bird," the janitor said. "She actually came out on top."

"On top? On top of *what?*" I asked.

"The big blowout. At that murder-mystery thingy they had in Orlando over the weekend."

My eyebrows met my hairline. "Blowout? Was there an explosion? Was anyone injured?"

"No bombs. More like a catfight, from what I read."

"Read?"

The janitor looked around and put his index finger to his lips. "Yeah. Well, I kind of, you know, accidently saw the HR file on the, uh, *incident.*"

"Oh my word! Tell me *everything* you know!"

The guy grinned. "Apparently, sometime during that retreat thing, Langsbury got fed up with this woman named Victoria and hauled off and sprayed her in the face with a can of Aquanet hairspray."

"She what?!"

"Yeah. In the report, Langsbury was quoted as saying 'Make it rain,' right before she blasted her."

As I waited for the janitor to stop laughing, I tried my best not to succumb to a giggling fit myself.

"The hairspray kind a temporarily blinded that Victoria woman," he said between wheezy chuckles. "But she came out swinging anyway. She tried to punch Langsbury out, but ended up smashing some other gal's nose instead."

"Clarice's?" I asked.

"That's the one!" the janitor said, and laughed.

"What else?"

The janitor looked up to the ashen sky for a moment and sucked in a breath.

"Well, there was something else about someone getting stabbed with a pencil. Can't remember exactly who did what. But I think one of the gals filed charges."

"Charges?"

"Yeah. Sorry, but that's as far as I got. The HR lady came back in her office so I dropped the file like a hot potato. I don't wanna get fired, you know."

"Geez," I muttered.

"Yeah." The janitor chuckled. "Who would've thought that old Langsbury could put up such a fight? She must weigh all of eighty pounds."

"Yeah. Who'd have thought? Thanks for the info."

"No problem. Have a good one." The janitor turned and continued on his route, pushing his cart down the open corridor.

I went back to the parking lot and plopped down in Maggie's driver's seat. I tried to envision Langsbury duking it out with Victoria. The thought of scrawny, ancient, bad-tempered Angela Langsbury chasing after bottle-blonde Victoria with a can of Aquanet made my lips curl with pleasure.

Victoria was no friend of mine. I didn't like her attitude or the company she kept. Somewhere in her fifties, Victoria always wore the dark-framed glasses and condescending expression of a snotty librarian. It was only later that I'd found out she actually *was* a librarian. That's when I'd also discovered she'd supplied that lowlife Finkerman with the names of folks with overdue library books. He'd used that intel to extort money from these folks to "clear their good names."

Poor Laverne had been one of their victims.

What a couple of scumbags.

I pictured Langsbury trapping Victoria in a corner somewhere and hosing her smug face down with hairspray until it ran down the lenses of her eyeglasses like thick, gooey rain.

For the second time that evening, a warm, satisfying, and slightly evil grin spread across my lips.

Good for you, Langsbury. Good for you.

Chapter Seven

"How was class?" Tom asked as I came through the front door. My answer was drowned out by the yips of a love-starved puppy.

"Snogs!"

I picked up the wriggling bundle of fluff and got a kiss on either cheek by both of my cute guys.

"Snogs?" Tom asked and made a sour face. "Were you calling the dog or blowing your nose?"

"What do you mean?"

"Snogs sounds gross. Like phlegm."

"Excuse me?" I said playfully. "Grosser than Sir Albert Snoggles, III? I don't *think* so!"

Tom grinned. "Okay. I'll let you have that one." He repeated his question. "So tell me, what did you do in class?"

I detected a tinge of persistence in Tom's usually laid-back tone. I studied him for a second. His smile seemed artificially tight. His eyes were focused on me like a TV cop's. But then again, he *was* a police lieutenant....

"Uh...nothing, Tom. Class was cancelled."

Tom's face softened a bit. "Good."

"What do you mean, *good?*"

"I didn't mean it like that. It's just that...well, while you were out, a lady called on the land line. She left a message saying she was your writing instructor."

"Angela Langsbury?"

"Yes." Tom sounded relieved. "I thought it was a prank call. I should have known better." He shook his head and laughed softly. "Only *you*, Val."

"What do you mean, only *me?*"

"Only *you* could have a murder mystery instructor named Angela Langsbury. You, my dear, are a magnet for the absurd."

Oh, boy. If you only knew the half of it.

In the five years since I'd returned from Germany to St. Pete, life's absurdities had followed me around, pestering the living daylights out of me like a swamp full of angry no-see-ums.

In that time, I'd been forced to falsify public records to claim the dead body of a stranger. (A stranger who'd later turned out to be my biological mother.) I'd been robbed by a dwarf looking for a disembodied finger. I'd chased down a hippie in a rogue RV to recover my mom's cremated remains after Tom traded them for a tiki hut. I'd competed with my adoptive mom Lucille and tied for "family fruitcake" of the year. I'd been sued for using a toothpick to lift the lid on a cop's bad toupee. I'd undergone relationship therapy from a dog psychologist. I'd been abducted by a serial killer disguised as Bigfoot. And two weeks ago, I'd been outwitted by the ceramic effigy of a man squatting on a toilet.

And now, I was the unwilling accomplice to a geriatric showgirl harboring a fugitive pig living in a compost bin.

Magnet for the absurd doesn't even scratch the surface.

"Magnet for the absurd, huh?" I said, and set Snogs down. I wrapped my arms around Tom's neck and winked. "So *that's* why you find me so irresistible."

Tom laughed. "That's got to be it." He winked a sea-green eye at me, then kissed me in a way that removed any lingering doubts about his intentions.

Which, by the way, turned out to be far from absurd. But then again, I've always been a sucker for a handsome blond with tight buns....

"DID YOU HEAR THE NEWS about Caddy's?" Tom asked as he washed up the supper dishes.

"Yeah. That guy Tim Amsel looks like a real scumbag," I said, and scraped my uneaten broccoli into the garbage can.

"Looks can be deceiving," Tom joked, and made a bandito mask out of the dish towel.

"Not *that* deceiving," I said dryly. "That guy's so gross he could go under cover in a pig farm—*without a disguise.*"

Tom didn't laugh. He dropped the dishtowel from his face and said, "Right," as if he hadn't heard me.

"Have you been to Caddy's lately?" he asked.

I put a clean glass away in the cupboard and closed the door. When I turned back to face him, Tom had his interrogating cop eyes trained on me again.

"I was there today. Why?"

"Nothing. Well...just...I'd rather you didn't go there again, okay?"

"Why not?"

"The owner, Greg Parsons, has been reported missing."

Something caught in my throat. "What do you mean, *missing?*"

"An employee called the station this afternoon. Parsons didn't come to work as scheduled."

"So?"

"The employee sounded pretty upset. She said Parsons has never shown up late since she's been working there. We're giving him forty-eight hours to turn up before we file an official missing person report."

"What do you think is—"

"Sorry, Val. That's all I can tell you right now."

"I understand. Can you tell me if the employee who called in the report was named Norma?"

Tom looked surprised, then nodded.

I blew out a breath. "Then something's up for sure, Tom. If Greg was just taking a day off, Norma would have known about it."

Tom chewed his lip for a moment and said, "Okay. Thanks for the tip."

"Sure. You know, I could—"

"Let's don't discuss it anymore, okay?"

"I wasn't. I was going to say that Goober's been missing a lot more than forty-eight hours, and nobody's filed a report on him."

"He's a grown man, Val. I'm sure he's just out having a good time in the old RV. He'll turn up."

"I'm sure you're right," I said half-heartedly.

I almost told Tom about finding the clue in the Skoal can. But he didn't seem that interested. Just like Winky, neither guy seemed that concerned about Goober.

Was it a guy thing?

Or was I just being a worry wart?

Chapter Eight

I waited until 9:00 a.m. to call Angela Langsbury back. I wasn't sure if she was an early-to-bed, early-to-rise kind of woman or not. As skeletal and ghostly pale as she was, she might have slept in a coffin and fed on the blood of students at night, for all I knew.

"Hello?" said a voice only a mother toad could love.

I recognized it immediately.

"Ms. Langsbury? It's me, Val. You called yesterday?"

"Uh...yeah. Fremden. I guess you know the writing class was cancelled."

"Yeah."

"Uh-huh. What do you know about it?"

"About what?" I asked, not wanting to get the tell-all janitor in trouble.

"Never mind. Listen, I need you to provide a deposition for me. As a character witness. Would you be able to do that?"

"Really? Is Victoria *suing* you?"

"So you *do* know."

Crap.

"Uh...a little bit. Listen. The whole hairspray thing? I get that. But nobody in their right mind would believe you stabbed her with a pencil."

"What?" Langsbury croaked. "I don't give a flip about *that*."

"Then what's the deposition for?"

"Victoria wants her eighteen hundred bucks back for the murder mystery weekend. I'm a *teacher*, for crying out loud. I don't have that kind of money lying around! Besides, I already spent it on a bikini wax and a ticket to Cozumel."

Too much information.

"Oh."

"So will you do it? Will you give a deposition?"

"For *what*, exactly?"

"I need you to back me up...you know, confirm that I made it clear in class there wouldn't be any refunds for the trip. Not for *any* reason."

I bit my lip and thought it over. Langsbury had her issues with Victoria. So did I.

I'd never gotten the chance to confront that jerk of a librarian for her part in hurting Laverne. Finkerman had sent Laverne a letter demanding ninety bucks to restore her standing as a good citizen and avoid legal issues arising from an overdue book. The thought that she might be considered a criminal had sent poor Laverne into a tizzy of worry. Helping Langsbury with a deposition could be my chance to even the score with smug-faced Victoria.

I racked my brain trying to recall if I'd heard Langsbury tell the class about her zero-refund policy for the retreat.

"Uh...I'm not sure, Mrs. Langsbury. I'm trying to recall..."

"Oh, come on, Val! Do me a solid, would you? I can't take this idiocy. Not on top of having my stupid brother-in-law squatting in my guest room. Twit thinks he owns half the planet, but he's too cheap to spring for a hotel. Just my rotten luck."

"Well, I—"

I was cut off by the sound of Langsbury yelling at someone. Thankfully, her ire wasn't aimed at me this time. Through the receiver, I heard her screech, "Tim, if you don't put out that cigar, I swear I'm gonna kick you all the way back to Chicago!"

What? Wait a minute....

A beat later, a sweet, toady voice said, "So, what do you say, Val? Could you be a love and help an old lady out?"

"Your brother-in-law wouldn't happen to be Tim Amsel, would it?"

Langsbury blew out a breath. "Unfortunately, yes."

"Hmmm. Well, you know, I just may remember something about you mentioning a no-refund policy. But to be clear, you'll owe me one for it."

"Owe you one *what?*"

"I'll let you know later."

Langsbury groaned. "I don't like the sound of that. But okay. What the hell. Hey, by the way, you wouldn't happen to have an extra room to let, would you?"

"Nope. I'm fresh out."

"Lucky you."

ON MY WAY OUT THE FRONT door, I turned and waved to Snogs. He returned my gesture with a yip and a pout. Trapped in his cage, poor Snogs looked like an incarcerated teddy bear.

"Sorry," I cooed as I backed out over the threshold. I grabbed the doorknob and bent over for one last wave to Snogs. As I did, my derriere made contact with something. I whipped around and nearly gasped. My nosy neighbor Nancy Meyers was standing cheek to jowl with me on my porch. I wondered how long she'd been there eavesdropping.

"What are you doing here?" I barked.

"Good morning to *you*, too," she said with a huff. She stuck her perpetually upturned nose a little higher in the air and tugged at the hem of her blouse with both hands. "I just wanted to remind you that September starts in a few days."

"Uh...thanks?" I eyed her up and down with raised eyebrows.

"Fremden! September is Spruce-Up Your Lawn Month! It's time to weed and feed. And plant winter annuals."

"Nancy, in case you haven't noticed, we don't *have* winter here."

If I'd actually slapped her across the face, I think Nancy would've worn the same expression.

"A green lawn is a *keen* lawn," she said. "We don't want people thinking our neighborhood is full of *riff-raff.*"

"Define riff-raff."

Nancy ignored my request and shot me a look that made me seriously suspect that *I* was *exactly* the kind of ne'er-do-well to whom she'd been referring.

"You know what I mean," she said.

"I'll think about putting in some flowers, okay?"

Nancy shot me a skeptical look and tried to peek through the door into my house. I closed it to a crack, just to tease her.

"Was there something else?" I asked.

"I was just wondering, Fremden. Does your new dog...uh...per chance...*grunt?*"

My suspicions that Nancy had a screw loose multiplied tenfold. "What?"

"I keep hearing grunts," she said. "Is that new mutt of yours a grunter?"

I shut the door behind me. The click of the lock was followed by a distinct grunt.

"There it is again!" Nancy said.

I glanced toward Laverne's place. A pink snout was sticking out from behind a Koonti palm.

Oh, crap on a cracker!

"It was *me*," I lied.

"You?" Nancy's piggish nose wiggled in dismay. If I hadn't been under duress, the irony would have made me burst out laughing.

"It sounded like it came from over—" Nancy's head started to turn toward the Laverne's place. I shot out a hand, put a palm on her puffy cheek, and firmly guided her face back toward me.

"Haven't you heard about the new craze?" I asked, scrambling to come up with an idea on the fly. "It's like...uh...*laughter* yoga, see? But it's called *grunt* aerobics."

Nancy stared at me blankly. "Grunt aerobics?"

"Yes. You see...uh...you grunt while you're working out. You should try it. It uh...builds lung capacity and...uh...wards off influenza."

To drive my lie home, I smiled, did a jumping jack, and grunted. "See?"

Nancy nodded approvingly. "Grunt aerobics. Very interesting."

I glanced over at the bushes by Laverne's place. Randolph was staring at us, open-mouthed, as if we were looney-tunes.

I shook my head softly.

Tom's right. I am totally *a magnet for the absurd.*

I INSTRUCTED NANCY in the fine art of grunt aerobics as I led her back across the street and to her own front door. She hung on every detail, and only let me go after I promised to fertilize my lawn by the upcoming weekend.

Before Nancy'd interrupted me, I'd been on my way to see Langsbury's attorney to give my deposition. I glanced down at my cellphone.

Crap! I should've already been there by now!

I made my excuses with Nancy, sprinted back across the road, jumped inside Maggie, hit the ignition, and reversed down the driveway like Mario Andretti. As I shifted into drive, I set my sights on Gulf Boulevard and punched Laverne's number on speed dial.

"Laverne! You're pig's out!"

"Randolph?"

"Uh...*yes!* Do you have any *other* pigs I don't know about?"

"No."

"Laverne, the point is, I saw Randolph in the bushes between our houses. Go get him and put him back in his pen, quick! Nancy Meyers almost saw him!"

"Oh, no!"

"And when you're done, go and talk to Jake. Maybe he can help you figure out what to do with Randolph. I can't help now. I'm on my way to meet an attorney."

"You're not suing me over Randolph, are you?"

"What? Geez, Louise!"

"Laverne."

"Yes, I know! I mean...no! I'm not suing you. I've got to go see someone about something else."

"If it's J.D., tell him I miss him."

"It's not J.D."

"Oh."

"Listen, Laverne. I don't think you understand the urgency here. You need to get Randolph back in his pen before Nancy turns him into a backyard barbeque."

"Randolph likes barbeque."

"He'll be on the spit."

"That's gross, Val. Randolph doesn't slobber."

I closed my eyes, took a deep breath to calm myself, and waited for the traffic on Gulf Boulevard to clear so I could hang a right.

"Laverne?" I asked, when my jaw had unclenched sufficiently that I could form words again.

"Yes."

"I'm sorry. I didn't mean to insult Randolph. But if he wanders around loose, he could get hit by a bus."

A loud gasp came across the receiver.

The line went dead.

Either Laverne finally got the message, or she'd been hit by a bus herself.

Chapter Nine

A s I motored east on Central Avenue toward downtown St. Petersburg, it struck me just how much the skyline had changed in the past five years. When I'd left for Germany, St. Pete had still been a sleepy little tourist town. The kind that attracted what we jokingly referred to as "newlyweds and nearly deads."

Back then, the neglected city parks had been crammed with hordes of seniors languishing away on green benches, earning St. Pete the unenviable moniker of "God's waiting room." But as I drove into town today, I could see St. Pete had switched gears. Big time. In fact, it had stretched its cosmopolitan wings far enough to garner the envy of Tampa, its larger, somewhat lackluster cousin across the bay.

But, like the handful of ancient seniors yet inhabiting the city's low-rent housing towers, other remnants of St. Pete's past still clung desperately to life.

The few thrift stores and junk shops still able to find venues had moved six to ten blocks further west down Central Avenue. Most now split the rent by sharing space with local artists and three-table coffee shops. Familiar restaurants, once the only choices among a handful of offerings, now faced so much competition they'd been forced to spruce up their menus and service or their tables remained empty throughout the day.

I checked the address I'd written down. I'd been right. The offices of Angela Langsbury's attorneys were in one of the smattering of old, gray skyscrapers that stuck out around downtown like a hobo's remaining rotten teeth. Constructed mostly in the 1960s, the dull, uninspired buildings didn't have enough ambition to stretch much beyond ten stories. As a result, they were quickly being overrun and dwarfed by the dozen or so posh new condo towers currently under various stages of construction.

I took a good look at the skyline and tried to memorize it. As fast as the city was changing, it would never look exactly this way again. The snapshot taken in my mind, I set my sights on a new goal—finding a parking space.

My run-in with Nancy, combined with an impromptu lesson in grunt aerobics, had set me back about fifteen minutes. Downtown was an easy, straight shot east from the beach on First Avenue South. I'd made good time. The trip had taken less than twenty minutes. Unfortunately, finding a parking spot added ten more. By the time I reached the offices of Gallworth & Haney, I was nearly half an hour late.

"Hi, I'm Val Fremden," I said to the receptionist as I burst through the door. "I have an appointment with Ms...uh...Dimdum."

"Ms. *Dimson* was expecting you," the receptionist said.

As I studied the face of the irritatingly attractive young woman, I had a feeling the raised eyebrow she was shooting at her computer screen was actually meant for me.

"Right. Sorry. I ran into traffic."

"Have a seat," the stunning blonde said sourly, as if she found my mere presence somehow disgusting.

I waited on a couch and pretended to read magazines for nearly twenty minutes. But lifestyles of the rich and ridiculous didn't interest me. I fiddled with my phone, but didn't have anyone in particular to call or text. In comparison to the portraits of the posh people lining the waiting room walls, my life, I realized, was kind of mediocre.

Geez. Maybe even sub-par....

The oppressive ostentatiousness of the room pressed down on me until it became unbearable.

I stood up to leave.

As I did, a buzzer sounded. A tinny voice came over a speaker in the ceiling.

"Ms. Dimson will see you now."

The receptionist's pretty but unpleasant face popped in the doorframe. Her pert, perfect lips parted and said, "Follow me."

I trailed behind the slim, beautifully dressed woman feeling like a slob who'd just crawled out of a dumpster. She led me down a hall and stopped in front of a door with a gold-plated nameplate. Etched in it was the name Darlene Dimson.

The receptionist rapped quickly three times, opened the door, and without another word, left me to fend for myself.

I took a tentative peek inside and nearly gasped. Darlene Dimson was one formidable-looking woman. Scary, even. She was thin and pale. Her narrow face featured a long, pointed nose offset by a pair of dark, sunken eyes like a raven's. Atop her head sat a mass of blood-red hair, fashioned in a knot that reminded me of a cinnamon bun. Or maybe a huge blood clot.

"Hello? Ms. Dimson?" I said. "Thanks so much for rearranging your schedule to see me."

"Right," she said sourly. "Come in. Let's not waste any more time, shall we?"

No doubt she was ticked off about my being late. I tried to make nice by complimenting the picture of a halfway decent-looking man in a silver frame on her desk.

"Who's the handsome guy?" I asked.

Dimson looked me up and down with those black, sunken bird eyes. "Timothy Amsel."

"Mr. Amsel has a son?"

The raven eyes narrowed and shot right through me. "You know him?"

"No. I just saw a picture of his father in the paper. You know, with the mayor."

Her face relaxed the slightest smidgen possibly discernable by the human eye. "Tim Amsel doesn't have a son. That's Mr. Amsel himself."

Really? What kind of egomaniacal jerk has a picture of himself that's thirty years out of date?

"It looks like a college graduation picture," I said. "What school did he attend?"

Dimson looked pained, as if she were in the middle of having a stroke.

"How about we stick with the deposition, Fresno?" she said.

"Fremden. Sure."

"I prepared the document. All I need you to do is sign it."

"Shouldn't I be interviewed? I mean, I thought I was supposed to..."

"You want to write your own deposition?" Dimson hissed. "*Fine.* Write it on your own time. I'm doing this pro bono." She checked her watch. "I've got another appointment to get to."

"Well...uh...."

As I fumbled for words, Dimson glared at me in disgust.

"Ugh! Just take this one with you, Frampton," she said. "If you don't like it, type up a new one. I really don't give a shh...sugar. Just make sure I have it back by Monday morning. The hearing is at eleven."

"Fremden. Well, I...uh...."

Dimson stood up and blew out a sigh. "Look, Framsen, I thought pre-preparing the document would be the easiest way, but you obviously have other ideas. Like I said, get it to me by Monday."

"Okay."

"I trust you can you find your way out."

"Yes."

And I can't wait to leave.

THE BEADY-EYED BROAD had given me the bum's rush. When I got back to my car, I still had an hour left on my meter. I considered walking the six blocks to Chocolateers for a chocolate-covered cherry fix. But then I realized J.D.'s offices were just around the corner. I needed to make some headway in finding Goober.

J.D. owed me a favor. It was high time to cash it in.

I tucked the deposition folder under Maggie's driver's seat and hotfooted it over to see Laverne's ex-boyfriend, Mr. J.D. Fellows, Esq.

It'd been a while since I'd been to his office, and I'd forgotten how posh it was. The furniture and art were even fancier than at Gallworth & Haney, but somehow it lacked the other place's cold ostentatiousness. Maybe it was because the receptionist was actually *nice*. She offered me a coffee, and before I'd had a chance to take a sip, J.D. came out to greet me wearing one of his immaculate, tailor-made Armani suits.

"You always make me feel like a fashion 'don't,'" I quipped.

J.D. rocked back on his heels and spread his arms out to his sides. "Not exactly the image that comes to mind of a guy who'd break into your house to steal a tacky figurine and a handful of marshmallow ghosts."

Normally the epitome of what one would expect from a top-drawer business professional, J.D.'s unusual candor surprised me so much I actually let out a little laugh.

"That's something new," I said.

"I'm working on it," J.D. said with a shrug. "Laverne says I'm too stiff. How'd I do?"

"Not bad. Is that a new suit?"

"Yes. As you may recall, Laverne sold three of my best suits in that ridiculous neighborhood yard sale of yours."

"Oh. Yeah. Sorry about that."

"Somewhere, some preschooler's looking good for kindergarten graduation," he joked. "At least Laverne gave me the entire fifteen dollars she got for them."

We exchanged eye rolls and burst out laughing.

"Life is weird," I said. "You know, never in a million years would I have put you and Laverne together. But somehow, you two click."

"Click*ed*," J.D. corrected. "As you know, we're not together anymore. But I hope to earn my way back into her good graces."

J.D. looked down at his Gucci loafers and shook his head. "But you're right, Val. I never would have put us together, either. But as Laverne says, the heart wants what the heart wants."

I blew out a breath between my pursed lips. "That it does."

I followed J.D. into his office and blinked twice. Every time I'd ever been in it, I felt as if I'd been transported into another dimension, where everything was off scale and out of whack. When he and I'd walked down the hallway, the top of J.D.'s silver-haired head had come to just above my elbow. But once he took his seat in his custom-made mahogany desk, he towered a good two feet over me as I sat cowered in the short-legged chair opposite him.

I wonder if this is how Alice felt when she was in Wonderland....

"I remember the first time I was here," I said to the mighty J.D. up in his impenetrable tower. "You helped me track down the heir to Glad and Tony's will."

"I remember, too. You wouldn't take no for an answer. You were spunkier then."

"And *you* were grumpier."

J.D. chuckled. "I suppose I was. Some changes are for the better. But not all of them. Take a look at *that* one."

J.D. pointed out the window and scowled.

"I used to be able to see the boats in the harbor," he grumbled. "Now all I can see is somebody's lousy balcony. That new Ovation condo tower killed my view."

"Sorry."

"What can you do?" J.D. shrugged and put away his sour face. "Anyway, what brings you here, Val?"

"I'm ready to cash in my You-Owe-Me. You said you'd help me find Goober, remember?"

"Yes. Of course. What have you got so far to go on?"

"Not much. Can I borrow a notepad?"

J.D.'s silver eyebrows shot up.

"Uh...sure," he said, and handed me a legal pad.

I took it, wrote out the word PObbLE, and handed it back to him. "Do you have any idea what that could mean?"

J.D. studied it a moment and sighed. "I'm an attorney, Val, not a cryptologist. I give up. What is it?"

"It's a note I found inside a gift Goober left me."

"What kind of gift?"

"Does it matter?"

J.D. shrugged. "It might."

"It was in a tobacco tin...hanging on a redneck dreamcatcher."

"A *redneck dreamcatcher?*"

"I didn't say it was a *nice* gift."

J.D. did his best to stifle a smirk. "Okay. What else do you have?"

"Well, I know Goober disappeared somewhere between Lake Wales and St. Pete nineteen days ago."

"Did he say anything to you the last time you saw him? Any suspicious behavior?"

"Not really. But I know he'd gotten a check for ten grand about a week before he disappeared."

J.D perked up and leaned across his desk toward me. "Ten grand? For what?"

"I don't know. I asked him, but he said if he told me, he'd have to disappear. And then...geez...well, he *did*."

"Strange. Did he say why he'd have to go?"

"No. Well, yeah. One thing. But it was a joke."

"What did he say?"

"He got a letter from the AARP. He said he had to go because they'd found him."

J.D. rested his head on his fist. "The AARP finds everybody eventually."

"That's what *I* told him."

"You have the tag number for the RV?"

"No. But I'll call Cold Cuts and get it from her."

"Okay. And what's Goober's real name again?"

"Gerald Jonohhovitz."

"Can you spell that?"

"Sure. But it may not matter. Tom's already run it through all kinds of databases. He didn't get a hit."

"Maybe he spelled it wrong."

I shrugged. "Maybe."

"Or maybe it's an alias."

"That's what I'm worried about. What if he's...you know, *running from the law?*"

J.D. leaned in toward me. "Well, then, that's where an attorney comes in handy. We cover both sides."

I nodded. "So what do we do now?"

"I recommend we interview Goober's other known associates."

"You mean friends?"

"Uh...sure. Winky, Jorge, anybody else you can think of."

"What should I ask them?"

"Don't worry about that. You set up the meetings...say tomorrow afternoon? We'll do it together."

"On a Saturday?"

"My social calendar's opened up since Laverne and I split up."

"Oh." I started to say something, but hesitated.

"Was there anything else?" J.D. asked.

"Just one more thing. Did you hear about Sunset Beach? Some developer wants to tear down Caddy's and Winky's donut shop and build a condo tower."

"Yes, I've heard."

"Aren't you upset? It'll be right next to your house. I was kind of hoping you could help me start the legal work for some kind of protest. You know, questioning the environmental ramifications?"

J.D. looked at me solemnly. "Sorry. I can't help you there."

My jaw tightened. "Why not?"

"It would be a conflict of interest."

"What are you talking about, J.D.?"

"I sold my house to Progress, Inc."

"What?!" I screeched.

"This Amsel fellow wanted it for a pre-construction office while he builds the place. As soon as my unit is done, I'll be moving to the Ovation right over there." J.D. nodded toward the window. "As they say, if you can't beat 'em, join 'em."

I picked my jaw up off the floor.

"J.D., where's your loyalty?"

J.D. sighed tiredly. "I don't get paid for loyalty, Val. I get paid for results. Set up the meetings, and let's see what we can do to find your pal Goober."

Chapter Ten

After spending the morning dealing with two different attorneys, I thought it was a pretty safe bet the low point for my day had already gone by.

I was wrong.

As I walked back to my car, a light-green slip of paper waved at me from my windshield.

Crap on a cracker!

Not only did I have a lousy parking ticket. Some jerk had reached inside Maggie and stolen my stash of green Tic-Tacs.

That's what I get for trusting people enough to leave the convertible top open.

I jerked opened the driver's side door and plopped down on the seat. I was so hopping mad I barely felt the molten heat of the red vinyl as it scorched my thighs. I reached down and felt under the seat for Langsbury's deposition folder.

Unbelievable! Some dirtbag took it, too!

For a brief second, I thought about running up and getting another copy from bird-faced Dimson. But I was out of quarters *and* patience. Besides, the freaking meter patrol vehicle was heading my way. I didn't need another twenty-five-dollar parking ticket. My good deed to get Langsbury off scot-free had cost me enough already.

It was time for that chocolate fix.

I turned the ignition and blew a noisy cloud of blue exhaust in the meter patrolman's face.

Look out, Chocolateers. Two dark-chocolate covered cherries are about to meet their fate.

WHEN I PULLED UP TO my house, I was surprised to see my neighbor Nancy outside without her binoculars. She was in her front yard, flailing around. She'd either had an aneurism or she was doing jumping jacks. As I cut the engine on Maggie, I could hear her grunting from across the street.

Oh my lord! She's doing grunt aerobics!

Nancy waved jazz hands at me mid-jumping jack. I waved back and checked my gut's ever-reliable guilt-o-meter.

Nothing. Not a jot.

I shot Nancy a grin and climbed out of the car. As the door slammed closed, I heard a hissing sound like a tire going flat.

"Pssst."

The noise was coming from the direction of my neighbor Jake's house. I looked over the hedge and spotted him. He was kneeling in the grass, waving at me. Jake dropped his hairy handful of dandelions, stood up, and ambled toward me like a bald chimpanzee dressed in a wife-beater t-shirt and shorts.

"I see Nancy's given you the 'Spruce-Up September' talk," I said as he approached.

"Yeah." Jake nodded in Nancy's direction. "I decided to pull some weeds and watch the show. I think the old girl's lost it."

I bit my lip and confessed. "I kind of told her there was such a thing as 'grunt aerobics.'"

Jake smiled at me like one evil genius to another. "Why?"

"Don't ask. Hey, did Laverne talk to you about finding a way to smuggle Randolph out of town?"

Jake glanced across the street again. "Is that Nancy's husband?"

"Uh...no. It's Laverne's pig. So, I take it she didn't talk to you."

"No. I think I would've remembered that conversation."

"Come with me." I led Jake inside my front door. "I'll call Laverne. It's time we got this whole pig thing wrapped up."

"Like a pig in a blanket," Jake joked.

I shot him some side-eye. "Uh, yeah. No."

"WELL, NOW I'VE SEEN everything," Jake said as he peered over the fence into Laverne's covert compost pen aka pig pen. "Hi, Randolph."

Randolph grunted.

"Do you think he actually knows his name?" I asked.

"Sure he does," Laverne said. "*Don't* you, Randolph?"

Randolph grunted again.

"She's right," Jake said. "Pigs are smart. And pretty social. It's been proven they can learn their names by the time they're just a few weeks old."

"How can they prove that?" I asked. "All a pig can say is 'oink.' It's easy to know your name if it's the only word your mom can say."

Jake sighed and rolled his eyes. "I meant the names *humans* give them, smarty pants."

"So, do you have much experience training pigs?" Laverne asked, as if she were conducting a job interview. "I don't want Randolph's feelings hurt. He's quite a tender little thing."

"I bet he is," I joked.

Jake ignored my comment. "What do you want him to learn?" he asked Laverne.

"Mostly that he needs to stay in his pen and not grunt, so Nancy Meyers won't find him."

Jake nodded as he thought it over. "Okay, I think I can help with that."

"And I wish he wouldn't beg for food all the time," Laverne added. "I worry he's eating too much. But he always seems so hungry. And he's so cute, it's hard to say 'no' to him."

Jake laughed. "Pigs are masters of deceit, Laverne."

Laverne's doe eyes doubled. "No!"

"Yep. Actually, they've been known to *intentionally* mislead other pigs away from a feeding spot, just so they can go back and get all the food for themselves."

"That's rather piggish," I said.

Jake shook his head at my lame joke. "I'll work on teaching Randolph to stay put, and reward him for not grunting. In the meantime, you two should figure out a date for him."

"You mean like on MatchMate?" Laverne asked. "Or would it be Matchpig? No. I'm sorry. I think he's much too young to be dating."

Jake's eyes met mine for a moment.

"Sorry Laverne," he said. "I wasn't clear. I meant you should decide on a date for him to go. Randolph's no pot-bellied pig."

"That's what I told Val," Laverne said, and crinkled her nose up at me.

"What I mean is, in a couple of months, he could outweigh us all," Jake said. "By the end of the year, you could saddle and ride him. Listen, I've got a buddy near Ocala who has a petting zoo. Maybe he could take him on."

"I'll have to see it first," Laverne said, tears welling in her eyes.

"Of course," Jake said softly. "How about we start tomorrow."

Randolph grunted happily, and we all nodded and agreed to the deal.

WHILE SNOGS DASHED around the backyard like dryer lint caught in a tornado, I put a call in to my old friend Cold Cuts about the tag numbers for Goober's RV.

"I take it that means you haven't found him yet," she said.

"Right."

"Well, when Goober picked it up, the tag number was GLAD ONE, but he could have changed it," she said.

"GLAD ONE? After my mom? That's really sweet," I said.

"It was the least I could do, seeing as how you let me keep the RV, even though I know it broke your heart a little to lose it."

"Thanks."

"So, we're still on for lunch tomorrow?"

What? Oh, crap! I forgot all about it!

"Absolutely," I said. "See you around noon?"

"Perfect. Gotta go."

I hung up and called J.D.

"Listen, J.D. The tag number for the RV is GLAD ONE. Unless Goober changed it. And I can't make it tomorrow for the interviews. Something came up. Will Sunday work for you?"

"Pathetically, yes," J.D. replied. "Like I said, my social calendar is wide open."

"Okay, then. My place at ten?"

"I can't wait."

Chapter Eleven

"So what did you do today?" Tom asked as he came through the door Friday evening.

Let's see...I taught our nosy neighbor grunt aerobics, met with a bird-faced attorney to save my writing instructor's bikini wax plans, talked with a dwarf about tracking down a missing derelict, got a parking ticket, got robbed, and had a heart-to-heart with Laverne about letting go of a stow-away pig.

"Nothing much. How about you? Has Greg from Caddy's shown up?"

"No. Not yet. But today I decided to take a look into this Tim Amsel guy. You were right. He's a real piece of work."

"What do you mean?"

"He's built up a pretty bad reputation over the years."

"Really? Like what?"

"He's had more than a few legal suits over shoddy workmanship on his building projects. And...well, something really odd."

"What?"

"I dunno...." Tom hesitated. "Either it's a huge coincidence, or something fishy's going on."

"What?"

"A few years ago, the guy who sold him property for a project down in Boca Raton went missing, too."

I sucked in a deep breath. "I don't get it, Tom. What would be in it for Amsel if the seller disappeared? He already has the property."

"Apparently, the guy in Boca owned the property mortgage-free. Amsel worked out a deal with him to provide owner financing."

"Why would the owner do that?"

"Amsel made it worth his while by giving him a pretty decent rate of return on the note."

"Is that illegal?"

"No. Not at all. But the thing is, according to the guy who investigated the case in Boca, the mortgage had an unusual stipulation. It said that if the seller died for any reason, the debt would be erased and the note would be automatically satisfied...like it had been paid in full."

"Oh."

"Val, do you know if Greg owned Caddy's outright?"

"No. You should ask Norma. She'd know."

"I can't. She's disappeared, too."

"What?"

"The investigators working the case found scuffmarks and footprints in the parking lot at Caddy's. They said it looked as if there'd been a struggle. That lot's made of crushed shell. They made some print castings, but they lacked any real defining detail. So far, all they could determine was that they came from two different individuals. One looked like a men's shoe size twelve. It's been confirmed that's the same size Greg wears. The other was slightly smaller. Possibly a man's size eight or a woman's size ten walking shoe."

"Geez, Tom. I wonder if those footprints could be Norma's."

Tom came up and rested both hands on my shoulders. "Do me a favor, okay? Keep this under your hat. I really shouldn't have told you."

"Then why *did* you?"

Tom looked at me as if I had a bug on my nose. "Because we're a *team*, Val. I don't like keeping secrets from you."

My gut guilt-o-meter spun off the charts.

"Okay," I said. "I guess there's something I should tell you, too."

"What?"

"Wait here. I'll be right back."

I slipped out from Tom's grip and padded to my office. I returned with the slip of paper that had the word PObbLE on it. As I approached him, Tom had a look on his face I'd never seen before.

I wasn't sure, but I thought it might have been *fear*.

"Uh...here. Look at this," I said, and handed him the paper.

Tom looked down at it, let out a breath, then laughed nervously. "You nearly gave me a heart attack, Val."

"What? Why?"

"I thought for a second this was a pregnancy test."

I burst out laughing. "No way. If it was, you'd have heard me screaming all the way from your desk at the police station."

Tom shook his head. "I have to admit, I'm relieved."

"I wouldn't worry too much about that," I said. "I think my time for having kids has come and gone."

Tom gave me a hug and a kiss, then asked, "So, what *is* this, then?"

"I found it inside the Skoal tin hanging from Goober's dreamcatcher."

Tom scrunched his face. "Huh. What does it mean?"

I shot Tom a look. "If I knew that, I wouldn't be asking *you* now, would I Sherlock?"

Tom grinned. "Fair enough. So, you haven't heard another word from him? No postcard or anything?"

"Nope. But while you're away fishing on Sunday, I'm going with J.D. to interview Jorge and Winky. He wants to see if they can remember anything that might be helpful."

"And what's on the agenda for tomorrow?"

"Cold Cuts is coming over for lunch. And she's probably going to have to bring Freddie with her. You know, Bill's dad."

"The crazy, naked fisherman guy?"

I winked and pulled the trigger on my finger gun. "That's the one. Care to join us?"

Tom gritted his teeth. "I'd love to. But I think my SUV needs a good scrubbing."

"Wash Maggie, too, and I'll let you off the hook."

Tom grinned. "Deal. So, is this the only clue you've got?"

"Yes, besides some random things I remember Goober saying."

"Like what?"

"It sounds kind of crazy, but Goober got a junk-mail letter from the AARP. I remember him saying it was a signal that it was time to move on. I dunno, Tom. It was almost like he was some kind of fugitive, and getting the AARP notice meant his location and identity had been uncovered."

"Hmmm." Tom placed his index finger over his upper lip like a moustache. "That's interesting. I mean, if he actually *was* on the run, the AARP thing could have been taken as a sign he'd been discovered. You know, those marketing companies have better tracking systems than NASA and the FBI combined."

I crinkled my nose. "I'm serious, Tom."

"So am I."

"You said Goober's name wasn't in your databases. Do you think Gerald Jonohhovitz could be an alias? That maybe Goober's some kind of spy or something?"

"I doubt it, Val. It's probably just a misspelling. Sorry, but I just can't picture Goober having enough brain cells to work for the CIA."

"Did you know Goober has two navels?"

Tom looked at me funny. "What?"

"You know how he never takes his shirt off, even to go swimming?"

"Uh...yeah, now that you mention it."

"I saw his belly once. When we were hiding out from those crazy RVers in Lake Wales. It looked like he had two navels, Tom. When I asked him about it, he said he was shot in stomach. That it was scars."

"Well, that's more plausible than him being a space alien," Tom quipped.

I punched Tom on the arm. "I'm trying to be serious, here. It would mean Goober was working in some kind of profession that could get him shot!"

"Geez! Take it easy, Val. Or it could have just been another one of his ludicrous stories."

I hated to admit it, but Tom had a point.

"Don't worry so much, Val. Like I said before, I think Goober's just off doing his thing. He'll turn up soon."

"I hope so."

I slumped onto a barstool at the kitchen counter. Tom came up behind me and wrapped his arms around me.

"I tell you what," he said. "As soon as I find Greg and get this case solved, I'll take some time off and we'll follow up on whatever clues you and J.D. dig up on Sunday."

"You'd do that?" I asked, squirming around to face him.

"Of course. Like I said, we're a team. Now, how about dinner. Are you hungry? I got the stuff to make broccoli and broiled pork chops."

Pork! I should tell Tom about Randolph!

I winced. "Well, I do have one more thing—"

"Don't tell me," Tom said. "You'd rather have the pork chops fried. But frying isn't good for us. But how about a drink before dinner?"

"Uh...sure. But I wanted to—"

"Try this," Tom said, and pulled a brown bottle from the fridge. He twisted off the cap and handed it to me.

As he leaned over and disappeared behind the fridge door to grab a bottle for himself, I took a sip. It tasted so bad I nearly spurted my mouthful through my nose.

"Gaaa!" I gargled. "What *is* this?"

"Kombucha," Tom said. "It's supposed to be good for you."

I looked at the label. It described the drink as, "*Green tea fermented with a symbiotic colony of bacteria and yeast.*"

What the frick?

"How is it?" Tom asked as he closed the fridge and opened his bottle.

"Tastes just like the description on the label," I said cheerfully. "Go on, take a big slug. I can't wait to see how you like it."

Chapter Twelve

"Hey there," Tom said.

I cracked open a bleary eye. I was still face-down in bed, not wanting the day to start. But the aroma of a freshly brewed cappuccino gave me just enough incentive to roll over.

Seeing Tom with his hair still tousled from sleep was almost enough to make me smile. The sight of two coffee cups in his hand pushed my lips over the edge.

"Hey," I squeaked in my morning voice. "May I say, you've never looked more handso—"

Before I could finish my sentence, I was French-kissed by a wet, pink slug. It was attached to a wriggling clump of fluff.

"Snoggles wanted to say good morning, too," Tom said with a grin.

"Ugh!" I groaned and sat up in bed. "I just got used to having *one* man around the house. I don't think I can take *two* morning people at once. It's against the law, isn't it?"

Tom laughed. "Here, maybe this will help." He handed me a cappuccino. Before I could stop him, Snogs licked the milky foam dripping from the side of my cup.

"See how handy he is?" Tom joked. He picked up Snogs and held him to his chest. "Come on, pup. Let's go."

"Wait! Where are you going?"

"I'm taking Snoggles for a walk so we can both avoid the wrath of the un-caffeinated kraken."

"Ha ha."

Tom leaned over and kissed me on the nose.

"Thanks for bearing the brunt of taking care of Snoggles," he said. "Enjoy your cappuccino in peace."

I snuggled back into the pillows and sighed.

"Thanks. I will."

I GOT OUT OF THE SHOWER to find Tom had prepared a sensible breakfast.

Oh joy.

It was a green smoothie and a yogurt cup topped with blueberries and banana slices. I guess my typical breakfast with Count Chocula was headed the way of dinner with Ben & Jerry.

"Thanks," I said, and took a sip of green goop. "Yummy."

"Glad you like it," Tom said.

"Aren't you having any?" I asked, eyeing the olive-colored glop in my glass.

"Already finished. Listen, after I get done with washing the cars this morning, I thought I'd stop by the grocery store and pick up the ingredients to make dinner. How does cabbage and white bean soup sound?"

"Gaseous," I mumbled.

"What?"

"*Delicious*. I said delicious."

"Good. I'm heading out. See you later this evening. Have fun with Cold Cuts and Crazy Man."

"Thanks."

After Tom left, I poured the green goo down the sink and made an effort to clean up the house. I knew Cold Cuts couldn't care less about such things. But oddly, this morning my gut guilt-o-meter seemed to be directly gauged to how clean the toilet bowl was.

I'D JUST USED UP THE last of the Ty D Bol when the doorbell rang. I smiled, put Snogs in his cage for the moment, and answered the door.

"There you are," I said. "It's been too long!"

"I know," said the cute, brown-haired bohemian standing in front of me.

Cold Cuts was dressed in a flowing, light-yellow cotton dress. It was the kind of outfit I always dreamed of wearing to the beach, but somehow ended up in shorts and a t-shirt instead. A chunky necklace of shells and driftwood hung around her slender neck.

"You remember Freddie, don't you?" she asked, more for Freddie's benefit than mine.

"Sure," I said. "I'm Val."

I smiled at the tall, surprisingly muscular old man standing beside Cold Cuts, holding her hand like a child. He was naked except for a pair of sweatpants, which were accessorized by a brown leather belt wrapped around his waist.

"Hi, Freddie," I said.

Freddie's wandering eyes zeroed in on mine.

"Albert," he said.

I eyed him up and down. "Okay, Albert. Please, come in."

Freddie wandered into the house.

"What's with the outfit?" I asked Cold Cuts.

She blew out a laugh. "Don't ask. Just be glad he's wearing *something*."

"Is his dementia worse? Does he think his name's Albert now?"

"Huh? Oh. No. I told him we were coming to visit Albert, your dog. It was the only way I could entice him into the car. Well, that and the promise of beanie-weenie casserole for lunch."

"Oh, dear. I'm afraid I don't have any of that."

"Don't worry. I brought my own supply."

Cold Cuts handed me a yellow, covered casserole dish. "Put this in the fridge. And don't eat any of the stuff. I put his meds in it."

"Sure. Y'all make yourselves at home."

Freddie spotted Snogs and bolted past me, making a beeline for his cage. He crouched on his knees next to it and asked, "Is he a bad doggy?"

"No, Freddie."

"Then why is he in prison?"

"Oh. He's not. He was just waiting for you."

I opened the cage and two new best friends made their acquaintances.

"How's he doing?" I asked Cold Cuts as the two played tug-of-war with a rubber hotdog.

"Dementia is a terrible and strange disease, Val," Cold Cuts said. "It's weird. Sometimes Freddie can quote Shakespeare, and sometimes, like today, he can't remember that shoes go on feet."

"Huh." I put the casserole in the fridge. "How are you holding up?"

"Pretty well, thanks."

"And the Sunset Sail-Away?"

"The resort is going gangbusters. That's why Bill couldn't make it. Too much work to do. We couldn't leave it all to the help."

"Is he still doing the yoga lessons?"

"Yes. And the sunset sails, too. They're his favorite part of the job."

"I could imagine running a beach resort would be fun, but overwhelming."

"Sometimes, yeah. The work is unending. You never get it all done. You just give up for the day. But the people who come there remind me that I live in paradise, you know? They come for a quick vacation. I get to *live* there. When you think about it, Val, we're truly blessed."

"I can't argue with that. So, where do you want to go for lunch?"

Cold Cuts' eyes glanced over at Freddie. "Oh. I can't take him anywhere in public. Not in *that* getup, anyway."

"Then how about pizza delivery?"

"Sounds great. Pepperoni?"

I grabbed my cellphone and hit speed dial.

"One pepperoni pizza in paradise coming up!"

"THEY MAKE A GOOD PAIR," I said and opened the pizza box. I took out a slice and nodded toward Freddie and Snogs, who were chasing each other around the dining room table.

"Yeah, they do. Kind of like us back in our Date Buster days."

"Oh, lord!" I said and nearly choked on a mouthful of pizza. "I remember Milly telling me about the first time she ever saw you. You were dressed like some rock-and-roll roadie in that rainbow Mohawk wig. Remember? Those fake piercings all over your face?"

"Oh...geez," Cold Cuts said. "Scary Kerry. How could I forget?"

"Milly said you made the horrible guy she was out on a date with disappear like magic. I remember thinking, whoever that woman is, I want to know her secret!"

"And now you do."

"Which is?"

Cold Cuts grinned and flicked her long, brown locks to the backside of her shoulders. "Don't take crap off of *anyone*, of course."

I laughed. "Ahh...the secret to a long and happy life finally revealed."

Cold Cuts jabbed a pointy piece of pizza at me. "And don't you forget it! Oh! That reminds me. Any news about Goober?"

"No. But I did find something that might be a clue. I've shown it to Tom, Winky and J.D., but nobody seems to be able to figure it out."

"Sounds intriguing. I love puzzles. Let me have a crack at it."

"Okay."

I padded to the desk in my home office and retrieved the slip of paper I'd found in the Skoal tin. As I stepped back into the hallway, I was nearly bowled over by Freddie. He was scooting along on his hands and knees with the rubber hotdog in his mouth. Snogs was hot on his heels.

"I think somebody's hungry," I said to Cold Cuts.

She looked over at Freddie gnawing on the plastic weenie. "I think you're right."

"Here," I said. "Have a look at this while I warm up Freddie's lunch."

I handed Cold Cuts the enigmatic clue.

"Pobble?" she asked.

"Yep."

I took the casserole dish from the fridge and popped it in the microwave.

"Is it a name?" Cold Cuts called from the sofa.

"I don't know. Could be."

"How about a place? Like Pobble Beach?"

"I think that's Pebble Beach."

"I know. I was just brainstorming."

"Brain storm?" I heard Freddie ask. He dropped the rubber hotdog and looked out the window. "I don't see any brains."

The buzzer on the microwave dinged, saving me from making an inappropriate comment. I poured the beanie-weenie into a bowl and carried it over to Freddie.

"Here, let me," Cold Cuts said, and took the bowl.

She sat beside Freddie on the couch. As she patiently helped him with his lunch, I decided to take Snogs for a potty break.

"Snogs!" I called. He didn't answer.

"He's here. Under the couch," Cold Cuts said.

I got on my hands and knees. Snogs was busy chewing away at something.

"What have you got there?" I asked.

Snogs spit out his treasure.

It was the little slip of paper from the Skoal tin.

"Snogs, no!" I cried.

I scooped up the soggy mess, which had been reduced to three gluey lumps.

"What is it?" Cold Cuts asked.

"Oh. He got ahold of the clue."

"Oh no! I'm sorry. It must have fallen from the coffee table. Val, I don't know what—"

"Don't worry about it," I said. "It's okay. I'll just set the pieces on the windowsill to dry out."

"Pieces?" Cold Cuts asked. "Gee. I feel like a heel. I should have put it somewhere out of reach."

"It's okay," I said. "You hear me? Just take care of Freddie. You've got enough to worry about."

"Okay. Still, I'm sorry."

I walked into the kitchen and smoothed out the three miniscule, soggy blobs of paper on the sunny window sill. When I turned around, Freddie was standing right behind me.

He stared over my shoulder. Then he opened his mouth. A slice of hotdog fell out, and he said, "Post office box."

"What's he talking about?" I asked Cold Cuts.

"I don't know," she answered. Cold Cuts joined us in the kitchen, carrying the empty casserole dish.

Freddie pointed to the window. "Post office box," he repeated.

"There's no mailbox in the backyard, Freddie," I said.

"Post office box," he said insistently, and pointed at the windowsill.

I glanced at the scraps of wet paper and did a double-take. Separated, the three pieces individual read: PO 99 37. Something squirmed inside my brain.

"Sorry about that," Cold Cuts said, and took Freddie by the hand. "He just spouts off random stuff sometimes."

"Don't be sorry. I think he just gave me an idea."

"What?"

"The last time I saw Goober was downtown at the post office. I wonder. Could he have left me a note in his post office box?"

"Well?" Cold Cuts asked. "What are we waiting for?"

TWENTY MINUTES LATER, Cold Cuts' van pulled up in front of the open-air post office on First Avenue North and Fourth Street in downtown St. Petersburg.

My gut flopped in anticipation as I stared through the van's window at row upon row of small, black post office boxes. They were all tucked away from the weather beneath the twenty-foot-high ceiling of the post office's open porch. The one-of-a-kind porch was supported by beautiful, arched columns decorated with Spanish-looking tilework. It was a rather auspicious-looking place to search for clues to a rather inauspicious-looking man.

"You go run and check it out," Cold Cuts said from the driver's seat. "I'll stay here with Freddie."

"Okay."

I opened the van door and sprinted up to the black boxes. At first glance, it was overwhelming. There seemed to be thousands of them. Each box was no bigger than a slice of bread. Adorning every single one was a number and a brass lock.

I glanced over at the very last one. It was number four thousand. That meant the box number couldn't be 9937. It had to be 3799. Yes! I ran over to the box and stared at it.

Crap! Now what?

I looked over at Cold Cuts and motioned toward the lobby. She nodded. I sprinted to the door and tried to yank it open. It wouldn't budge. A sign on the window informed me that Saturday hours of operation were from 9 a.m. to 1 p.m. I checked my watch. It was five after one.

Crap on a cracker!

"It's closed," I said to Cold Cuts as I climbed into the van. "I guess it'll have to wait until Monday."

"YOU SURE YOU CAN'T come in?" I asked Cold Cuts as we sat in the van in my driveway.

"Yes. We've got to get back. Freddie doesn't like being gone from home too long."

I looked in the backseat. Freddie was sitting on his hands like a naughty kid waiting to see the principal. "I understand." I leaned in for a hug. "See you again soon. It was great catching up."

I waved goodbye, and as the van made its way down the street I realized that some things never changed. Cold Cuts was still the same fun-loving, brave-hearted woman she always had been, ever ready for a laugh and whatever adventure came her way.

I sighed as she and Freddie disappeared out of view, only to be replaced by the sight of a sweaty, Spandex-clad Nancy doing grunt aerobics in her front yard.

"Who was that?" she asked in between grunts.

"Some old friends," I said.

"You want to form a grunt aerobics club?" she asked.

"Not today."

I made a hasty retreat inside. When I walked into the kitchen, I saw Cold Cuts' yellow casserole dish.

Dang it!

I grabbed my phone and gave her a ring.

"Cold Cuts! You forgot your dish."

"Huh? Freddie, stop that! Sorry. The dish? Just keep it for now. I'll see you again soon. Come down and see me in Sarasota, okay?"

"Okay."

"I gotta go. Freddie, stop that!"

She clicked off the phone. I thought about what Tom had said about taking time off after the Caddy's case to help me hunt for Goober. If I found him myself, we could take that time for a vacation down at the Sunset Sail-Away Resort instead.

I made a wish, and as a talisman to seal the deal, I put Cold Cuts' casserole dish in the trunk of my car. That way, I wouldn't forget it when we headed down to see them soon. As I closed the trunk, I spotted J.D.'s white Mercedes pull up in Laverne's driveway.

I smiled and hoped the talisman would work for them, too, and the unlikely pair would find a way to reconcile their irreconcilable differences after all.

Chapter Thirteen

I made sure the bottle I grabbed out of the fridge was a beer, and popped it open. Then I flopped on a bar stool and watched the show. Tom was standing at the kitchen counter, chopping broccoli like a mad teppanyaki master.

"What'd that broccoli ever do to you?" I asked.

"Huh? Oh. Just taking out a little frustration."

"Why? What's happened?"

Tom blew out a breath and set his knife down.

"Greg Parsons became an official missing person case today."

"Oh."

"That's not it. I told my boss yesterday about Amsel's connection to the guy who went missing in Boca. Well, I got a call from him today saying to leave Amsel out of the investigation and to focus on other suspects."

"Why?"

"He didn't say outright, but I think the mayor's putting pressure on him. Seems that our mayor's a big fan of the Randy Towers project and doesn't want any 'undue bad press' effecting its 'forward movement.'"

"That's not fair. Isn't Amsel your main suspect?"

"Well, no. He's one of them. But the main focus of attention right now is his head waitress, Norma. She's involved in this somehow. But whether she's the perpetrator or a victim, we just don't know at this point."

"Does this mean Amsel's totally out of the investigation?"

"No. We're just supposed to focus on finding other 'more viable' suspects first."

"Who's more viable than Amsel?"

"That's what we're supposed to get off our duffs and find out," Tom said sourly. "I dunno, Val. I've got a bad feeling about Amsel, given his shady past."

"Then you should pursue it. You taught me once that your gut has better instincts than your brain. You told me gut instinct solves more cases than anything else."

"I know. And I still agree with that, Val. But as of right now, when it comes to Amsel, my hands are kind of tied."

I shot Tom a sympathetic frown.

Well, my *hands aren't.*

AFTER DINNER, WHILE Tom took Snogs for an evening walk to let off steam and broccoli-induced gas, I gave old lady Lansbury a call. Last time we talked, she'd told me Amsel was her brother in law, and he was staying with her. If I knew her address, I could tail him. The trouble was, I couldn't think of a very good reason to ask for her address.

"Yello?" Langsbury croaked into the phone.

"Hi. Uh...Mrs. Langsbury? It's Val. I ran into a snag with the deposition Ms. Dimson prepared."

"What do you mean?"

"I took it with me to read over, but someone stole the folder from my car. I thought I might drop by tomorrow and get another copy from you?"

"I don't have one."

"Oh. Uh...do you know where I could get one?"

"Sheesh, Val. It isn't some big mystery. Call Dimson."

"Oh. Sure," I laughed weakly. "Why didn't I think of that?"

"Yeah, that's what I'm wondering."

"Sorry to bother you. Have a nice weekend!"

I clicked off the phone before I humiliated myself any further. I could've asked Tom to look up her address, but then he'd have gotten suspicious. I glanced at the clock. I figured I still had around ten minutes before he'd be back with Snogs.

I made a split decision—as in I split over to Laverne's place.

When I rapped on her front door, Laverne opened it clad in a gold lame lounging outfit I'd only ever seen the likes of in a vintage *James Bond* movie. She held a glass of champagne in her right hand.

"Hiya, honey! What's up?"

"Hi, Laverne. Could you do me a favor? My teacher's retiring and I wanted to get her a gift. Do you know how could I get her address?"

Laverne's horsey head cocked sideways. "Well, just go to a dress store, sugar."

"Not a dre—" I began, then gave up on complicated explanations. "I mean...I need to find *the address* where she lives, Laverne. So I can have the gift delivered."

Laverne grinned. "Easy-peasy, honey. You got her phone number?"

"Uh...yeah."

"Come on in." Laverne waved me into her living room, which was so chock-a-block with tacky Vegas memorabilia that my fingers twitched for my Hammer of Justice.

Man, I could do some damage in here.

"Land line or cell phone?" Laverne asked as she sashayed over to a laptop open on her dining room table.

"Uh...I'm not sure. Land line, I think."

"With a land line, you can get anything. J.D taught me that, didn't you, sugar?"

Oh my gawd. I forgot J.D. was there!

I whirled around and tried my darndest to look surprised. "Hi, J.D!"

"Hello, Val," he said through slightly pursed lips. "Nice of you to drop by."

I winced. "Sorry. I didn't mean to interrupt your...uh...plans."

"Not to worry!" Laverne said. "Sit down. I'll show you how to do it."

I sat down in front of her computer. Laverne pushed the power button with the tip of a red lacquered nail. J.D. and I exchanged tense, silent faces as we waited for the screen to boot up. I felt like the bratty kid sister that two teenagers had been forced to take along on a hot date.

I started to get up from the chair. "Listen, I really don't want to bother you. This can wait."

"Nonsense!" Laverne said as the screen flashed to life. "Now, just enter the password."

"Uh...shouldn't you do that?" I asked.

"Why? You can do it. You need to learn how!"

I looked at J.D. His shoulders slumped. If he hadn't had a cocktail in his hands, I think he would have slapped his forehead.

"Uh...you sure you want me to put in your password?" I asked Laverne.

"Absolutely, honey."

"Okay. What is it?"

Laverne leaned close to my ear and whispered, "I don't know."

Really?

"Laverne, if you don't want me to know your password, why don't you just type it in yourself?"

"I trust you honey. Don't worry about it!"

"So, what's the password?"

"I don't know."

I was already chomping at the bit, anxious to leave the scene of their senior-citizen love nest booty call. Laverne's silly game was getting on my last nerve.

"Come on, Laverne!"

"Look, let me spell it for you, honey," Laverne said patiently. "You ready?"

"Yes."

"I-D-O-N-T-K-N-O-W."

It was *my* turn to slap my forehead. I turned to look at Laverne. "That's either the most idiotic or most brilliant password I've ever heard."

"That's our Laverne," J.D. said, and raised his drink at me.

Laverne beamed her pearly dentures at us.

"Okay, so now what?" I asked.

"Get on Find-a-Fool dot com and type in her phone number," Laverne said.

I did as instructed. "Yep. There she is. But there's no address listed."

"Must be a cell phone," J.D. said. "Does she own her place?"

"I'm not sure."

"Go to Pinellas House dot com and input her name," J.D. instructed.

"Is this legal?" I asked J.D.

"It's all part of open source intelligence. Who are you looking for, anyway?"

"Angela Langsbury. My murder mystery instructor."

J.D. groaned. I wasn't sure if it was from the absurdity of the whole situation or if he'd been forced to eat something Laverne had cooked.

"Bingo!" I said. "There's the history of her buying the place, and the address."

I scribbled it down on a piece of paper and was about to shut down the site when something caught my eye.

"Wait a second. It says here that two weeks ago, a quit-claim deed for the property was issued to Timothy Amsel."

"Who's that?" Laverne asked.

"Langsbury's brother in law. That's weird. She told me she couldn't stand him.

Laverne smiled at J.D. "Well, honey, people do strange things for love all the time."

"*I'll* say," J.D. remarked, and took a huge swig of his drink.

Chapter Fourteen

When I woke up Sunday morning, Tom had disappeared. But unlike Goober, Greg, and Norma, I knew where he'd gone. He'd had plans this morning to meet a buddy of his at Pass-a-Grille Beach so they could get an early start on some offshore fishing.

That meant I had the place to myself.

Ahhhhhh!

I laid around in bed until I couldn't stand it anymore, then I padded to the kitchen, made myself a cappuccino, and climbed up on the countertop to sneak the last twin-pack of Pop-Tarts I'd been hiding behind a flour canister in the top cupboard.

Tom's penchant for healthy eating had me absolutely jonesing for some junk food. I drooled as the blueberry tarts toasted, and bided my time by giving Snogs his morning overdose of cuddling. But as soon as the pastries popped up, Snogs was back on the floor and I was flopped on the couch, chewing on Pop Tarts, slurping cappuccino and scanning the pages of *St. Petersburg Times*.

Ironically, the front-page news was about the paper itself. The *St. Petersburg Times* was merging with the paper across the bay, the *Tampa Tribune*. From now on, the new paper would be called the *Tampa Bay Times*.

What happened to the "St. Petersburg" part? Geez! Would the entire history of my town be erased before I was in my grave?

"I hate change!" I grumbled to Snogs. He yipped conciliatorily, and jumped up high enough to lick my knee, which was sticking off the couch. I took a sip of cappuccino and turned the page. What I saw next soured my mood enough to curdle cream.

It was a picture of that pig-faced Tim Amsel. He was grinning, taking a mock swing with a sledgehammer at one of Caddy's porch posts! The caption read, "Demolition to begin next week."

My jaw locked tighter than an Easter-Sunday girdle.

"Oh, no it isn't! Not if *I* can help it!" I yelled, and flung the paper onto the floor, where Snogs gladly snapped it up like it was some sort of game.

But it wasn't a game. Even worse, I had no idea how I could possibly fight the system, especially now that J.D. had said he couldn't help me.

I glanced at the clock. It was 9:06 a.m. J.D. would be here in less than an hour to go with me to interview Winky and Jorge about Goober.

So much for my lazy Sunday.

I jumped up, got a quick shower, slipped on a sundress and headed out to give Snogs a morning walk. As we toddled down the driveway, I noticed that J.D.'s white Mercedes was still parked at Laverne's. A smiled began to form on my lips, but got waylaid by a nearby grunt.

Oh no! Randolph's loose again!

I scanned the bushes around Laverne's house for a chubby little pig face. I found one, but it was across the street. Nancy was out doing jumping jacks on her front lawn again.

Good grief. I've created a monster...that grunts.

"Nice day for grunt aerobics," she called out, red-faced and breathless.

"*Every* day is a good day for *that*," I said cheerily, and flashed Nancy a grin.

Hoo boy, Val. You're getting way too much sadistic pleasure from this....

AT 10:00 A.M. ON THE dot, J.D. appeared at my door looking dapper...and a bit sheepish.

"Good morning, Val."

I eyed him up and down.

"Hungry?" I asked.

"No."

"Sleepy?"

"No."

"Dopey?"

"*No!*"

I smirked. "Should I go on?"

J.D. rolled his eyes. "Okay. Let's get this over with. I spent the night with Laverne, okay?"

I did a poor job stifling a grin. "I thought you two broke up."

"We did."

"So, are you back together now?"

J.D. pursed his lips. "I'm not sure. She said she's been seeing this guy named Randolph. What kind of idiot is named *Randolph* anyway?"

"Well, it might—"

"Never mind," J.D. said, cutting me off. "You know, I'm not sure if Laverne invited me over to try and get back together, or so she could have one last chance to poison me."

I flinched. "Don't tell me you *ate* something over there!"

"Are you kidding? No. Well, not really. Just a piece of toast. And a fried egg. They seemed safe enough."

"Huh," I said, stepping outside. I locked the door and turned to J.D. "You know, you and I may have something in common, then."

"What's that?"

"I think Tom's trying to poison me, too. With a long, slow ingestion of broccoli."

J.D. turned his nose up. "Yuck."

"My sentiments exactly. So should we get going? Let's head to Winky's first."

"Good. I could use a real cup of coffee."

"Okay, then," I said, pulling the door closed behind me. "The sooner we start, the sooner we can find Goober."

"And the sooner we start, the sooner we'll get this over with."

"That's the spirit," I smirked. "Why don't we take my car, J.D.? I wouldn't want to get yours all sandy. Laverne's always telling me how persnickety you are."

"She is?"

"Yeah."

J.D. grimaced. "Oh, crap."

"HOWDY, Y'ALL," WINKY called to us through the service window as we walked up to the little concrete bunker known as Winnie and Winky's Bait & Donut Shop.

J.D. and I picked out the most reliable-looking table and chairs from amongst a handful of offerings that all appeared to have been rescued from a dumpster at some point. A minute or so later, Winky was at our sides, serving us hot, fresh coffee in Styrofoam cups.

"What happened to the ceramic mugs?" I asked.

"Shhh! They's all busted," Winky whispered, and shifted his eyes toward the shack. "You ain't the only one around here likes to smash things to smithereens."

"Hey Val and J.D.!" Winnie called from the service window. She shot Winky a look that made him jump like a scalded cat. "Y'all want a peanut-butter bomb?"

"Sure, make it two," I said, before J.D. could object.

"You've got to try one," I said to J.D. as he stared at me with a skeptical look on his face. "They're filled with custard crème and topped with peanut butter icing sprinkled with bacon bits. You haven't lived until you've had one."

"Yes," J.D. deadpanned. "I'm sure that my life up to now has just been a pointless sham."

"I'll fetch 'em," Winky said. "But I got to tell you, not ever'thang's hunky-dory here at the shop."

"You mean the proposed constru—" I began.

"Me an' Winnie's on the outs about the weddin'," Winky said, cutting me off.

"Oh. Why?" I asked.

"She wants to have a bunch a corny gay men at the reception. I mean, I got nothin' against any kind a folks, but I don't want no pure strangers at our shindig. I want it to be for friends and family only, you know what I mean?"

"I can understand that," I said.

"Val, talk some sense into her, would ya?" Winky pleaded.

"Uh...okay. Send her out with the donuts and I'll see what I can do."

"Here you go, on the house," Winnie said as she set the peanut-butter bombs on the table.

J.D. carefully picked one up employing a dainty pinch of his fingers. He sniffed it. He took a tentative nibble. The whites of his eyes doubled. He took a huge bite.

"Dear lord in heaven," he said, and looked up at Winnie's beaming face. "Do you have any more of these? I'll take all you've got—in a to-go bag."

Winnie laughed. "Sure thing, J.D. Glad you like 'em!"

"Like them? No," J.D. said. "I'm in love."

I grinned at the fastidious little attorney. J.D. was acting totally out of character. Maybe he actually *was* loosening up. Winnie turned to leave. I grabbed her arm.

"Winnie, what's with the corny gay men?" I asked.

"Corny gay men?"

"Winky said you want them at the reception."

"He said *what?*" Winnie's cute button nose crinkled like a pug's. A second later, her face smoothed out again. She shook her head. "That ding-dong. I didn't say corny gay men. I said Cornish game hens. You know, them fancy little chickens you serve whole?"

I held back a smirk. It wasn't easy.

"Oh. Sure," I said. "Well, maybe you should explain that to him before he calls off the wedding on account of it."

"Oh, he's not calling off *this* wedding," Winnie said. "Over my dead body!" Winnie stomped off into the shack, bellowing Winky's name.

"I wish all the world's problems were that easy to solve," J.D. said. "You going to eat yours?"

J.D.'s donut was gone.

"I most certainly am," I said, and swatted at J.D.'s hand. "Keep your mitts off!"

"Can't blame a guy for trying," he said, as Winky came stumbling out of the shop.

"Thanks for settin' Winnie straight on that one, Val. I don't know what you said, but it worked. She just told me she'd cancel them Cornish fellers if she could serve midget chickens for the reception dinner." Winky glanced over at J.D. "No offense intended."

J.D. grinned and shook his head. "None taken." He took a sip of coffee and cleared his throat. "So, why don't we get down to business. Winky, do you recall anything strange about Goober's actions in the days prior to his disappearance?"

"Hmmm. Lemme thank," he said. Winky turned a chair backwards and pulled it up to the table. He straddled it, laid his forearms across the top of the backrest, and nested his freckled face on top of his arms.

"You know, old Goober always did act a bit odd. Always comin' up with them schemes and stuff. You know? Like that pet crematorium gig. Remember?"

"How could I forget?" I said. "But I think what J.D. means is, did Goober ever tell you anything weird, like he had to leave town because someone was after him? Something like that?"

"Naw. Not really. He never had no visitors. Not even no bill collectors nor nothin'. I think there must a been good money in what he done for a livin'."

The check for ten grand. Winky knows something about it!

"Really?" I asked. "What did he do for a living?"

"Val, you know yourself. Goober was a natural-born fartiste."

My face collapsed like a two-dollar beach chair.

"Okay," I said, my hopes fading. "Anything else?"

"Yeah. I always wondered. How does a feller learn how to fart at will? I been practicin' all my life and never figured it out."

"I think our work here is done," J.D. said. He stood up so quickly his chair fell backward onto the concrete floor.

"All righty, then," Winky said. "But looks like their work's just gettin' started."

Winky nodded toward the beach. I turned in that direction and spotted two men carrying a big sign nailed to two fence posts. On the sign was an image of an ugly, boxy condo tower and the words, "Future Home of Randy Towers, brought to you by Progress Inc."

My jaw dropped as the men leaned the sign against the side of Caddy's beach bar and went inside. My fingers twitched for my Hammer of Justice. Good thing I didn't have it on me. I'd never find Goober if I was behind bars.

"Let's get out of here," I said.

"Just let me get the donuts first," J.D. said. He walked over to the service window with a twenty dollar bill, but couldn't reach the counter.

"No one ever thinks of the little people," he said sourly.

"Winnie!" I called out. "We're ready for the donuts."

She appeared in the window. I grabbed the twenty from J.D. and handed it to her

"This is too much," she said.

"Then you're charging too little," J.D. said.

Winnie stuck her head out the service window, spotted J.D. and beamed a proud smile at him. "Thank you, sir."

"You're welcome," J.D. said, and patted the sack in his hand. "These are delicious."

Winnie and Winky waved at us the entire time as we made our way across the sand to the parking lot.

"Odd," J.D. said. "Winky didn't seem bothered at all about his place being slated for demolition."

"No. He's not much for worrying."

"Takes it all philosophically, huh?"

"Well, I wouldn't say that. The only philosophical question I've ever heard him pondered is, 'What would happen if the whole world farted at once?'"

J.D. laughed so hard he farted himself.

"Excuse me," he said, his face as red as a beet. "I should have known better than to eat breakfast at Laverne's."

Chapter Fifteen

"How far is it to Jorge's place?" J.D. asked.

"Another ten minutes, give or take a traffic light," I said. "Why? You in a hurry?"

"No. I'm okay."

I glanced over at him in the passenger seat. "You look sweaty. Should I put the top up and turn on the AC?"

"I'm fine. I'm curious. Why couldn't Jorge have met us at Winky's donut establishment?"

"He offered to. But Goober used to live at Jorge's place. I was thinking we could check out his old room for clues."

"Oh. That makes sense."

I turned off Central Avenue onto Thirty-Fourth Street, also known as U.S. 19. We tooled past a few miles of ugly strip centers and chain stores. When I hit a pothole right past the Toyota dealership, J.D. groaned.

"You okay?" I asked.

"Yeah."

I sped through the green light and maneuvered onto the fancy new stretch of US 19. Like an interstate overpass, the new road bypassed the next fifteen miles of strip centers all the way to Palm Harbor. We weren't going the entire distance, but for J.D. it was still a trip too far.

"I'm not gonna make it, Val," J.D. said.

I looked over at him. He was the color of cream of broccoli soup. Sweat stained the pits of his once crisp, pink Polo shirt.

"Geez, J.D.! Are you having a heart attack? Don't die on me!"

"No...no heart attack," J.D. panted. "Food poisoning. Laverne's....need men's room. Now."

"There's not another exit for five or six miles. Can you make it?"

"I don't have much choice," he groaned.

J.D.'s gut gurgled loud enough to hear over Maggie's rumbling glass-packs. Having been a victim of Laverne's cooking myself, I knew we'd never make it in time.

"I'm pulling over," I said, and maneuvered Maggie into the emergency lane. I slammed on the brakes.

J.D. let out a flappy fart and a moan.

"Awgggh! I can't hold it in. What have you got that I could...you know...."

"Hold on."

I jumped out of the car, popped the trunk and scrounged around for something. My hand landed on Cold Cuts' yellow casserole dish. I grabbed it and handed it to J.D.

"Here. Use this," I said.

J.D. didn't blink twice. He grabbed the pot and started unbuckling his pants. I ran over to the driver's side, hit the ignition and then the switch to raise the convertible top on the car.

"Good luck," I said, and left him to it.

"Nearughguh," J.D. replied.

I walked to the back of the car and tried not to look as Maggie's top slowly rose up in the air, then fell down onto the frame, mercifully shielding me from the view of J.D., pants down, squatting in a casserole dish on the passenger floorboard.

I waited by the roadside a few minutes, being windswept by vehicles as they flew past us on the US 19 overpass. Finally, I yelled, "There's a box of tissues on the floorboard somewhere."

"Found 'em," J.D. said weakly.

I called back to him. "Should I—"

"Just give me another minute, please."

I winced. "Okay."

I waved off a truck full of construction workers that stopped to help, and tried to look cheerful and un-needy to others passing by. Finally, J.D. emerged from the passenger side of the car holding the yellow casserole dish in his hand.

"What should I do with this?" he asked.

If only Finkerman hadn't moved his office I'd have the perfect plan for it...

"Uh...I vote we just leave it here on the side of the road."

"Right."

J.D. set the dish on the pavement behind Maggie and climbed back into the passenger seat. I got in and started to fasten the clips to secure the ragtop, but a certain odor stopped me in my tracks. I glanced over at J.D.

"Mind if I put the top back down?"

J.D.'s face was the mottled greenish-red of a half-ripe tomato. He kept his eyes on the road straight ahead and said, "I think that's a judicious idea."

"MAY I USE YOUR RESTROOM?" J.D. asked as Jorge answered the door.

"Uh...sure. Come on in."

Jorge's place was a modest, 1950s ranch house like mine, only larger. It had a master bed and bath suite on one end, and two bedrooms and a bath on the other. The kitchen and living room were located in the center of the house.

I'd only been there twice before. Once was to celebrate Jorge's forti-
eth day of sobriety. The other was to celebrate his six-month mark without a drink.

Back then, Winnie and Winky had been living in the master suite.
Jorge had taken one of the smaller bedrooms on the other end, next to
Goober. He'd furnished the room with family mementos and a heart-
flinching collection of photos of his wife and kids who'd been killed in
a traffic accident. Mixed in among them were a few photos of Jorge and
his buddies during his former glory days on the police force.

It reminded me that, not too long ago, it had seemed that Jorge's
best days were behind him.

But sobriety and Sherryl had changed all that.

The photos of Jorge's deceased wife and children were still around
the house, but now they were joined by happy photos of him together
with Sherryl and her family. The whole house had a much lighter vibe.

"So where's Goober's room?" J.D. asked when he emerged from using the facilities.

"Look for the one with the 'Keep Out' sign," I joked.

"Oh. We took that down," Jorge said. "Come on, I'll show you."
As he led us to the room, he added, "I don't think you'll find much of
Goober left in here. Sorry, but we've been doing some renovations."

When he opened the door to Goober's old room, it was apparent
that Jorge and Sherryl were in the midst of plotting some diabolical
plan. Either that, or they were putting together something from IKEA.

"What *is* all this?" I asked.

"Well, I was going to tell you next time we all got together," he said.
"But...well, it's a crib."

"A crib?"

"Sherryl's pregnant."

"Oh my goodness!" I cried out. I gave Jorge a huge bear hug. "Congratulations! You know, I should have guessed when I saw the new
minivan out front."

Jorge rolled his brown eyes. "We kind of eloped last week." He showed me his wedding band. "Do me a favor, though. Keep it a secret for now. I haven't told my mother yet."

"I'm sure she'll be absolutely thrilled," I gushed.

"You think?" he asked hopefully.

"Absolutely."

Jorge sighed with apparent relief.

"Congratulations," J.D. said. He cleared his throat and asked, "So, Jorge, tell me what you've done to alter the room."

"Well, pretty much everything. We scrubbed it, painted it, put up new curtains."

"Did you find anything unusual when you were cleaning out the room?"

"Nada. Nothing."

"That's disappointing," J.D. said. "Has Goober had any mail delivered since he's been gone?"

"No. But He never used this address. He had a post office box downtown."

"Right," I said. "I'm going to check that out tomorrow, when the post office opens."

"Did he ever mention anything about traveling?" J.D. asked. "Any hobbies? Clubs? Professional associations?"

"Oh! He once told me he used to be a sociology professor," I said.

"Where?" J.D. asked.

"Who knows?" I said. "Goober told me teaching public school was the hardest time he ever did."

"So you think he might have been incarcerated at one time?" J.D. asked.

I shrugged. "Or he could have been joking. He loved to joke."

"Listen," Jorge said. "I'm sorry, but I've got to go pick up Sherryl."

"Okay," I said. "Let me know if you think of anything else."

"I will."

"You ready to go, J.D.?"

"Yes. Thanks for your time, Jorge. Good luck to you and Sherryl."

"Thanks."

J.D. took me by the elbow and led me toward the front door.

"I don't mean to be rude, but I want to go home and get a shower. Immediately."

"I totally understand."

As we climbed back into the car, J.D. turned to face me. "Val, promise me you won't mention a word of this to Laverne. It may be the difference between her choosing me or Randolph."

"J.D., Randolph is a pig."

J.D. pursed his lips. "Most men are."

"No I mean he's a hoof-footed, snout-faced pig."

J.D. nearly fell out of his seat. "What?"

I shook my head. "Laverne really didn't tell you? Randolph's her pet pig. She's got it in the backyard. We're hiding it so nosy Nancy won't turn it into pork chops."

"I would never allow that to happen," he said.

I smiled. "Look at you, coming to Laverne's rescue! You really *have* changed, J.D. You're a prince!"

"No," J.D. said tiredly. "I'm just Jewish."

Chapter Sixteen

J ust when I thought my day couldn't possibly turn out to be crappier than J.D.'s was, the universe had to go and prove me wrong.

After our visit to Jorge, I'd dropped poor J.D. off at his ugly orange house on Sunset Beach so he could "freshen up" before he caught a taxi back to Laverne's place. So, he was out of the picture when I arrived home.

Lucky him.

That made me the lone witnesses to the three-ring circus of stupidity playing out in front of my house on Bimini Circle.

As I drove up, I spotted Laverne running full-tilt along the sidewalk like an ancient praying mantis in heels. She was chasing a squealing, frolicking Randolph, who appeared to be having the time of his life.

Hot on Laverne's heels was a huffing, red-faced Nancy Meyers, swinging a fishing net attached to a ten-foot pole. Ape-man Jake brought up the rear, galloping along behind Nancy, half-heartedly twirling a rather limp-looking lasso.

It was a conga line of lunatics being led by a pig in aviator goggles.

Nearly every molecule of my being begged me to just keeping on driving past the scene.

But Nancy was gaining on Laverne, and I just couldn't leave the poor old gal to handle the wrath of the Knick-Knack Nazi all on her own.

I jammed Maggie into park in the middle of the street, jerked open the door and bolted out to join the maniacal chase. As I ran toward the unfolding disaster, something bounced up and down in the breast pocket of my shirt.

It was one of Winnie's peanut-butter bombs. I'd filched it from J.D.'s sackful while he was otherwise indisposed.

Wait a minute! I'm packing a pig lure!

I pulled the donut from my pocket and waved it in the air. Randolph's little snout went up. He stopped dead in his tracks, sniffed the air again and locked in on me. Laverne took a flying leap at him, but Randolph scrambled away just in time, and made a beeline right for me.

Great, Val. Now what?

Before I could answer that burning question, Randolph plowed into my shin and bowled me over in the middle of my lawn like a lone nine pin.

"Arrggghh!" I bellowed as I tumbled sideways onto the ground.

Randolph pounced on the donut. I pounced on him.

"You got him!" Laverne screeched. She added to her announcements of the obvious with the classic, "Don't let him go!"

"I wasn't planning on it," I grunted as I wrestled with Randolph in the grass, trying to maintain a grip on his round, porcine belly.

Laverne was panting like a chicken in a hot house as she skittered to a stop next to me. Her gold high heels glinted in the grass mere inches from my face.

High heels? Again? Really, Laverne?

"Why is he wearing goggles?" I asked, for lack of a better conversation starter. The effort caused me to nearly lose my grip on Randolph. I squirmed around until I was lying on the lawn sideways, spooning with a squealing pig in spectacles.

"He likes goggles," Laverne said with a proud grin.

She looked up and spotted Nancy heading toward us. Laverne's doe eyes doubled in size. "Oh Val! Now Nancy's gonna make me get rid of him!"

As if on cue, Nancy's ugly, mannish feet in ugly, mannish sandals appeared in my peripheral vision.

"Hush, Laverne," I said. "Let me do the talking."

"What's going on here?" Nancy demanded. "This is against every city ordinance in the book! You can't have a pig here!"

"Darn. You found out," I said, trying to look cheerfully outsmarted while lying in the grass with my arms around a pig. "It was supposed to be a surprise...for *you*."

I rolled over and pulled Randolph onto my lap. To my surprise, he grunted and nestled there peacefully. Maybe the sugar from the donut had kicked in and given him some kind of high.

Nancy eyed me suspiciously. "A surprise? For me? What are you talking about, Fremden?"

"Why, Spiff-Up September, of course," I said, trying to buy myself time to come up with a better lie.

"*Spruce*-Up September," Nancy corrected. "What about it?"

"Well...," I looked to Laverne and Jake for help, but from the expressions on their faces, I was totally on my own. "We...uh...we all thought we'd celebrate it with a...with a...*Hawaiian-style luau*."

I shot my sketchy, less-than-dynamic duo a look. "*Didn't* we?"

Laverne and Jake looked at me, then nodded at Nancy as their gaping mouths morphed into weak smiles.

"That's right," Jake said, apparently snapping into coherence. He hung his head dramatically. "But now the pig-roast surprise is ruined."

"Pig roast?" Laverne gasped. She gulped and stared at me wide-eyed.

I looked into Laverne's eyes, shook my head almost imperceptibly, then turned to Nancy.

"You were going to be the surprise guest of honor, Nancy. Laverne was raising the pig herself so we could have the best meat available. But if you don't want a luau in your honor, we'll get rid of the pig today."

Nancy looked as if she'd just swallowed a bratwurst whole. "Oh," she coughed. "Well, there's no need to be hasty."

"No, you're right," I said, and made a show of petting Randolph, who grunted contentedly. "Let's forget the whole thing."

"No!" Nancy nearly shouted. "I mean, when were you planning on having this surprise luau?"

"Uh...Tuesda—" I began, but Jake shook his head. "I mean Thurs—" Laverne shook her head. "Friday?"

Both of my accomplices nodded.

"Friday night," I said.

"Five days from now," Nancy said. "Well, I guess it won't be too much against the rules to keep the pig a few more days. And since it's not a surprise anymore, I have a most excellent idea. Why don't we have the luau at my place? I just got the shuffleboard court resurfaced and put new cushions on the patio furniture."

Nancy eyed us like a drill sergeant. No one dared speak.

"It is settled then," she said. "My place. Eighteen-hundred hours. Sharp."

"That's a lot of hours!" Laverne said.

"She means six o'clock," I said, then looked to Nancy for confirmation.

"Precisely," Nancy said. "So it is our plan, ja?"

I gave Jake and Laverne a hard stare. "Sure," I said. "We'd *all* be happy with that."

I didn't see how we were in any position to argue. Me especially, since I was sitting cross-legged on the ground with my arms wrapped around the belly of a pig wearing aviator goggles.

Besides, with any luck, the luau would never happen anyway.

TOM CAME HOME FROM his fishing expedition empty handed, except for a sackful of Big Bobby's barbeque. It smelled like hog heaven. And, because it wasn't on our healthy menu, it had me salivating like one of Pavlov's mangy dogs.

The thought of a meal without broccoli in it made my soul smile. I kissed Tom on the lips as he walked into the kitchen, and snatched the bag from his hands.

"Sorry, no fish," Tom said.

"We'll make do," I quipped, and opened the bag.

Tom touched my arm.

"Val. I *did* catch something. And it's kind of concerning."

"What? The flu?" I joked, my mind blurred by thoughts of juicy spare ribs.

"No. This."

I turned to make a joke, but stopped when I saw the concern on Tom's face.

"What is it?" I asked.

Tom set a clear plastic baggie on the counter. Inside was what looked to be a man's silver I.D. bracelet. I noticed a red Caduceus medical symbol etched into the left side of the smooth name plate.

"It's a life-alert bracelet," Tom said. "I snagged it trolling the bottom for flounder."

"I guess that's better than an old boot," I said.

Tom's face went deadly serious. "Val, I could have pulled up an arm with it. This bracelet was around someone's wrist at some point. It has saw marks on it. Like someone's been dismembered. A dead body could be out there in the Gulf right now."

The thought made my nose crinkle. "Maybe, but I doubt it."

"What? Why?"

"I think those twinkling green eyes of yours may finally need some cheater glasses, Tom. That's a novelty bracelet."

"What do you mean, novelty?" Tom asked, and picked up the baggie.

I handed him the eyeglasses I bought off a rack at a drugstore. "Take a closer look at the medical symbol. The staff has two L's wrapped around it instead of snakes. The L's stand for 'loser.' The script on the bracelet says, 'Notify authorities in case this person ever gets a life.'"

Tom shook his head. "You're right. It's a joke bracelet."

"Don't tell me you've never seen one?"

Tom shook his head. "I haven't."

"You need to get out more. They're all over eBay. It's a favorite tourist joke at Caddy's. Whenever he gets in one of his joking moods, Greg pulls this prank where he—"

I stopped myself mid-sentence and stared at Tom.

"Greg!" I grabbed the bag from Tom's hand. "Oh my word! This could be Greg's! He wore it a lot. It was like his standing joke."

Tom's eyes locked on mine. "And now he could be lying in a watery grave."

Chapter Seventeen

"When was the last time anyone saw Greg?" I asked Tom as he got ready for work. As usual, Monday morning had struck too early yet again.

"Not since early Thursday morning," he answered, and checked the fastener on his gun holster. "Parsons closed the bar down at two. The bartender working that night said he left around two-thirty. He was supposed to return for the afternoon shift around three that afternoon, but he never showed up."

"That's what Norma told me, too. I mean, that Greg was supposed to be in at three o'clock. And now you say no one can find her, either."

I eyed the baggie still on the kitchen counter. "What are you going to do with the bracelet?"

"Well, with Greg's case upgraded to a missing person report on Saturday, I'll file the bracelet as potential evidence."

"*Potential* evidence?"

"It's a novelty bracelet Val. Like you said, they made millions of them."

"But...." I argued.

"Don't worry. I'm still sending it over to forensics. Maybe the lab can find DNA or fingerprints on it. But I wouldn't hold my breath. It's not likely, given that it's been swimming around in saltwater for who knows how long."

I bit my lip and frowned. "Right."

"Okay. I gotta go," Tom said. He kissed me goodbye, stuck a foot out the front door, then turned around. "Oh. With the bracelet and everything, I forgot to ask you. How'd it go yesterday with J.D. and your search for Goober?"

I tried not grimace at the thought of J.D. taking a dump in a casserole dish. I decided a short, one-word answer would suffice.

"Crappy."

"Well, try not to get in too much trouble today, okay? I've got enough on my plate with Parsons and now the Jeen case."

"Jeen?"

"That's Norma's last name."

"Oh."

Tom shot me a mock smug look. "Finally, something you didn't know already. Listen, I really gotta go. Don't forget to walk Snogs."

"I won't."

At the sound of his name, Snogs came flying at us like a harpoon made from a dust cloth. Tom lifted him up and set him in my arms.

"You watch out for her, you hear me, Snogs?"

I laughed, kissed Tom again and closed the door. As the lock clicked into place, something pinged in my brain. I jerked open the door and called after Tom.

"Hey. Wait a minute. You called him Snogs! I thought you hated that name."

Tom pondered my words for a moment, then winked a sea-green eye at me.

"Huh. What do you know? I guess it kind of grew on me after all. Kind 'a like someone else I know."

I RANG UP GALLWORTH & Haney and got the snotty blonde receptionist.

"Hi. I was just calling to see if I could stop by and sign another copy of the deposition for Angela Langsbury."

"No," the woman huffed. "Your services are no longer needed. Ms. Dimson has acquired everything she needs, and is, in fact, headed to court as we speak."

Well, la-tee-da. I guess I'm too late for her again. Too bad.

"Well, good for her," I said, and hung up the phone. I felt more relieved than guilty. I had one less thing on my to-do list for today, and no longer having to go to Dimson's office lowered the dress code for the day significantly. My planned dress and heels got demoted to sandals, a jean skirt and a comfy t-shirt. As far as I was concerned, the whole thing was a win-win.

I got dressed, grabbed my purse, and tiptoed guiltily by Snogs in his cage. As I closed the front door behind me, a glint of sunlight caught my eye. It was arcing off one of the beer cans dangling from Goober's dreamcatcher hanging in my office window.

I bit my lip. I knew I should have been writing. But since class had been cancelled last Thursday, I hadn't touched my computer. Besides, right now I had a more important mission. Goober was still missing, and I needed to track him down.

The only useful clues I had were the post office box number Freddie helped me figure out, and the address on the postcard Goober'd sent me. Goober once told me he'd been a sociology teacher, but that info was pretty much useless. It could have been a fabrication. And I had no desire to search the entire US public and private school systems on the off chance they'd hired a nutty professor with a walrus moustache. Besides, who could even say what name he would have given them.

No. Right now, it was better to focus on the post office box clue. My plan for today was to head downtown and check it out. As I walked to my car, I waved to Nancy, who was in her front yard, jogging in place with weights in her hands.

That woman is a grunting aerobics machine!

"I see you're at it again," I called out.

"I (grunt) want to be in top shape for the (grunt) luau pool party!" she called from across the street. "I ordered (grunt) enough flowers so everyone can get laid."

My brain screeched to a halt.

What?

"Oh," I said. "Hawaiian leis, right."

I climbed into Maggie, hit the ignition, and wondered how long it had been since Nancy had gotten...a ring of flowers placed around her neck.

"I'D LIKE TO ENQUIRE about the owner of post office box number 3799," I said to the postman behind the service counter at the downtown post office.

He eyed me suspiciously. "What exactly do you want to know?"

"Uh...I'd like to know if the owner left instructions or perhaps another key? You see, I've...uh...lost mine."

"Oh. Sure, lady. Hold on."

The tired-looking clerk came back and slapped a form on the counter between us. "You'll need to fill this out. In triplicate."

"Um...okay. I'll just do it over there," I said, and pointed toward the narrow strip of counter designed for patrons to rest their elbows and packages on while they waited in line.

"Fine," he said dryly. "It'll probably take a couple of weeks to process the information. In the meantime, I just thought I'd let you know that falsifying federal documents is an offense punishable by fines, imprisonment, or both."

Something in my throat collapsed.

"Right," I croaked. "Thank you, sir. Is it okay if I...uh...take these with me and fill them out at home?"

The clerk peered over his bifocals and sighed. "Sure. Knock yourself out."

I backed out of the post office like a wanted criminal. As soon as I made it out alive, I ran to my car, jumped in it, and called Winky.

"What are you doing right now?" I asked.

"Uh...usin' the toilet."

"Ugh! Call me back when you're done!"

"Naw. It's all over but the paperwork." I heard a toilet flush. "What can I do you for?"

"I want to keep an eye on the post office and see if anybody comes to check Goober's box."

"You mean like a stakeout?" he asked, his voice rising at the end.

"No."

"Dang."

"Well, I mean, yeah. Like a stakeout."

"When?"

"Right now."

"All right!" Winky cheered. "Listen, Val, I ain't got no car. It's in the shop. But I can take a beach trolley. Be there in half an hour, give or take an hour."

"Okay," I sighed. "I've got another stop to make anyway. Meet you at the post office at say, eleven o'clock?"

"Eleven o'clock."

"Yes."

"Eleven o'clock," Winky repeated.

"Why do you keep saying that?"

"'Cause you told me to say eleven o'clock."

Maybe this isn't such a good idea after all....

"Listen, Winky, why don't we just—"

"Hold up a second. Here you go, mister trolley man."

I blanched. "You're already on a trolley?"

"Yep."

No turning back now.
"Okay, then, Winky. See you soon."

Chapter Eighteen

I was parked across the street from the post office in downtown St. Pete, waiting on Winky to arrive by trolley. I was wiping the sweat from my upper lip when I spied Angela Langsbury in my rearview mirror. She was hobbling down the street, her arm in a sling, her neck in a brace. I jumped out of Maggie and ran over to check on her.

"Geez, Mrs. Langsbury," I said, taking her arm. "I didn't realize you'd gotten injured in that scuffle."

Langsbury stopped limping and rolled her eyes at me. "I'm *not*, Fremden. It was Dimson's idea for me to wear this getup. Said it would garner sympathy with the judge."

"Oh." I let go of her arm.

"Thanks for the deposition, kid. Between these stupid props and your testimony, I got off the hook for the eighteen hundred bucks." Langsbury chuckled to herself. "You should've seen Victoria's flabbergasted face. Priceless."

"Uh... But I didn't—"

"Pretty clever of you, too, saying I'd even offered Victoria an early-bird discount. Gave the whole thing a ring of authenticity."

How ironic, considering there was nothing authentic about it.

Langsbury tugged at the fake neck brace. "Yeah, I'd say you got the makings of a great fiction writer, kid."

"Uh...thanks."

Dimson had forged my deposition, but I couldn't see any reason to argue the point now. If I told Langsbury it wasn't me, she'd no longer owe me a favor. I wasn't ready to let that go. I might need it before all this business with her slimy brother-in-law was over. Langsbury might be off the hook with Victoria, but Timothy Amsel wasn't off my hook. Not by a long shot.

"Glad I could help out, Mrs. Langsbury. I was wondering, how well do you know Timothy Amsel?"

"Better than I care too."

"Do you think he's capable of doing something...uh...*untoward?*"

Langsbury's beady eyes gleamed. "Absolutely. You know something, don't you! Tell me!"

"You aren't...uh...planning on moving into a nursing home or anything, are you?"

"What? No! Why would you ask that?"

I gave the old woman the once-over. As thin, pale, and busted-up looking as she appeared, she could have been a posterchild for the Grim Reaper.

"Amsel filed a quit-claim deed on your house."

"He *what!*" Langsbury shouted so loud she nearly fell over sideways. "I'll kill him!"

"I'm working on an even better plan, if you're interested."

Langsbury's thin lip curled upward. "Does it involve slow, painful suffering?"

"Maybe. You up for it?"

Langsbury glanced around to make sure no one was looking, then swung her bandaged arm out like a chicken and danced a jig on the sidewalk.

"Bring it on, kid. As you can see, I'm as fit as a fiddle."

"HOW MUCH LONGER WE gonna sit out here in this heat?" Winky asked, and wiped his red face with the front of his threadbare t-shirt.

"I don't know." I shifted my sweaty thighs in Maggie's driver's seat. "Until someone goes to Goober's post office box, I guess."

"Lord a mighty. Look here, Val. I done got me a St. Pete swimmin' pool."

I glanced over at Winky. He stuck a finger in his sweat-filled navel, causing the perspiration collected within it to spill out onto his belly.

Okay. I'm outta here.

"The two-hour limit on this parking spot is almost up," I said. "Let's go. If only there was some way of getting a note to Goober...you know, slipping one in his post office box or something. Then we could get in touch with him without having to stake out his box."

Winky cocked his freckled head at me like a quizzical, ginger-haired bulldog.

"I got an idea," he said.

Great. I can't wait to hear this *one.*

"What?" I asked, and braced myself for the idiotic onslaught.

"Why don't you mail him a letter to his post office box?"

The sharp sting of realizing my own colossal stupidity made the hair on the back of my neck stand up, despite the broiling heat.

"Oh. Well...right, of course I could do that," I said. "I was saving it...as a last resort."

"Uh-huh," Winky said.

Humiliation seared my burning cheeks. I glanced in the rearview mirror and nearly gasped. Not only was I officially a dingbat. Tthe August heat and humidity had melted my makeup. I looked like Mrs. Potato Head after a five-minute stint in a microwave oven.

"Okay. Plan B it is," I said, and handed Winky the envelope on which I'd scribbled Langsbury's address last night at Laverne's. "We've got this other place to stake out. You know where it is?"

Winky read the envelope. "Shore do. Take a turn down this here alley."

"I did as instructed and cut through the alley between First Street North and Central Avenue.

As I cruised slowly by a fragrant dumpster, Winky hollered, "Stop the car!"

I slammed on the brakes, but since we were only going about four miles an hour, the effect was melodramatic.

"What?" I asked.

"That car there."

I glanced at the rusty, baby-blue, 1980s-era Chevy Chevette parked up against the back of a shop wall.

"Wow," I deadpanned. "What a classic."

Winky looked at me like I was crazy. "Don't you recognize it? That's Goober's car!"

"What?" I squealed. "Oh my lord! Let's go check it out!"

In my mad scramble to get out of the car, my elbow mashed the horn on Maggie's steering wheel. A second later, a head popped up in the Chevy's front seat. It wasn't Goober. This guy had hair.

Frizzy, reddish-brown hair.

A tall, skinny, beak-nosed man unfolded himself from the driver's side door. He looked like a stink bug wearing a suit filched from a dirty-clothes hamper. Both his expression and hairdo reminded me of someone who might have recently been attacked by birds.

Somewhere beneath all that grunge, a familiar face peeked through. My jaw hit the asphalt.

It was my old nemesis, Ferrol Finkerman.

"WHAT IN THE WORLD ARE you doing in Goober's car?" I yelled at Finkerman.

"Geez, Fremden," Finkerman said sourly. "Slow down. I didn't know it was a goober car. And anyway, what, pray tell, is a goober car? An Uber without wheels?"

"Not a goober car. *Goober's* car. It belongs to our friend Goober. What are you doing with it?"

"Nothing. I found it here and, well, you know the rules. Possession is nine-tenths of the law. I just...took up temporary residence."

"You're *living* in it?"

Finkerman shrugged. "Well, everybody's gotta live somewhere."

"I lived in the bed of a pick 'em up truck for three months," Winky said. "Had a topper and everything!"

"Sweet," Finkerman deadpanned.

"Why are you living in a car?" I asked.

"Funny story," Finkerman said. He tried to laugh, but it came out more like a wheeze. "I got in a little hot water over that whole overdue library book thing. My idiot nephew Fargo, you remember him?"

"Yes."

"He sent one of my letters to the wife of a circuit judge. Come to find out you were right, Fremden. Soliciting a fee to make a fake legal problem go away qualifies as extortion. Who knew?"

"*You* should have, that's who. You're an attorney, after all!"

"Not anymore. I kind of got, well...disbarred."

"Oh, don't you worry none," Winky said. "When I lost my job, I got disbarred to, but I cheered up directly."

"Winky, that's despaired...and I don't think you used quite the right syntax."

"Sin tax?" Winky asked. "There's a tax on sin now?"

"Only in Georgia and parts of Tennessee," Finkerman quipped.

"Well, at least you haven't lost your sense of humor," I said. "How long have you been...uh...living in the Chevy?"

"Since Thursday. They repo'd my Hummer."

"Yeah. I think I saw that go down." I didn't bother to hide the grin creeping across my face. "So, what will you do now?"

"Not sure," Finkerman said. "At the moment, my options are rather slim. I need to lay low...bill collectors and all. Still, you can't get blood out of a turnip."

"Or integrity out of a Finkerman," I said.

"When's this Goober guy getting back?" Finkerman asked. "I could stay here and 'guard' his vehicle while he's gone. For a small fee, of course."

I shook my head. "You never know when to quit, do you?"

Winky tugged on my sleeve. "Val, I think he just said he did. You know, quit. Attorneyin' and all."

I held in a sigh. "Right."

I walked over and peeked inside the Chevette. It was full to the brim with clothes, blankets, food wrappers and whatever else, I didn't want to know. If Goober's Chevy had held any clues to his where-abouts, they'd been buried or obliterated by Finkerman's unsanctioned inhabitation.

"I think we should take the Chevy back to my place," I said.

"I've got a set a spare tires at the donut shack," Winky said. "You could take me to get 'em."

"Don't bother," Finkerman said. "It's not going anywhere." He lift-ed the hood and held it open for our inspection. "Take a look."

"Dang," Winky said. "Looks like they done got the battery, the dis-tributor cap, and a few other hoozy-whatsits."

Finkerman let go and the hood slammed shut. "So, what do you think of my gracious offer to guard this little beauty for you?"

"Not much," I said. "You already let them steal the tires and engine right out from under you."

"Technically, they stole the engine right out from *in front* of me. Actually, it was like that when I got here. Otherwise, I'd have hotwired the thing and driven somewhere that didn't offer the aromatic allure of week-old dumpster."

I pondered my options. They were pretty slim.

"Okay," I said. "I guess it won't hurt if you stay another night or two. But don't leave without telling me. I may want to search the vehicle. I'll need you to sort out what junk is yours and which is Goober's."

"Not a problem," Finkerman said, and held out a thin, insectoid hand. "You owe me for five days service."

"What?" I practically screeched.

"Like I said, I've been guarding the car since Thursday."

"Five days. This ought to cover it." I handed Finkerman a fiver.

He took it and tucked it inside his rumpled suit jacket. "Your graciousness knows no bounds, Fremden."

"Neither does your gall, Finkerman. Come on, Winky, let's go."

"Nice seeing you," Finkerman quipped as we walked away.

"Why do you think Goober left his car there?" I asked Winky as we climbed into Maggie.

"I don't rightly know. But they wasn't any parking tickets on it. Maybe it's a kind 'a secret spot. You know, one that don't get checked by the police."

I shifted into drive and cruised toward the end of the alley.

"Huh. That make sense, I guess. It would explain how Finkerman could stay there so long without being run off."

"Yep." Winky agreed. "Or, you know, it bein' a secret spot all hid away and such, it could be that's where Goober got hisself abducted by aliens."

I closed my eyes and took a breath.

"Right, Winky. Or it could be that."

Chapter Nineteen

After leaving Finkerman in a downtown alley as the official, live-in bodyguard of Goober's old Chevette, I'd planned to head over to Langsbury's place with Winky and see what we could find out about Amsel. But Winky had to get back to work, so I dropped him off at the donut shop.

I made a quick pit stop at home to grab a floppy sun hat and sunglasses as a disguise before I went to stake out Langsbury's place by myself. But once I stepped inside my front door, real life derailed my well-laid plans.

First, I had to let Snogs out for a wee. While I waited on him to do his business, I thought I might as well write a letter to Goober to mail when I left.

I sat at my desk and dashed off a less-than gracious note to Goober, telling him that absconding without a word to his whereabouts was a rather jerky thing to do. After signing it, I decided to include my phone number, just in case he'd lost his cellphone. When I'd misplaced mine last year, I'd realized I hadn't known a single soul's phone number by heart anymore. Not even Tom's.

With Snogs relieved and the letter to Goober done, I searched around for an envelope to mail it in. That's when it dawned on me that Winky still had the envelope I'd used to scribble down old lady Langsbury's address. I started to give him a call to get it, but then again, I wasn't sure I could count on him to accurately relay the information.

I blew out a breath and glanced at the newspaper lying on the kitchen counter. The new banner on the *Tampa Bay Times* informed me that it was Monday. That meant it was my night to make dinner.

Crap on a cracker.

I picked up the newspaper and skipped to the local business page. A new picture of Amsel made my stomach turn. He had one foot on the head of a shovel, digging it into the sand next to Caddy's. The smug grin on his ugly mug made me want to puke. I ripped the section out and called for Snogs.

"Here boy!"

Snogs came running up. I put the newsprint on the floor and a toe on Amsel's face. "I've gotta run. Do your business right here, okay?"

Snogs yipped.

It sounded like "I'll do my best," to me.

I tousled the pup's head and glanced at the clock on the kitchen wall. It read 3:39 p.m. If I left immediately, I'd have just enough time to swing by the donut shop, grab the envelope from Winky, then stop at the grocery store, pick up some semi-healthy food from the Publix deli, slap it into some serving dishes, and hide the take-out containers in the trash before Tom got home.

I grabbed my keys and made a mad dash for the door.

This healthy, home-cooked meal plan is going to be the death of me....

I WAS IN THE GARAGE stuffing the deli containers into the trash bin when I heard Tom's SUV pull up in the driveway. I scrambled back inside, yanked on an apron, and did my best Doris Day impression.

"Honey, you're home!"

Tom eyed me skeptically, then cracked a weak smile. "Hey."

"Geez, Tom. You look beat."

"Thanks." Tom kissed me absently on the lips, took off his gun holster, and eyed the fake home-cooked meal laid out on the dining room table. "Huh."

"You okay?" I asked.

"Yeah. Just exhausted. You're lucky you don't work like I do. You get to sit around and write all day. I can't imagine what that's like."

Me either, buddy.

"Any news about Greg and Norma?" I asked.

"Nothing much. It's weird."

Tom pulled a bottle of beer out of the fridge and offered it to me. I took it. He fished out another for himself.

"What's weird?" I asked.

Tom popped the top on his beer and took a sip. "I dunno. My gut tells me Amsel's our guy. But thanks to orders from higher up, I can't touch him. And maybe they're right, because the evidence keeps pointing elsewhere."

I fiddled with the label on my beer. "Like where, elsewhere?"

"To Bigfoot," Tom quipped tiredly.

"Yeah, right," I said.

"You know I shouldn't be telling you anything."

"Why? What would happen if you did?"

"I could get reprimanded. Sued. Fired. Beheaded."

"Fine. Don't tell me anything. Just don't joke about it, either. I know Greg and Norma. They're friends, sort of."

Tom wrapped an arm around my waist and pulled me close. "Sorry. I'm just frustrated. I feel like my hands are tied. And whoever did this, well, she *does* have big feet."

I shifted out of Tom's embrace. "*She?* You mean big feet like *Norma?*"

"I mean any woman who wears size ten Birkenstocks."

I shook my head. "It just can't be Norma, Tom."

Tom looked me in the eyes and shrugged. "If the shoe fits, Val."

"How do you know the perpetrator wore Birkenstocks? You can't leave me hanging like that. I thought you said we were a team."

Tom locked eyes with me for a moment and said, "Okay. But what I'm going to show you stays between you and me."

Tom led me to the couch and sat down next to me.

"Okay. Look at this," he said, and opened a folder. He handed me a photo of footprints in the sand. "We found this trail of footprints. See those long gouges there?"

"Yeah."

"It looks like someone or something was dragged across the sand from Caddy's out to the beach."

"I see."

"What's weird is, on either side of the trail were sets of what appear to be identical women's shoeprints. Large ones. Like size ten or bigger."

"So, what are you saying?"

"Nothing but exactly what I just said."

"That Greg was abducted and dragged out to sea by a pair of Amazon women?"

"I'd say that's a stretch, Val. And I've already said too much." He took the picture from me, put it back in the folder and closed it. "Let's eat. I'm so hungry I could eat a rubber chicken breast."

"Good. Because that's exactly what we're having."

Chapter Twenty

As I drove down Central Avenue toward downtown on Tuesday morning, I rehashed the plan in my mind that I'd come up with last night. I was going to mail Goober's letter at *his* post office. That way, I could show that skeptical mail clerk that I was legit. After all, why would I send a letter to someone's post office box if I wasn't officially allowed to have access to it?

My upper lip snarled involuntarily.

Crud. That doesn't make any sense at all.

Like messages from a dream written down in the middle of the night, in the light of day, my idea no longer held water. Or, should I say, Tanqueray.

Last night, after three gin and tonics, the idea of handing that dubious postal clerk a letter addressed to Goober's box had sounded like a brilliant plan. But as I paused as the light on Sixteenth Street, it suddenly sounded like crap.

Double crap. On a cracker, even.

Geez, Val! Why would anyone send a letter to a post office box they supposedly were allowed to access themselves?

I blew out a breath and resigned myself to Plan B. When I pulled up in front of the post office, I skipped going inside the lobby. Instead, I slipped Goober's letter into the mail slot outside. Yesterday, the postal clerk had been suspicious, but he'd let me off without making a citizen's arrest. There was no use tempting fate again. Ending up in federal prison didn't sound too appealing.

Neither did the other choice I was left contemplating. In fact, this last-resort option was so unappealing, I actually decided to visit Finkerman as a delay tactic. Besides, his new office *was* conveniently located just around the corner...in a baby-blue Chevy Chevette.

I turned off First Street and cruised down the alley to Goober's car. As a courtesy, I "rang the bell" by tapping lightly on Maggie's horn. Finkerman's frizzy head slowly rose up from the seat like Dracula emerging from his coffin.

I was about to make a snarky remark when, to my surprise, another nappy head rose up beside him in the passenger seat. Disgust shot through my gut when I actually recognized the other face.

What's wrong with my life, that I know every miscreant and deviant in town?

Finkerman's passenger was Victoria, the snotty twit who'd lost her catfight and lawsuit with old lady Langsbury. Victoria put on her librarian glasses. She blinked, spotted me, and sneered.

No surprise there.

From the looks of her, Victoria hadn't quite recovered from her Aquanet run-in with Langsbury. As I watched from my automotive spectator seat, she and Finkerman appeared to have some kind of argument. After a minute or so, Finkerman got out of the car. Alone.

"Geez, Finkerman. You raising a family in there? What are you doing hanging around with *Victoria?*"

Finkerman shrugged. "You know how it goes. I was working with her on a case. One thing led to another and...well, let's just say her husband didn't take too kindly to our...uh...*partnership.*"

"Really?" I deadpanned. "Who would've ever seen that one coming?"

Finkerman sighed. "If you've just come here to rub salt in my wounds, mission accomplished."

I opened my mouth to deliver a zinger worthy of a whole box of Morton, but closed it again. Unbelievably, my stupid Southern guilt-o-meter had caused my heart to ping with something along the lines of sympathy—for *Finkerman*, no less!

"Are you two okay?" I asked.

"Yeah. We were counting on a payout yesterday. Eighteen hundred bucks. But it fell through."

Don't do it, Val. Just smile and walk away. Don't do it! Please don't do it!

"Maybe I can help," I said, and mentally kicked myself in the behind.

"Yeah?" Finkerman said. His face read disbelief. I'm sure mine did, too.

"I thought maybe, since you've got some free time, you could help me out on this investigation thing I'm doing," I said.

"Really?"

As Finkerman's jaw made the slow return trip to the base of his skull, I forced a smile, loathing myself more with each word that passed from my lips.

"Yeah. I've got a few legal questions. You could help me, and I could help you."

Finkerman managed to scrounge a smug look from amongst the sorry ruins of his current situation.

"Well, I normally charge five hundred an hour," he said.

I sneered. "How about we say, uh...five bucks a question."

Finkerman laughed his sick, piranha-mouthed chortle. "Yeah, right."

"Okay. Never mind." I turned to go.

"Wait!" he practically screamed. "Since you've been a good client—"

I turned back around and shot him a dirty look.

"Well, I mean, since you kept your word and didn't rat me out for the library book scam, I guess we could work something out."

"Okay. What's your best advice on how to locate missing people? People that maybe don't want to get found."

"Easy. Follow the money trail."

"Money trail?"

"Basic stuff, Fremden. Check for credit card receipts. Where they stopped to get gas...restaurants, hotels, stuff like that."

"What if they were traveling incognito? In an RV?"

Finkerman held out a thin, insectoid arm. "Five bucks first. For answering the first question."

I rolled my eyes and fished a tenner out of my purse. Finkerman grabbed for it, but I held it back like bait.

"This is all I got," I said. "Answer the second question, too."

Finkerman blew out a breath. "Someone traveling in an RV can be trickier. I'd start by checking out RV parks for the vehicle. But you're up against two obstacles."

"What?" I asked.

"RVs are mobile. And nowadays, the economy's so bad, half the country's living in something with wheels."

I glanced over at Victoria and handed Finkerman the ten dollar bill.

"Good point," I said.

My mind flashed back to five years ago, when I'd been about ten bucks away from living in Maggie. "You still have your cellphone, Finkerman?"

"Yeah. Prepaid. For the next three days, anyway."

"Okay. Keep it handy. I might need you."

I handed Finkerman a twenty. He nearly gasped.

"What's this for?" he asked.

"Let's just call it 'prepaid.' You owe me one."

"Actually, I owe you four."

"Four?"

"We agreed on five bucks a pop. I may be a lot of things, Fremden, but I live by one creed. Everyone works for the terms they negotiate for themselves."

I smirked. "So then, how much is Victoria charging?"

Finkerman's narrow, angular face registered a startled surprise. Then it cracked into a grin.

He threw back his frizzy head and burst into a laugh that, for the first time since I'd known him, actually sounded genuine.

Chapter Twenty-One

I leaned back in my desk and stared at the dreamcatcher postcard Goober had sent me nearly a month ago.

Where in blue blazes could he be?

With the letter to Goober in the mail, I was stuck waiting for a reply from him. The trouble was, I was notoriously bad at waiting. Besides, I didn't know for absolute certain if 3799 was even *his* post office box. It could've belonged to *anybody*. If that were the case, I'd be waiting forever for a reply that would never come.

I sighed and thought about my conversation with Finkerman. He'd advised me to follow the money trail. But Goober had an active aversion to using credit cards. "Too traceable," I remembered him saying once. Based on that, I was pretty sure he didn't have one. That ruled out running a credit check.

As far as chasing down the RV went, I could've started calling every RV park from Key West to Tennessee in the hopes of getting lucky. But the odds of finding him were about as good as chasing down a cockroach in a junkyard.

I sat up in my chair and blew out a long breath. I couldn't put it off any longer. There was absolutely, positively no getting around it.

Goober had left me with one last, dreaded option.

I turned the dreamcatcher postcard over in my hand and studied the postmark.

Greenville, Florida.

Goober'd mailed his card from the same podunk town where my adoptive mother, Lucille Jolly Short, lived. Did he do that so people would think the postcard came from *her* and not *him*? If so, why would he care? Was someone after Goober? Or....

A nagging thought tied a knot in my stomach.

Did Goober go to Greenville so he could leave a clue to his where-abouts with my mother?

Goober'd never met my mother. So, being unaffiliated with her "charms," it was theoretically possible that he *had* braved a visit to her.

Dread gnawed at the knot in my gut.

What if he *had* dropped by to see her? Would he have introduced himself as my friend Goober? Maybe. But he could've shown up on her doorstep as *anybody*. After all, he was traveling in an RV crammed with Cold Cut's crazy disguises. Who would Goober have told Lucille he was? According to Tom, even the name Goober went by, Gerald Jono-hhovitz, wasn't real.

I could call my mother to find out, but that would involve calling my mother....

I stared up at the corner of the ceiling, hoping a better idea might be stuck in a dusty cobweb up there. Or maybe a black widow spider would swing down, bite me, and put me out of my misery....

I put a mental X through the thought of calling my mother and pinned the postcard back on the corkboard on the wall.

There has to be some other way....

I STUCK A LEG OUT OF the hammock and kicked the ground to get it swinging again. With Snogs sleeping on my belly, I took a sip of Tanqueray and tonic and watched the diamonds dance on the choppy surface of the Intracoastal Waterway that lined the edge of my back-yard.

Goober hadn't been the most industrious of men. I was trying to get into his mindset.

Where would a lazy man with a low work ethic and a high IQ go to disappear?

"To the moon!" a voice screeched, providing a timely, if unlikely, answer.

I sat up in the hammock and saw Laverne run across her yard in hot pursuit of Randolph.

"Hey!" I yelled. "What's going on over there?"

"Gosh darn it!" Laverne bellowed, then dove into the grass.

Grunting ensued from both parties. Finally, Laverne stood up. I could see her arms were wrapped around Randolph. His little pig belly looked swollen.

"Everything all right?" I asked.

"No! This little rapscallion ate the pineapple upside down cake I was making for the luau!"

"Oh."

I snickered, plied a limp, sleepy Snogs from my stomach, and crawled out of the hammock. As I toted Snogs over to the picket fence, I couldn't help but giggle. Randolph's contented face was the polar opposite of Laverne's frustrated scowl.

"It's not the end of the world, Laverne. You have plenty of time to make another cake."

Laverne pouted. "You don't understand, Val. It was a *special* cake. I used up the last of my secret ingredient making it."

"Secret ingredient? What are you talking about?"

Laverne looked around, as if to make sure no one could overhear her.

"Krassco," she whispered.

"Krassco? What's that?"

"You don't know about Krassco? Hold on. I'll show you."

Laverne set Randolph down and disappeared inside her house. I put Snogs in the grass and looked up Krassco on my phone while the pup sniffed at the pig between the pickets in the fence. What came up on my Google search made me swallow my spit.

No. It couldn't be.

Laverne returned, toting a rusty, gallon-sized tin can.

Oh my lord. It is.

Laverne handed me the tin. It was so greasy it slipped out of my hands. Before I could stop him, Snogs dove for the can. He sniffed it, yelped, tucked in his tail, and ran off.

I picked up the can, still reeling in disbelief.

"Laverne, they haven't made this stuff since 1938. Krassco's a ration from World War II."

"Huh. Well, no *wonder* I can't find it anywhere. Not even at the Dollar Store anymore."

"Laverne, we're talking seventy-year-old pig lard here!"

Laverne's face shot through with panic. "Shh! Not so loud! Randolph might hear you! I know what it is. But I was raised on Krassco, Val. It's my favorite."

"Laverne, I don't think you get it."

I pointed at the greasy words stamped onto the metal, Army-surplus can. "This stuff expired in *nineteen forty-eight!*"

Laverne tutted and shook her head.

"Oh Val, you know you can't trust those expiration dates."

WITH THE LONG-RUNNING mystery of Laverne's deadly baked goods solved, I turned my attention to the remaining four crises at hand.

One, Caddy's was slated for demolition next week by Timothy Amsel. Two, Greg Parsons, the owner, had disappeared. Three, head waitress Norma Jeen was missing, and considered either a victim or a prime suspect. Four, Goober was also MIA.

Tom had warned me to keep clear of the first three. Those were his domain, and I had to trust him on that. So, there was only one thing left for the crazy gerbil living in my addled brain to do.

Find Goober.

And that meant....

I let out a groan that could be heard in Mexico City.

I have to call my mother.

I fixed a gin and tonic and downed it. I fixed another and dialed her number before I lost my nerve.

"Hey, Mom."

"Vallie? Is that you?"

"Yes."

"It's been so long I hardly recognized your voice."

"Right. Mom, what's that whirring sound?"

"I'm here at Betty Jean's Feed and Beauty. Hold up a second."

I heard Mom yell, "*Elmira!* Can you reach back there and turn my drier off for a second?"

The whirring sound stopped.

"What's up with you?" she asked. "Are you in trouble?"

"No. Just calling to say, 'hi.'"

"Uh-huh. Well then, hi." Then she yelled, "*Elmira!* You can turn my drier back on!"

"Wait!" I said. "Mom, I was wondering...have you maybe gotten...uh...a visit from some strange man lately?"

"Well, yeah. Not me, really. But Dale." Mom giggled. "Dale said some feller turned up at the door calling him a bastard."

I blanched. "What?"

Mom laughed. "Funniest story to hit Jackson County in years, Vallie."

"What happened?"

"Awe, nothing much. Turns out it was all a misunderstandin'. Poor feller come knockin' on our door. Said he was from the New Will Angelical Order of the Southern Methodist United in Spirit Church. Well, a course Dale let him in."

"Of course."

"Well, that's when this feller went to tellin' Dale he was a bastard. You know it ain't like Dale to get all hot under the collar. But he did."

"Really?"

"Yep. Dale actually left that feller standin' in the doorway and went and turned down the volume on the TV to tell me about it. Well, you know I jumped up outta my chair to give that feller a piece of my mind."

No surprise there.

"Geez, Mom. What happened?"

"Come to find out, Dale's hearing aid was on the blink. Poor feller was telling Dale he was a *pastor*, not a bastard."

I waited while Mom laughed over the phone line for a full minute.

"Ah...whooo!" she finally bellowed after catching her breath. "Cracks me up ever' time I tell it."

"So what happened to the pastor? Did you let him in?"

"Naw. We sent him on his way. He *was* a Methodist, after all." Mom paused a beat and said, "Why, thanky, Elmira."

"What's going on?"

"Oh, that new girl Elmira just brought me a glass of water. You'd be proud of little Greenville, Val. We got us one a them rainbow people workin' up at the beauty salon."

"You mean a gay person?"

"Huh? I mean a woman with a rainbow afro."

My gut flopped.

"What's she look like, mom?"

"Well, if you ask me, she ain't gonna win no beauty contest anytime soon, but she can tease hair like nobody's business. She got poor old Alberta's thin hair all blowed up like an extra-large strawberry cotton candy. It was a downright miracle, if you ask me."

"What's she look like, mom?" I asked again, trying not to sound the least bit impatient.

"I ain't one to judge, you know that, Valliant."

Yeah, right. "I know, Mom."

"Well, let's see. She's kinda tall and square-shouldered. And bless her heart, Elmira's got a five o'clock shadow. But after fifty-five, what woman don't? Anyway, poor thing. She ain't too long for this world. Seems like every time I'm in here the ambulance comes and hauls her away for somethin' or another."

"What's wrong with her?"

"Don't rightly know. You know I ain't one to pry. But there ain't no tellin' how much time any of us's got left on this Earth, Valliant."

"No, Mom."

"So, you comin' to visit me before it's too late and the Lord calls me home to my reward?"

"Yes. How does tomorrow sound?"

"Well, if that's the best you can do, I guess I'll have to live with it."

Chapter Twenty-Two

As I clicked off the phone, the full weight of what I'd just done slammed into me like a ton of hicks.

There was no turning back. I'd gone and done it.

I'd told my mother I'd visit her.

Tomorrow.

Ugh! Why? Why? Why did I do that to myself?

I tossed my phone on the couch and slunk off to my home office. I scanned the corners for the cobwebs I'd seen earlier.

Where's a black-widow spider when you need one most?

Assisted suicide apparently off the table, I heaved a sigh and plopped into my desk chair. I leaned over and opened the blinds to let in more light. As I gazed wistfully at the dangling beer cans on Goober's redneck dreamcatcher, a movement from outside caught my eye. It was my missing-link neighbor Jake. He was crossing the street, carrying a shovel over his shoulder.

I zipped out the front door after him.

"What are you doing?" I called out as he stepped onto the sidewalk in front of Nancy's house.

"For the luau," he yelled back, and patted the shovel handle. "Gonna dig a pig-roasting pit in the ground. Nancy asked me to."

I sprinted up to him and glanced over at Nancy's place to make sure she wasn't spying on us.

"But Jake, the whole thing is bogus. It's all a joke."

"Not according to Nancy. I mean, what was I supposed to say to her when she asked me to dig the pit? No? We have to at least make it *look* authentic...you know...like it's really gonna happen. At least until we get Roscoe out of here."

"Randolph. And you're right. So, how big a hole are you gonna dig?"

"About the size of a small grave."

A glimmer of hope flashed across my mind.

Maybe I could jump in there when he's done. Jake could bury me alive. Then I'd be off the hook for Greenville....

"But it's only Tuesday," I said. "What's the rush?"

"Roasting a pig in a pit takes a minimum of twenty-four hours. I googled it. Plus, I got appointments coming up in the next few days. I'm gonna be busy."

"But it's not really gonna happen!"

Jake's lips twisted up on one side.

"Maybe it should, Val. If Nancy gets wind this whole thing was a joke on *her*, no telling what kind of nasty new regulations she'll come up with to torture us."

"Geez. Maybe you're right. Do you think we should, you know, order a pig and just go along with the plan?"

"Honestly? Yeah. Nancy's doing most of the work now, anyway. And I can't take another onslaught of nastygrams. You know I caught her yesterday in my front yard with a ruler? She was measuring my grass blades!"

"Okay, okay. I'm on it. Any idea where I can get one?"

"A ruler?"

"A pig."

"You mean besides Laverne's backyard?"

"Har har."

"How about a butcher? Or a restaurant, maybe?"

"Vance!" I practically shouted, startling Jake so badly he ducked and nearly dropped his shovel.

"Is she behind me?" he whispered.

"Who?"

"Nancy!"

"No."

"Geez!" he grumbled. "I thought Vance was some secret code-word for Nancy! Don't scare me like that!"

"Sorry. Vance is the husband of my friend Milly. He owns a restaurant. He could hook us up with a pig. I'm sure of it."

"Good. Then that's settled."

Jake's spine went ramrod straight. "Uh-oh," he whispered. "I see Nancy's binoculars between the blinds. I better go dig that poor pig's grave before she starts digging mine."

IT WASN'T EVEN NOON yet and my day had already shot completely off the crazy charts.

I was officially in cahoots with Ferrol Finkerman, of all people. I'd uncovered Laverne's deadly culinary plot and saved the world from Krassco. I'd downed two gin and tonics and made a date with the devil in Greenville. And now, I was about to order a real pig for a fake luau.

Tom's wrong. I'm not a magnet for the absurd. I'm a magnet for the insane!

I shook my head at my reflection in the bathroom mirror, then walked to the kitchen, picked up my cellphone and punched speed dial.

"Hey, Milly."

"Val! What's up?"

"Nothing much."

Milly laughed. "Yeah, right."

"I need a favor."

"Okay....?"

"Do you think Vance could get me a pig?"

Milly snorted. "A pig?"

"Yeah. A pig."

"But you've already got one. He's named Tom, remember?"

"Ha ha. Very funny. I'm dead serious, Milly. You see, I'm trying to save Randolph from the Knick-Knack Nazi by throwing a fake luau."

"Oh. Well, why didn't you just say so in the first place?" Milly waited a beat, then said, "Geez, Val! What the heck is going on over there?"

"Don't ask. Do you think Vance can get me a small pig to roast in a fire pit or not?"

"Well, sure, I guess. When do you need it?"

"Uh...Thursday?"

"I'll call him. Where do you want it delivered?"

"Well, I might still be out of town. Better send it to Nancy Meyers' place across the street from mine. I don't know her number offhand, but it's the green house with the military-precision lawn and bushes trimmed into ninety-degree square boxes."

"Okay. I'll do my best. Hey. I know it's last minute, but are you free for lunch? I'd love to hear the rest of this story. Sounds like your life's a zoo, as usual."

"Yeah. And now I've got a pig to add to my collection. Listen, I'd love to get together with you. But not today. I've got loads to do. Besides, I'm too nervous to eat."

"Why?"

"I'm going to Greenville tomorrow."

Milly's playful voice dropped three octaves.

"Oh. Geez, Val. What happened? Did your mom finally kick the bucket?"

"No. That would require too much effort on her part."

Milly burst out laughing. "Oh, come on, Val. Meet me at Ming Ming's for sushi. I don't want your last meal to be fried chicken gizzards and moonshine."

"Actually, moonshine sounds pretty good about now."

"WHOA!" MILLY SAID, her green eyes bulging. "Has Tom kept you locked away in a closet and starved you or something?"

I looked up from my plate at the cute, button-nosed blonde sitting across the table from me at Ming Ming's. I tried to answer her, but my mouth was stuffed to capacity with sea-creature roll.

"Sorry," I mumbled and nearly choked. "Tom's on this health-food kick."

"Is it working?"

"If you count kicking my butt, yeah. Broccoli and tofu. I tell you, Milly, I can't take much more of it!"

Milly tilted her head and looked down at my thighs. "Could have fooled me."

"Thanks. Yet another thing to envy you for."

"Envy *me*? For what?"

"You mean besides the fact that you're gorgeous and slim? Well, let's see. Maybe just because you have your total act together?"

"Val, what are you talking about?"

"You've got the whole storybook, Milly. You're married to Vance. He's handsome. Owns his own pub. You live in a fabulous Tudor mansion. You've worked your way up to manager at Griffith & Maas. And—this is what I particularly hate about you—you don't even have cellulite!"

Milly laughed. "I do, too, but I'm not saying where. And you haven't done too shabbily for yourself, either, Val."

"Yeah. Right. Here I am, Ms. Novelist, with one lousy short story published in a Polk County paper. I'm shacked up with Tom, and I live in an old hoarder's house I inherited from my parents. How can you stand the glare from my meteoric rise to stardom?"

"Val, there's only one thing holding you back. You're afraid to fully commit to anything."

"Ouch."

Along with her poison arrow of truth, Milly shot me a sarcastic, yet somehow sympathetic smile.

"Val, making a commitment means you have to quit waiting around for something better to come along. You have to dive in and claim your prizes. The only thing that ever gets 'better' is *you*."

"Geez, Milly. How can I still be so screwed up at age fifty? I thought I'd have it all figured out by now."

"Have what all figured out?"

"Life. You know, like one of those wise guru men on a mountain top."

Milly laughed. "Yeah. Good luck with that. Val, don't you know by now? Being wise isn't about knowing everything. It's about knowing how good you've got it—while you've *still* got it."

"Geez. Does that include my mother Lucille?"

Milly crinkled her button nose. "Well, you've got me there, Val."

Chapter Twenty-Three

When I arrived home from lunch with Milly, Winky was sitting on my doorstep, looking like the only kid in the playground who didn't get picked for dodge ball.

As I pulled into the driveway, he stood up and ambled over. I put Maggie in park and killed the engine.

"What are you doing here?" I asked.

"Awe, Winnie's in one a her moods again," Winky whined. "I figured I'd best give her some woman space. So I come by to see you. You know anything about women, Val?"

Really?

"Not much," I said. "I've only had fifty years of experience. So, what'd you do?"

"*Me?*" Winky said, and reared back defensively. "Nothin'!"

"Then what happened?" I asked as I climbed out of the car.

"Confound if I know."

"*Something* had to set her off, Winky."

"Only one thing I can think of. You know how she's always workin' on new recipes?"

"Yeah."

"Well, I tasted somethin' she was workin' on, and it was godawful!"

"You didn't tell her that, did you?"

"No. Not directly. I ain't crazy, you know! But then she went and asked me if I thought her new recipe could win this dad-burned contest thang she's all hyped up about."

My eyebrows scrunched together in anticipation of the coming reply. "And you said?"

"I told her I wouldn't feed them cookies she baked to our dogs Nancy Drew and Hardy Boy. I'm tellin' ya Val, I've licked the bottom of shoes that had more flavor."

I shook my head. "You didn't really say that to Winnie, did you?"

Winky pouted. "Well, it was the truth! I don't know why she's got to where she's so cranky all the time. I tell you, she's ornerier'n a bulldog with a busted lip. I done skedaddled outta the donut shop a'for she throwed me out."

Winky seemed more dejected than angry, and a pang of pity pierced my heart.

"Come on in," I said. "Let's have a beer. You can lay low here a while. I'm sure it'll all blow over."

"Thanky, Val."

Winky followed me into the kitchen. I pulled two beers out of the fridge and handed him one.

"Maybe you should send her some flowers," I said. "Relationships are work. You don't want to lose Winnie. If you did, all you'll have left is that trailer of yours."

"Trailer shmailer." Winky shook his freckled head. "Thangs ain't what makes people rich, Val. It's how many folks you get to call your friends."

I smiled and patted Winky on the back. "You're right about that, my friend. Want to stay for dinner?"

Winky's freckled nose twitched. "You and Tom still on that health kick thang?"

"Yeah."

"Well then, I might just have to graciously decline."

I GUESS IT WAS BOUND to happen. Still, I never saw it coming.

Winky and I were stretched out in recliners in the backyard. We were taking turns teaching Snogs how to howl at the rising moon, and making faces behind Tom's back as he barbequed a package of fake tofu dogs on the grille.

"Smells delicious," I lied, then whispered to Winky, "At least the fumes are keeping the mosquitoes away."

"Yeah," Winky said loud enough for Tom's benefit. "Cain't beat the aroma of honest-to-goodness bona fide bean curd."

"Speaking of curds, I'm going to visit my mother," I said.

Tom turned around. His forehead was lined with concern. "Is she sick?"

"No," I sighed.

Tom's face morphed into a grin. "Are you?"

"Ha ha," I replied sourly.

Tom turned back to roasting wieners and asked, "What brought this on all of a sudden?"

I crinkled my nose and pondered my options.

Should I tell Tom and Winky that I suspected Goober might be in Greenville working as my mother's transvestite beautician? What if I got up there and Elmira turned out to just be some random weirdo with a rainbow Mohawk? I'd never live that one down! But if I said nothing about it and we just happened to go up there and stumble on Goober together...well, I could claim the credit for finding him and not face total and complete humiliation.

The solution was clear. I'd tell Tom a lie I knew he'd believe.

"She kind of guilted me into it," I said.

Tom laughed. "*There's* a new one."

As he removed the seared tofu wieners from the grille, I got up and touched Tom on the arm.

"Tom, I was hoping you could go with me tomorrow."

He looked surprised. "*Tomorrow?* I can't."

"Why not?"

"You know that's too short a notice. I have to work in the morning."

"But..."

Tom grinned and laid on his lousy impersonation of a Southern accent. "But you be sure and give yore momma an' Dale a big ol' hug and kiss from me."

"Thanks," I said.

Tom handed me a hotdog. "Consolation prize."

I sniffed the fake tube steak and crinkled my nose.

"Tom, I don't think Maggie can make the trip. If you can't go, can I at least take your 4Runner?"

"Well, I—" Tom began.

"*I* know!" Winky bellowed. "*I'll* go with you, Val! Yore momma likes me. And we can take my truck."

"There you go," Tom said with a devious wink. "Problem solved."

I opened my mouth to object, but a pig squeal beat me to it.

I turned in the direction of Laverne's place just in time to see a portly little pig come flying over the picket fence. Randolph grunted at the three of us, squealed again, and made a beeline for the front yard.

Oh, crap!

"Catch him!" I hollered, and tossed my tofu dog on the ground. I took off after Randolph, Tom and Winky hot on my heels.

As I rounded the corner of the house, the scene playing out in front of me stopped me dead in my tracks. Tom and Winky bumbled into the back of me, and we all tumbled onto the grass like three drunken stooges.

It was just as well. If I'd have remained standing, I'd have fallen on the ground from laughter.

Across the street, Krassco was claiming its last victim.

Apparently, the pineapple upside-down time-bomb cake Laverne had baked using the last remnants of WWII grease had made its way through Randolph's digestive system. There, it had detonated and released a chain-reaction diarrhea explosion of epic proportions.

Tom, Winky and I watched in awe as Randolph bucked and twirled around in the middle of Nancy Meyer's front yard, squirting pig poop from his posterior like a sprinkler head possessed by demons.

"What in blue blazes has got into that pig?" Winky asked.

I bit my lip. I knew the answer, but I couldn't say. Laverne had sworn me to secrecy over her secret ingredient. Her supply of Krassco was finished and could do no more harm. So I didn't see any reason to spill the beans now. Besides, I hated the idea of Laverne ending up in some kind of lawsuit over it. Over the years, at least half the people I knew had fallen victim to her Krassco-laced culinary disasters.

"There's no telling," I said. Which, in a way, wasn't a lie, since I couldn't tell them.

Winky rolled over, sat up and admired the show. "You know, if'n he had him a little saddle and a monkey on his back, we'd have us a min'ature rodeo."

Tom shook his head and whistled. "Gives new meaning to the term rear-jet propulsion."

"Shore do," Winky said. "Never thought I'd ever see me a pig fly."

Nancy's front door flew open and banged against the wall. Framed in the porchlight, I could see the Knick-Knack Nazi in an olive-grey nightgown. A helmet of curlers framed her head. In one hand, she wielded a rolling pin.

"Hush!" I warned the guys.

We hunkered down on our hands and knees and held our breath as Nancy took a cautious step into her front yard. A second later, she was mowed down by an enthusiastically ejected stream of excrement from Randolph's AK47-like sphincter.

"Uh-oh," Winky said. "Looks like the pig poop's done hit the fan."

"I suggest a hasty retreat," Tom said.

"Roger that," I said.

We spun around on our hands and knees like a trio of synchronized lawn crabs, then scrambled along the side of the house as fast as we could. As we dashed through the grass, Winky snorted like a pig with laughter. It was all I could do to keep from wetting my pants as we crawled toward the hidden sanctuary of the backyard.

As we rounded the corner out of Nancy's sight, I took a tiny bit of comfort in the fact that now, at least, I had a real reason to visit my mother.

It had suddenly become a most excellent time to leave town.

Chapter Twenty-Four

"Good luck and god speed," Tom joked as he headed out the door for work Wednesday morning. He wrapped his arms around my waist and kissed me on the nose. "You know you're allowed to stay longer than one day at your mom's, Val. I can take care of Snogs."

"I know," I sighed. "But one day ought to be plenty of time for mom's backhanded compliments to destroy my entire self-worth."

Tom laughed. "Don't be so hard on her. *Or* yourself. Try to have fun, okay?"

"Just remember me how I look now," I said.

Tom's head cocked to one side. "How's that?"

"With my dignity still somewhat intact."

Tom shook his head. "See you tomorrow."

Tom climbed into his 4Runner and I watched him drive away. I was about to shut the front door when I saw Winky pull up. I was certain Tom had driven past him. And I was even *more* certain Tom was laughing his butt off.

Winky was driving the ridiculous, souped-up hearse he'd bought Winnie for her birthday.

Let the destruction of my dignity begin.

Winky pulled the long, black vehicle onto the grass by the side of the road, giving me and all my neighbors a good look at the custom flames painted along the front side-panels. He revved the V8 engine and honked the horn, just in case someone had missed the sideshow.

Anyone watching could be forgiven for thinking Winky was a limousine driver here to escort me to hell.

I grabbed my suitcase, locked the door, and marched down the driveway to my doom, one lone thought whispering in my ear.

Unbelievably, this is one occasion where I probably actually would *be better off dead.*

WE WERE ZOOMING ALONG on I-275 and had just passed the exit sign for Dade City when I fished my cellphone out of my purse.

"Who you callin'?" Winky asked.

"Laverne. I want to find out what had happened with Randolph and Nancy last night. I figure we're far enough away to be out of earshot of the screaming."

Winky grinned. "And the smell."

"Laverne? I'm on my way to my mom's. Just wanted to check on you and Randolph."

"You haven't heard?" Laverne asked.

My gut sunk. "Heard what?"

"Nancy came over last night. She caught Randolph in her yard and—"

The line went dead.

"Hello? Hello?" I yelled into the phone, then turned to Winky. "Crap. Nancy caught Randolph last night."

Winky winced. "Did she skin the critter alive?"

"I don't know. Poor Laverne!"

"Don't you worry, Val-Pal. We should get us some reception again once we get towards Ocala."

"Geez. I hope Randolph's okay."

"Speakin' a pigs, you hungry?"

"I beg your pardon?"

"I could go for me a pulled-pork sammich."

"Oh." Visions of diarrhea blasting out of Randolph's sphincter did nothing to fuel my appetite. "No. I'm not hungry."

"You don't look too happy to be goin' to see your mamma. What you got against her anyways?"

"Nothing. She's just not what you'd call a very 'motherly' mother."

"Well, she give birth to ya, didn't she?"

"Uh...*no*."

"Oh. That's right. She only took you in and raised you as her own."

Crap. When you put it that way....

"I dunno, Winky. It's the way she talks to me. Like there's an unspoken 'idiot' at the end of each sentence."

Winky grinned. "Well, she *is* talkin' to *you*."

"One more comment like that and you'll be eating a knuckle sandwich. And I don't mean pig knuckles."

Winky smirked. "At least you come by it honest, Val."

"What do you mean?"

"You're a chip off the old block."

I was about to feed Winky my fist full of knuckles when my phone rang.

"Looks like we got reception," Winky said.

"It's Laverne!" I grabbed the phone. "Laverne? We got cut off. What happened? Did Nancy knock Randolph out with her rolling pin?"

"What? No, honey. She was as pleased as punch."

"Huh?"

"Nancy brought Randolph home and gave me a big old thank-you hug."

"Laverne, have you been drinking?"

"Well, yes. I had a two cups of coffee and a glass of orange juice. Why?"

"Ugh! Laverne, I thought Nancy would have flipped her lid over having her yard sprayed down with pig crap!"

"You know, I would have thought so, too, honey. But not Nancy. She thought it was part of our surprise for Spruce-Up September!"

"Huh?"

"Nancy told me she used to live in a small village in Germany. Apparently, every fall the farmers sprayed the fields with pig poop. She said it made her feel right at home."

"Even the smell?"

"Especially the smell."

"Go figure. Thanks, Laverne."

I clicked off the phone and turned to Winky.

"What'd she say?" he asked.

"One man's poop is another man's treasure."

Winky shrugged. "Gee, Val. I could a tole you that."

I'D PLANNED ON KEEPING it a secret until we arrived in Greenville, but I was desperate for a change of subject. If Winky didn't stop naming every NASCAR driver Big Gulp cup he had in his collection, I was going to crawl into the back of the hearse and die.

"Winky, I think Goober may be living in Greenville and working at my mom's beauty parlor."

Winky stopped mid "Dale Earnhardt" and stared at me.

"What in tarnation? How you figure that?"

"I just got a gut feeling when I was talking to my mom yesterday. There's a woman there with a rainbow Mohawk."

Winky shot me a look. "You on drugs?"

"No. It's a long story. I'll show you when we get there. Anyway, I was wondering. Did Goober ever show you his navel?"

"Now I *know* you're on drugs!"

"I'm serious. I saw it once. It looks like he's got two, actually. He said he got shot in the stomach and the scar looks like a second navel."

"Well, I don't know nothin' about that. But it's kind a cool, if you think about it."

"What do you mean?"

"I mean like, if Goober was some kind of secret agent man, like in the movies."

"With Goober, who knows? I can't decide if he's a genius or just bonkers. But if you think about it, I guess we're all a bit of both."

"Huh. I ain't too sure about that, Val. If Goober's a genius, he keeps it better hid than a Baptist's liquor cabinet."

I sighed. For once, Winky *did* have a point. And it wasn't on top of his head.

Chapter Twenty-Five

It was just before 3:00 p.m. when Winky veered the flaming black hearse off westbound I-10 and headed north toward Greenville.

"Take a right when we get to US 90," I said.

"Don't you wanna go see your mom first?"

"No."

Dread had already formed a grapefruit-sized knot in my stomach.

"I wanna put that off as long as possible, Winky. Let's go right to the beauty parlor first. Mom said Betty Jean's Feed and Beauty was just outside of town."

Winky hung a right and we drove past dense patches of towering, longleaf pines, the forest floor beneath them colored rust with a thick, even blanket of shed needles.

Every half mile or so, we'd see a thinned out area of pines under-storied with dogwoods and clumps of azalea bushes as big as minivans. Tucked up amongst these casual country "yards" sat modest houses erected beside family junk middens comprised of several generations of abandoned cars, appliances and other disused household paraphernalia.

"This place looks nice," Winky commented. "Love me some wide-open spaces."

"Yup," I agreed. "Close to nowhere, and yet right up against the highway. You can't beat it."

About three miles out, I spotted a collection of trucks, tractors, and dusty Ford sedans pulled up beside an odd structure that seemed to be the aftermath of soldering together a trailer, several metal storage sheds, and a small warehouse.

A one-word sign painted on the apex of the warehouse read, "Feed." Around these parts, that could mean lots of things. But seeing as there was an ambulance pulled up in front of it, I figured it was most likely a restaurant.

We were about to drive by it when I spotted an old Minnie Winnie. It was parked off to the side of the trailer end of the cobbled-together buildings.

"Winky! Stop! Turn in here!"

Winky jacked the steering wheel on the hearse and we nearly flipped into a ditch. He managed to straighten out the rear end as it fishtailed on the red clay shoulder, then pulled over into a patch of weeds just outside the main lot.

"Geez, Val! You ought to give a feller better notice than that!"

"I would have, if I'd known myself. Look! I think that's Goober's RV!"

I pointed toward the Minnie Winnie.

"I'll be. That looks like her, all right."

We climbed out of the hearse for a closer look. As we walked by the ambulance, two EMTs came out of the trailer hauling someone in a stretcher. Right before they tucked her into the back, I caught a glimpse of rainbow hair.

"Winky! Geez, Louise! I think that's Goober."

"Where?"

"In the ambulance. I didn't want to say anything earlier because my mom has a tendency to...uh...*exaggerate*, but she told me that the woman who does her hair wasn't long for this world."

Winky gave me a sad face. "Bless her heart. But what's that got to do with Goober?"

The ambulance's lights lit up. The engine roared, and it took off toward the highway.

"Crap! I don't have time to explain. Just follow that ambulance! I'll tell you about it on the way!"

AS IT TURNED OUT, I had plenty of time to explain.

The nearest hospital, Madison County Memorial, was thirteen miles down US 90. As we flew along behind the ambulance, I hoped whatever poor soul was in it didn't look out the back window. They'd be shocked into a heart attack to see they were being followed by the devil's own paddy wagon.

"So why we chasing this ambulance again?" Winky asked.

"Because I think Goober's in there. I didn't want to tell you in case it wasn't true. But it looks like he may be really sick. My mother said Elmira's been in and out of the hospital for months."

"Who's Elmira?"

"Goober. In disguise. I think."

"I been on some wild goose chases, Val. But this here one done took the cake."

I bit my lip. "Well, if it's not Goober, we haven't lost anything."

"'Cept half a tank a dieseline."

"I just wonder why he wouldn't call us. Especially if he was so sick."

"Some folks is just like that," Winky said. "You got your dog folks who want the whole family round to see 'em pass on. Then you got your cat folks who wander off and you never know 'zackly what happened to 'em till somebody finds the body."

"That's real comforting, Winky."

"I do my best."

We followed the ambulance onto Marion Street. The hospital finally came into view.

"Looks like we're here," I said.

"Whew!" Winky said. "Good thing I filled up in Lake City. We'd be running on fumes."

The ambulance pulled up to the emergency room. Its doors flew open and the EMTs rushed the patient into the hospital.

"What do we do now?" Winky asked.

I glanced around and caught sight of a small crowd of people staring at our vehicle in horror.

"First off," I said, "we need to find someplace to park this thing so we don't scare the bejeebers out of everybody."

"HELLO, I'M HERE TO see a patient who's just been admitted," I said to the woman at the hospital reception desk.

"Name?"

"Val Fremden."

She peered at a computer screen through her bifocals. "I don't see it on the list."

"Oh. Sorry. That's *my* name. I meant um...Goober. But he goes by...uh...Elmira."

Geez! Double crap on a cracker!

The receptionist scanned the list again without missing a beat. "Sorry. I don't see anyone named 'Goober' or 'Elmira.'"

"How about "Gerald Jonohhovitz."

"Oh. Yeah. Room 304. You family?"

I wrapped an arm around Winky's shoulder and pulled him to my side. "We're all the family he's got."

"Look, I can't let you in unless you're related. Hospital regulations."

"I'm his wife," I blurted.

"You are?" Winky gasped.

I shut my eyes and wished my freckled friend would disappear. But when I opened them again, I saw my magic genie hadn't granted me squat. I pulled Winky to the side of the reception desk.

"Winky," I whispered. "I'm trying to get us in to see Goober."

"Does Tom know you're married?"

"No. I mean, no, I'm not...ugh! Forget it. Winky, you stay here in the waiting room. I'm going to find some way to sneak into room 304."

"What am I supposed to do?"

"Find a vending machine."

"What for?"

"An RC and a moon pie, okay?"

Winky's left eyebrow shot up. "Roger that."

I left Winky reaching for his wallet and slunk down a hallway in search of room 304. When I got to the nurses' station, I was stopped by an orderly.

"You can't go in there," he said. "Not without a visitor's badge."

"Where do I get one?" I asked.

He hitched a thumb toward the nurse's station. "Over there. But nobody's there right now. They must be busy."

"Okay, I'll wait here," I said, and sat in a chair and smiled at him demurely.

He shrugged and disappeared into an elevator. As soon as the doors closed behind him, I shot up out of the chair, grabbed a lab coat off a nurse's chair, and hid my face behind a clipboard.

Room 304 was the fourth door on the left. I slipped inside and nearly fainted. The patient with the rainbow Mohawk no longer had a moustache, and his bushy eyebrows were thinned out.

But it was Goober all right.

And he was hooked up to more blinking and buzzing medical contraptions than I'd ever seen. Not even on a season finale of *General Hospital*.

Chapter Twenty-Six

"Oh, Goober," I whispered sadly as I stood over his hospital bed. "Are you okay, buddy?"

I fought back tears as the respirator covering Goober's mouth moved mechanically up and down, pumping oxygen into his lungs. My poor friend was unconscious. He was thin and terribly pale, but at least he looked peaceful.

The sound of footsteps coming down the hall pricked my senses. I wasn't supposed to be in the room with Goober. The footsteps stopped in front of his room. The door started to open....

Crap!

I scrambled into the bathroom, hid behind the door, and eavesdropped on the doctors as they discussed Goober's case.

"This is 304...must be the brain tumor," a man's voice said.

A brain tumor! Oh no!

"Yeah. Says here his blood pressure is failing," a woman said.

"That means he's probably in the final stages. Cardiac arrest is imminent."

"How long has he got?"

"No telling. Minutes. Hours, tops."

I bit down hard on my bottom lip. *No! That can't be right!*

"Should we resuscitate when he goes?" the woman asked.

"No. The chart says he's signed a 'no-ro' order. But he's an organ donor, so we should leave the respirator on."

"What parts do we harvest first?"

"I dunno. Let's go check the cafeteria menu," the man quipped. "I heard today's special is liver and onions."

You horrible, callous dirtbags!

"You're so bad!" the woman laughed. "Let's go get some coffee. I feel like a zombie. I've been awake since three."

I heard the door squeak open, then click closed. I peeked out, made sure the dastardly pair were gone, and ran over to Goober's side.

He looked so weak. So fragile. I touched his arm, lay my head on his shoulder, and started bawling my eyes out.

"Oh, Goober," I cried. "Why didn't you *tell* us you were ill, you silly peanut head?"

I felt his shoulder move. I wondered if maybe he could feel my presence. I hugged him tight, then someone said, "What's going on here?"

I lifted my head, thinking I'd been caught by a nurse. But to my surprise, the respirator was gone from Goober's face.

"Goober!"

He stared at me until his faraway eyes came into focus, then said, "Val? What the heck are you doing here?"

"Goober! You're still alive!"

"Of course I'm still alive. How'd you find me?"

"They said you were terminal!"

"Who?"

"The doctors. They just left...."

"Oh. Don't believe those quacks. I'm perfectly fine."

I touched Goober's arm tenderly. "It's okay. You don't have to put on a brave face for me."

One of Goober's plucked eyebrows shot up on his billiard-ball pate. "Does this face look brave to you? Val, this is a gig."

"A gig?"

"Yeah. I get paid fifteen bucks an hour to be a fake patient for medical students."

"Wha...?"

"Today I'm patient 304. Inoperable brain tumor." He turned his head and pointed to some purple lines drawn above his left ear.

"Whuh?" I sniffed, still in shock.

Goober laughed and pulled the tape from his fake IV.

"See? Easiest money I ever made. And as a bonus, I get to ride in an ambulance. I lay around on my butt and get paid, Val. It's paradise!"

"Paradise?"

"Well, there are a few drawbacks. The free lunch sucks. And these marks where the surgeon's supposed to cut? The darn ink they use won't wash off for days."

As I stared at the surreal vision of Goober in a hospital gown, his bald head marked up like Frankenstein, the icy shock I'd been feeling suddenly melted. It'd been replaced by a conflicting blend of relief and anger.

I could have throttled Goober for scaring me so. But then again, the overwhelming relief that he was actually okay swamped my anger like a tsunami. I was too happy to care about anything other than the fact that Goober wasn't going to die anytime soon. Not unless it was at my own hands.

"It's so good to see you," I said.

"Likewise." Goober grinned. "Bring any of the other loonies with you?"

As if on cue, the door to Goober's hospital room burst open. Winky ran in.

"Goober!" he hollered. "Is that you?"

"In the flesh," Goober said.

"Well, I'll be." Winky ambled over to Goober's side, hugged him, and handed him a teddy bear.

"Thanks, pal." Goober shot me a knowing smile. "It's just what I always wanted."

Goober glanced at the clock on the wall. "I get off in twenty minutes. What say I meet you two down in the cafeteria?"

"I hope they won't be serving liver and onions," I said.

"You ain't gonna wear that gown thangy there with yore butt hangin' out, are you?" Winky asked.

"No. I won't be needing it anymore. I just got a clean bill of health."

"Can I have the dirty one, then?"

Goober sat up and smiled. "Sure. I don't see why not."

"THIS IS THE BEST DANG chicken-fried pork chop I ever laid lips to. You want a bite?" Winky asked, and jabbed a fork full of fried meat in my face.

I waved it away. "No thanks."

"What? You ain't hungry?"

"Pork is kind of off the menu right now. Besides, what does 'chicken-fried' mean anyhow?"

"There you are," a falsetto voice sounded to my left.

I looked up and saw a tall, gangly woman in a canary-yellow pantsuit. Atop her otherwise bald head was a crooked, rainbow-hued Mohawk.

"Well, hi there, purty lady," Winky said. "You must be Val's sister Angie."

The woman laughed.

"Winky, that's Goober," I said.

Winky's chin met his neck. He cocked his head, stared at her sideways and said, "Is *not*."

"Is too," the woman said, this time in Goober's voice.

Winky nearly swallowed his tongue. "What in tarnation are you doin' in *that* getup?"

"Teasing old white ladies' hair, mostly," Goober deadpanned. He plopped into the cafeteria chair beside me, his eye on Winky's plate. "I see you chose the chef special."

"Yep. Mighty tasty. You want a bite."

"I prefer to limit my diet to things I can identify."

A wry grin crept across my lips. I'd really missed Goober and his droll sense of humor.

"I'm glad to see you're still the same," I said to him.

Goober smiled. "Still up to your old sleuthing tricks, I see. How'd you find me?"

"Your reputation preceded you," I said. "You're just too good with a teasing comb."

"Yes," Goober sighed. "It's the true artists who are so often plagued by unwanted fame."

"Goober," Winky asked, disbelief still marring his freckled face, "If'n that really *is* you, what in god's good golly are you doing here...dressed like that...working at a *beauty parlor?*"

Goober ran his thumb and index finger absently along his upper lip, smoothing down the ghost of the wooly brown moustache that usually inhabited the space. A warm, comforting feeling enveloped me as I watched him perform his familiar ritual. It was as if no time at all had passed since we'd seen each other last.

"Well, long story short, I parked the RV beside Betty Jean's Beauty and Feed store nearly a month ago, and it wouldn't start again," Goober explained. "After a week or so, I ran out of clean clothes. I started dipping into Cold Cuts' disguises...then Betty Jean put a 'Help Wanted' sign in the window...and, as they say, the rest is history."

"What about this stupid medical gig of yours?" I asked.

Goober shrugged. "Hey, teasing hair doesn't pay as much as you might think."

"But why did you leave...and not tell us where you were going?"

"Because at the time, I didn't know myself. Then life got busy. You know how it is. And you wouldn't believe how many women in this county need a wash-n-set every week."

"But why did you leave in the first place?" I insisted.

"I told you, Val. The AARP found me."

"So what?"

"Well, once *they* know where you live, it's not long before '*the others*' do, too."

I studied the half-strange, half-familiar face of the tranny sitting next to me. Dressed in a practically glowing yellow pantsuit and sporting a rainbow Mohawk, Goober wasn't exactly "blending into the scenery." But then again, he *had* plucked his bushy eyebrows. They now looked like a pair of starving caterpillars mating on his forehead.

Is Goober a spy, a master of disguise, or a raving lunatic?

"What '*others*' are you talking about?" I asked. "The CIA? FBI? KGB?"

"No," Goober said.

"Little green Martian mens?" Winky asked, wide-eyed.

Goober shook his head. "Negatory."

"What then?" I asked.

Goober shrugged. "Relatives."

"Oh," Winky and I said simultaneously.

I nodded in sympathy and said, "Well, that makes perfect sense."

Chapter Twenty-Seven

"Nice ride," Goober said as he climbed into the backseat of Winky's flame-covered hearse.

"Thanky," Winky beamed from behind the steering wheel. He turned to me and asked, "Where we off to next?"

"I guess we can take Goober back to the feed store place. There's no use in him having to suffer through a visit with my mother."

"That's true," Winky agreed. "Not with his health problems and all."

Goober and I shared a secret eye roll as Winky shifted into drive and headed back to US 90.

"I don't mind meeting your mother," Goober said. "But it would be good to have Winky take a look under the hood of the Minnie Winnie first. I'd like to get her in working order, in case I need to make a quick getaway."

"I doubt you'd have to worry about that," I said. "The only way your relatives would find you in Greenville is if they lived there themselves. This place makes the middle of nowhere look like New York City."

"Why'd you drive that thing instead of your Chevy, anyways?" Winky asked.

"You've obviously never owned a Chevette," Goober said. "Riding a bicycle made of macaroni in the rain would probably be more reliable."

"I heard that," Winky said, and let out one of his psychotic, wood-pecker laughs.

I watched the sarcastic lines in Goober's face soften into a smile. My own lips followed suit.

"How'd the Chevette end up in the ally by the post office?" I asked.

"No real mystery to it. It died on me there," Goober said.

"So you actually *did* come back to St. Pete after rescuing me from that RV park in Lake Wales."

"No," Goober said. "I'd already left the Chevy at the post office before I went to Lake Wales. You see, I got a call from Tom saying you'd locked your keys in Maggie's trunk and were stranded in some hillbilly campground. He asked if I could drive over with the spare set, and I thought, why not? It might be fun to give camping another try myself. So I got the spare keys for Maggie and called Cold Cuts about borrowing the old Minnie Winnie. She agreed. So, I took a Greyhound bus down to Sarasota and picked it up."

"That was really nice of you," I said.

"Yeah," Goober said. "As they say, no good deed goes unpunished."

"What you mean by that?" Winky asked.

"Well, by the time I got to the trailer park Val was staying at, she'd settled in and was making the best of it. I didn't want to spoil her fun, so I put on a disguise I found in the back of the RV and blended into the crowd myself."

Goober poked me on the shoulder. "Little did I know Val here was gonna go poison some poor old man and turn the whole RV park into a giant redneck revenge rally."

I swatted him on the arm. "Goober! You know I didn't have anything to do with Woggles' death."

He looked over at Winky and waggled his eyebrows. "Yeah. That's what they all say."

I shook my head at the two clowns. Winky let off another round of Woody Woodpecker impressions. He turned right, wiped his tears with his t-shirt, and hit the brakes. "Looks like we made it back in one piece."

"Miracles never cease," Goober said.

The cobbled-together feed and beauty store was on our right. Winky pulled the hearse up beside Glad's old Minnie Winnie, cut the ignition, and hopped out of the car.

"Let's just have us a look-see."

Goober popped the hood. Winky lifted it and let out a long whistle.

"Looks like the pistons done blowed," Winky said. "Gonna cost a fortune to fix it."

"Will this cover it?" Goober asked.

He reached into his pocket and pulled out a wad of bills thick enough to make a Rockerfeller choke on a glass of hundred-year-old bourbon.

Winky glanced at it and said, "Pro'lly."

"Okay," Goober said. "Let me go inside and tell Betty Jean I'm taking the rest of the day off. Wednesday's a slow day anyway. Nobody wants a wash-n-set this far out from the weekend."

As Goober disappeared into the trailer, I turned to Winky and said, "I think Goober's like Howard Hughes."

"Yep. I could see that. He *do* like his pancakes."

"Winky, that's Howard *Johnson's*. What I mean is, I think Goober's rich...and maybe a bit *eccentric*."

"You tryin' to tell me he's a crazy-rich redneck?"

"Uh...yes."

Winky grinned and nodded. "Well, Val, it takes one to know one."

I pondered Winky's statement while he fiddled around under the hood of the RV. He was right. We were all a bit redneck. And we were all rich. Some of us had more money than others. But the friendship, loyalty, and love we shared were luxuries no amount of money could buy.

I WAS HURTLING DOWN a country road in a flaming hearse, on my way to have my self-esteem obliterated by a woman who found me on the side of the road. My chauffeur was a freckle-faced, redneck donut maker. In the backseat, a fugitive tranny with purple Frankenstein marks on his bald head was slipping out of a yellow pantsuit and into a pair of Winky's orange coveralls.

Yep. Life just doesn't get any better than this.

"Thanks for changing clothes, Goober," I said, trying to keep my eyes on the road. "I'm not sure my mother could take the shock of finding out that her *hair*dresser is also a *cross*-dresser."

"No worries," Goober grunted and he wrestled around in the backseat trying to put on the coveralls.

"I don't mean to be nosy," I said to Goober, "but I'm dying to know. How'd you get all that money?"

"What money?"

"What money? That wad of bills you just showed Winky! That check stub for ten grand I saw at the post office?"

"Oh. *That* money. Royalties."

"I knew it!" Winky yelled. "Yore a king or somethin' ain't you!"

"Hardly," Goober said. "I invented something NASA wanted big-time, okay?"

"And that was your annual check?" I asked.

"Not exactly."

"Monthly?"

Goober sniffed. "Weekly."

"Geez, Goober!" I practically screeched. "If you get all that money, why do you live like some hapless hobo?"

Goober leaned forward until the chin on his bald head rested on the bench seat between me and Winky. It looked like a bowling ball that'd been attacked by kids wielding purple crayons.

"I dunno," he said. "Being rich is boring. Sure, the money comes in handy sometimes. But then, well, people start acting funny when they know you're loaded."

"Acting funny?" Winky said. "You mean like they start tellin' jokes and stuff?"

"I don't think he meant funny ha ha," I said. "More like funny *strange*."

"Right," Goober said. "Most people are just weird when it comes to money. That's why I had to leave St. Pete. Every time the AARP finds me, I know my deadbeat relatives are only days behind."

"I get that," I said. "But why live like a bum?"

Goober cocked his head toward me. "It has its advantages."

"Like what?"

"Well, when you go out with a homeless guy, after the date, you can drop him off anywhere."

Winky shot out a staccato laugh.

"Get serious!" I grumbled.

"Okay," Goober said. "Here's one. No one pays attention to transients, Val. It's the best way to remain invisible."

"That's not true," I argued.

"Okay," Goober said. "There was a guy standing by the traffic light we passed back in Monroe. What did he look like?"

"I dunno."

"My point exactly. Being a transient, you can hide in plain sight."

"But then why go and do outrageous things...like your Le Petomaine fartist gig in downtown St. Pete? Or being a hair-teasing tranny in a rainbow Mohawk? Why couldn't you just...I dunno...work a normal job in the feed store like a regular guy?"

Goober lifted his head from the seat and shrugged. "Too much manual labor involved. Besides, can't a guy have fun if he wants?"

"Fun?"

"Yeah. Working in the beauty shop, I get to hear the latest gossip. I know the dirt on everyone in town. See that gal over there?"

Goober pointed to a plump woman coming out of a Li'l Champ convenience store.

"Yeah," I said.

"She has a two-carton-a-day habit."

"Cigarettes?" I asked.

"Little Debbies."

"You don't say," Winky said. "What kind?"

Chapter Twenty-Eight

"Better drink 'em now, boys," I said. "Mom doesn't allow beer in the house."

Goober's mention of a fat lady's penchant for Little Debbies had stirred Winky's appetite something fierce. He'd jerked the steering wheel on the hearse like a berserk chimpanzee, and before I knew it, had hung a U-turn on US 90 and lurched into the parking lot of the Li'l Champ convenience store in a cloud of orange dust.

My forehead had almost hit the dash as he'd slammed on the brakes, but I hadn't objected. In fact, I'd been glad. I'd been in no hurry whatsoever to get to our final destination, and a visit with my mother always went down better with a dose of liquid courage.

After making a quick run inside for provisions, the three of us stood out in the parking lot, chugging back a shared six-pack of Pabst Blue Ribbon. I didn't know if it was the beer or what, but sandwiched in amongst the monster trucks, ATVs and cobbled-together junkers around us, I didn't feel so conspicuous anymore about leaning on a flame-covered hearse.

"So, what's been going on in your neck of the woods while I've been gone?" Goober asked.

I glanced over at him. That conspicuous feeling started to creep back in again. The orange coveralls Goober'd borrowed from Winky only came down to his shins. Paired with his red converse sneakers, purple surgery marks and that rainbow Mohawk, Goober looked like a clown from some poor kid's birthday party that had gone horribly awry.

"Lose the Mohawk," I said.

"What? You're not into diversity?" Goober joked.

"Lose it. Please?" I begged.

"Okay." He grinned, looked in the side-view mirror and began peeling the strip of wig from his shiny pate.

"Well, Laverne's went and got herself a pet pig," Winky said between gulps of beer. "Named him Randolph."

"Randolph," Goober said, trying the word out on his tongue as if he could taste the bacon within it. "Sensible name for a Sus scrofa domesticus."

"He ain't *that* messy," Winky said. "Besides, Laverne keeps him outside now."

"At least until the fake luau on Friday," I said. "Which, by the way, has actually turned into a *real* luau."

"Good," Goober said, and flung the Mohawk into the hearse through an open window. "Nothing worse than a fake luau, I always say."

"And Caddy's is going to be torn down to build condos," I said.

That got Goober's attention. He scowled. "So, in other words, business as usual on the Florida Suncoast."

"I'm afraid so. I'd laugh at the stupidity of it all if it weren't for the fact that people have gone missing in the deal."

"What people?" Goober asked.

"Greg Parsons, for one," Winky said.

"Greg as in the owner of Caddy's?" Goober asked.

"Yes," I said. "And Norma, too."

"Geez." Goober's face grew serious for the first time. "What happened?"

"If we knew that, they wouldn't be missing now, would they?" Winky said.

Goober sighed. "True enough. I guess that was the beer talking."

"I wish *my* beer could do the talking," I bemoaned. "I never know what to say to my mother."

Winky belched. "Why don't you just say 'Hi, mom'?"

"Gee, Winky," I said sourly. "Why didn't I think of that?"

WE WERE ON OUR WAY to mom's place with a few beers under our belts when I realized I should probably call Tom and let him know the news.

"Tom?"

"Hey! You made it there okay, I see."

"Yes. And we found Goober!"

"You *what?* You're kidding!"

"Nope. He was working as a tranny at my mom's beauty parlor."

Tom was silent for a beat. "What's wrong with me that I'm not even surprised by that?"

I laughed. "I guess it comes with the territory when you're part of *this* crew."

"He's all right, then?" Tom asked.

"Yes. He gave us a scare, but...never mind. It's all good. I'll explain when we get back tomorrow."

"He's coming back with you?"

"I...I guess so. I just assumed he would."

"Good. Tell him I said 'hi.'"

"I will. How are things going with your case? Any news on the whereabouts of Greg and Norma?"

"Nothing definitive."

"What's that mean?"

"I was going to wait and tell you when you got back. But...we found something floating in the surf this morning. It appears to be a human thigh bone."

"Geez! Greg's?"

"Too soon to tell. And another thing. Demolition on Caddy's starts Monday morning."

"Crap. Isn't there *any* way to shut Amsel down?"

"You can't stop progress, Val."

"That's not progress! I wear, Tom. If I have to, I'll stand on the beach and fight the bulldozers tooth and nail."

"Save your strength for your mother. You're gonna need it."

"Ugh. Tell me something I don't already know."

"Be good. See you tomorrow."

"Okay."

When I hung up the phone, Goober said, "Pardon my eavesdropping, but what's so bad about your mom, anyway?"

"Besides the fact that she has a mind rusted shut by entrenched opinions?"

Goober laughed. "Whose mother doesn't?"

"No, really. My mother is a psychological force not to be reckoned with, Goober. She could have been downright diabolical if she'd had any ambition. Why do you think we call her husband 'The Hostage'?"

"Sheesh!" Goober said, his eyebrows an inch higher than normal.

"Speak of the devil, we're here," Winky said. He lurched the hearse into mom's dirt driveway.

A plump woman wearing a faded house dress, a frizzy perm and a bulldog scowl came out and stood on the porch.

"'Bout time you got here!" she bellowed.

I looked at the guys and said, "Welcome to my world."

Chapter Twenty-Nine

Goober's caterpillar eyebrows shot up another inch. "*That's* your mom?"

"Yeah. You do her hair at the beauty parlor," I said as I opened the passenger door on the hearse.

"Yes. I most certainly *do*. My condolences."

"Thanks." I froze in place. "Wait. *Why?*"

"Oh...no reason," Goober said, and climbed out of the hearse behind me.

"I see you done traded in another one," Mom grumbled from the run-down porch tacked onto the faded, ranch-style house.

"What?" I asked her.

She nodded her frizzy head toward Goober. "That ain't Tom."

"No, Mom. It's Goober."

"That one what up and disappeared?"

"Yes, Mom."

"Well, what are y'all waitin' for?" she barked. "Get inside a'fore you let all the AC out."

We followed Mom inside. She waved a ham-hock sized arm at a plaid couch that nearly matched the hideous chair of Tom's that I'd laid waste to last month with my Hammer of Justice.

Huh. Maybe that's why I hated that chair so much....

"Y'all have a seat," Mom said.

Goober headed for a brown recliner and was about to make butt-fall when Mom yelled, "Not there!"

He made a hasty reversal and joined me and Winky on the ugly couch. The three of us watched like mesmerized puppies as Mom backed her sizeable derriere up to the brown recliner, leaned backward, and let gravity take her the rest of the way down. The worn-out recliner creaked in protest. Its groans echoed off the dusty knick-knacks and wood-paneled walls surrounding us.

I breathed in the smell of the place. It was comfortingly familiar, even if it *was* an odor best described as the comingling of stale farts, old cheese, and Jergens hand lotion. I probably would've been more embarrassed if I hadn't been so mortified about the old pictures of me hanging on the walls.

Mixed in among a hodgepodge of classic Olan Mills family portraits, images of me could be found in various stages of my life, including without teeth, without boobs, and without hope.

"Nice place you've got here," Goober said without the slightest bit of irony.

He really is *a good friend.*

"Hrrmph," Mom grunted. "You know how it is. When you got kids, you got nothin' else."

"Mom, you haven't had any kids in here for thirty years."

"No thanks to you, Valliant. Couldn't see fit to make me a grand-baby."

For a second, I thought about showing her a picture of Snogs. But I knew it wouldn't fly. "Sorry, Mom."

"Y'all hungry?" Mom asked.

"I thought we'd all go out to eat," I offered, mostly because I didn't feel like having to scrounge through the leftovers in her refrigerator and then wash all the containers. "Where's the Hosta...husband.... Uh...where's Dale, Mom?"

"He's off in that blamed golf cart with Tiny McMullen."

"I remember that feller," Winky said. "He's the one what fixed Tom's 4Runner when we had that axle-dent when we was up here last."

"Yep," Mom said. "That's right. Too bad Tom ain't here, too. Val, you ain't no prize poultry no more. It's time you learned how to hold onto a man."

"I told you, Mom. We're still together. He just couldn't come. He's working on a missing person case."

Mom eyed me skeptically. "Uh-huh. I'd say *he's* the one's gone missin'."

I rolled my eyes. "Do you think Tiny might be able to take a look at Goober's RV?"

"I don't know, Vallie. Ask him yoreself. They just pulled up."

I ran out the front door to greet Dale. He'd come into my life after I was grown, but he'd been worth the wait. Unlike my mother, I'd never heard him say an unkind word about anyone. The poor little guy was as blind as he was kind. With glasses as thick as coke bottles, Dale never saw me coming.

I wrapped my arms around him. "Hi, Dale!"

"Is that you, Val?" he asked.

"Yes, sir."

"Well I'll be," he said, and hugged me tight against him. "It's so good to see you."

"You, too."

"You remember Tiny McMullen, don't you?"

"Sure." I shook hands with a man so tall and big around he probably wouldn't fit inside a large chest freezer. Then I worried about why I would make such an odd observation.

"Howdy, Dale, Howdy, Tiny," Winky's voice sounded behind me.

"I see he's still out," Tiny whispered to me.

"Huh?" Then I remembered at our last visit. I'd told Tiny we were transporting Winky to Chattahoochee mental hospital. It had been a joke. But it had apparently stuck. "Oh! Yes. He's all better now."

Tiny eyed Winky, then the flaming hearse, and asked, "That your vehicle?"

"Yep," Winky answered.

"She's a beaut. Mind if I look under the hood?"

"Be glad to show you, Tiny. She's got herself a diesel V8, you know."

Tiny shook his enormous head and grunted appreciatively. "I'll be."

"Maybe when you two are done we could run up to Betty Jean's Beauty & Feed and have a look at my RV," Goober said from the porch. "It needs some major work."

Winky shot a knowing look at Tiny. "Busted pistons."

"You don't say," Tiny said with a grin. "That's my favorite kind."

"TINY SURE LOVES WORKING on engines, doesn't he?" I asked Mom as we stood on the front porch and watched the guys climb into the hearse. "Sure you don't want to go along for the ride?"

"Nope," Mom said. "I'll just wait right here."

"Me, too."

Mom shot me a look. "I got dibs on the bathroom."

Crap!

"Well, hurry up."

"You cain't hurry perfection," Mom said, and hobbled down the hallway.

Great.

Some women had synchronized periods. My mother and I had synchronized bowels. Whenever I needed to go, you could bet the farm that she did, too. Her place only had one toilet, and she always beat me to it without fail.

"SO, HOW'VE YOU BEEN Mom?" I asked, and handed her a glass of iced tea.

"Meh. Fair to middlin'. I come into this world with nothin', Val, and as you can see, I still got most of it left."

"Mom!"

"But at least I'm better off than you. I still got Dale."

"Mom, I really *am* still with Tom."

"You ain't married. You ever plannin' to?"

"No plans as yet. I want to take it slow. I don't want to make another big mistake."

"Don't get me wrong, Valliant. Tom ain't no mistake. I like him."

"You *do?*"

"Sure. I've learnt over the years to never underestimate the value of a man who bathes regular."

I took a sip of sweet tea and sucked my teeth.

"Yeah. Well, Mom, you're right. Tom *does* have *that* going for him."

Chapter Thirty

I was lost in the pine woods alone. The pounding of heavy footsteps drew nearer. Some horrid creature was after me! The sound of its panting and growling grew louder as it got nearer...ever nearer.

I held my breath and braved a peek through a scrub palm. Gadzooks! It was a huge brown bear! Its eyes locked on me. Suddenly, it began to barrel toward me, crashing through the scrub, causing the earth underneath me to reverberate with each pounding step.

I tried to get up and run but my legs were paralyzed! Before I could move, the bear leapt on top of me. It threw back its hideous head and let out a horrible, gravely howl. It put its nose up against mine. The hairs on its head were frizzed like a bad perm. I could feel the hot saliva draining from the bear's lips onto my face. It opened its mouth and let out a roar not unlike the sound of a toilet flushing....

I awoke with a start. In the moonlight filtering through the dust particles, I could see I was in my mother's living room. I'd fallen asleep on the couch.

I sat up on one elbow and wiped the drool from my chin. Someone had covered me with a blanket. Lying beside me was a teddy bear. The same one Winky had given Goober at the hospital.

Slow, heavy footsteps echoed down the hall. A door creaked closed. I sighed and leaned back onto the pillow. I pulled the stuffed bear to my chest, smiled, and closed my eyes.

I WOKE AGAIN SOME TIME later, feeling as if I had gotten a new lease on life. With the help of Winky and Goober, I'd survived the evening with my mother. All I had to do now was get through breakfast and I was home free.

I stumbled into the kitchen and scooped a whole cup of Folgers into a filter, poured a carafe of water into the Mr. Coffee machine, and hit the "on" switch.

So far, so good.

But I should have known my luck wouldn't hold.

Goober was the first to emerge from the guest room down the hall, where he and Winky had shared a full-sized bed for the night.

"Morning," he said, and rubbed his bald pate.

"Morning," I said. "Coffee?"

"Please and thank you, ma'am." He shook his head. "You know, Val, I had no idea Lucille was your mom."

"Yesterday you offered me your condolences. Why? What did you hear about her?"

"Well, it's probably just old-lady gossip, but I heard she can be a tad self-absorbed."

"You think?" I deadpanned.

Goober snickered. "I heard she missed her best friend's wedding because she was getting her hair done."

"That's a totally true story. What else did you hear?"

"Well, I know this for a fact, because I do her hair. Your mother's got a bald spot on the back of her head as big as a goose egg."

"What from? She's not sick is she?"

"No. Just scrubbed it off sitting in that Barcalounger all day."

"Oh my word! She'd be mortified to know that."

Goober started to say something, but was interrupted by a round of sneezing that sounded like an asthmatic donkey.

"That would be my mother. She's prone to sneezing spells."

"Is she allergic?" Goober asked.

"Yeah. To cleaning, I think."

Goober looked around. "Well, from the looks of this place, I think *that's* a true story as well."

I TOOK MY TIME GETTING dressed while Mom and Winky sat at the dining room table drinking coffee. The three of us were waiting on Dale and Goober to get back from IGA. They'd taken the golf cart there to get donuts.

As I walked back into the dining room, Winky was finishing up a story I was kind of glad I'd missed.

"But that's the honest truth, Mrs. Short," he said. "I didn't bite the feller. I just closed my mouth and his ear was in it."

"It could a happened to anyone," Mom said in the conciliatory tone she usually reserved for the elderly folks at her church.

"So, how's yore momma?" Mom asked Winky.

"She ain't been the same since she lost her false teeth in that leaf-blower incident."

"Is that a fact," Mom said, shaking her head.

"Yeah, she loved them choppers. She got herself a new set, but they wasn't never the same. After that, she kind a lost her confidence, you know? The spunk went out of her like a fart out of a whoopee cushion."

"It's a hard thing when a woman's looks start to fade," Mom said. She shot me a look. "Ain't it, Val?"

I felt what was left of my self-worth implode. "Absolutely," I said, and wished I had some gin to pour in my coffee.

The sight of the golf cart pulling up in the front yard made me nearly jump for joy. Until I saw Goober, that is. He was wearing that yellow pantsuit and that darned Mohawk. He made it to the door before I had time to stop him.

"Elmira?" Mom asked as he came through to the dining room. "What are *you* doing here?"

Winky laughed. "Goober, you sure make one ugly woman."

"Goober?" Mom asked. "You? You're Elmira? From the beauty shop?"

Oh, crap! Now Mom's going to think he's a cross dresser.

"Yes, I am one and the same," Goober said. He set the box of donuts on the table and bowed with a flourish.

"Are you leaving today with Val?" she asked, a horrified look on her face.

"Yes, ma'am. Tiny said he can tow the RV back to St. Pete for me."

I closed my eyes. *Oh, no. Here comes the judge....*

"Well, I sure am sorry to hear that," Mom said in a tone that sounded genuine. "I hate to see you go."

My eyes flew open with surprise.

"Why, thank you, Mrs. Short," Goober said.

Mom opened the box of donuts, picked out a cruller, and took a huge bite. "Goober, darlin'," she said sweetly, "could you do me a favor and tease my hair up real good one more time before you go?"

THE TV WAS BLARING out *The Price is Right* at ten million decibels, but Mom actually got out of her Barcalounger to see us off this time. She and Dale stood with me on the front porch and we watched Goober and Winky help Tiny McMullen secure the Minnie Winnie to Tiny's tow truck. The fellows had already said their goodbyes to Mom and Dale.

"Well, I guess we'll be going," I said.

"It was great to see you again," Dale said.

"You, too, Dale." He gave me a hug and went back inside.

"Why you got to run off?" Mom asked.

"I told you. I've got that luau party tomorrow."

"You and your fancy city life. Whoever heard of giving a luau for a pig?"

"It's not exactly *for* a pig," I said, then realized it actually *was*. The whole stupid thing had been concocted to save Randolph's hide.

I'm living my life around the needs of my neighbor's pet pig! Geez! I need to start setting better priorities!

"So long, Mom." I started to step off the porch. Mom grabbed me by the arm and pulled me to one side.

"I just want you to know something, Vallie. I liked Tom better'n Goober. Even though I got to admit, that man can tease hair like nobody's business."

She patted her hair, which, thanks to Goober, was the size and shape of a honeydew melon.

"Mom, like I told you. I'm not *with* Goober. I'm still with *Tom*."

"Good. 'Cause I like to think of you settled Val. In your own place and all."

"Thanks, m—"

Mom turned and yelled inside the house. "Dale! Keep yore hands off my crullers! You hear me?"

She turned back to me. "You should be with somebody you love and respect, Vallie. You know. Like me n' Dale."

"Right, Mom."

"That Tom feller. You better hold onto him. You ain't getting' any younger, Vallie. And that behind of yours ain't getting any smaller."

That's like the sow calling the piglet fat. Just how much of this was I supposed to take?

"Well, you know what Mom? You've got a bunch of ner—"

Mom's eyes narrowed to slits. "What, Vallie? I've got a bunch a what?"

I crumpled. "You've got a bunch of family that loves you."

Mom blew out a breath and shrugged. "Yeah. Tell me something I don't know."

Chapter Thirty-One

As always, it was an odd, mashed-up feeling to watch my mom as she stood on the front porch, shrinking down to the size of an ant in the rearview mirror. Or maybe, in her case, to the size of a dung beetle.

The child in me was leaving home. The adult in me was escaping prison. I was sad. I was happy. I was turned inside-out from confliction.

I guess it showed on my face.

"Nothing feels quite as double-edged as cutting your losses," Goober said to me from the backseat of the hearse.

My furrowed brow released its pensive grip. I turned in my seat to face Goober. "That's it *exactly*. How did you know?"

Goober grinned and shrugged. "Like I said, I've got relatives, too."

I smiled, then sighed and looked past Goober out the back window to the cloud of orange dust rising up from the road. It nearly obliterated the view of Tiny McMullen's tow truck as it followed behind us, pulling the old RV.

"I guess nobody's all good or all evil," I said.

"Tell that to my preacher," Winky said, elbowing me. "He's always askin' us, 'When Jesus comes, you want to be in the smoking or non-smoking section?'"

I grinned at Goober, then turned back around in my seat, content to watch the countryside as the hearse wound its way toward the interstate.

"SHOULD WE STOP FOR lunch in Lake City?" I asked when we were about twenty miles from the junction of I-10 and I-75.

"We could go to Taco Schnell," Goober said.

"Don't you ever get tired of tacos?" I asked him.

"Negatory."

I thought about the broccoli salad Tom was probably preparing for tonight's dinner. "Taco Schnell sounds good to me."

"Why not," Winky said. "The hearse needs gas. If we go there, we can kill two birds with one stone."

"Nice one, Winky," I said.

"What?" he asked. "I been meanin' to try Taco Schnell. To tell the truth, I think Winnie might be addicted to it. She picks up lunch for us nearly every day. She gets me KFC but she always eats Taco Schnell."

"Why do you get KFC instead?" I asked.

"I ain't too big on ethnic food."

"Right."

"But if my gal Winnie likes it so much, maybe I should try to like it, too. That stuff must be good for your digestion. After lunch, Winnie goes directly to the toilet. I hear her flushin' it three or four times."

"You really *haven't* eaten at Taco Schnell, have you?" Goober said. "It's tasty. But they *do* put the 'schnell' in gastric momentum."

"And they got parkin' for tractor trailers," Winky said.

"Yes," Goober said. "And there's that, too."

"I AIN'T EAT HERE IN a coon's age," Tiny said as we grabbed our bags of tacos and headed for a table. "Not since my Aunt Vera got herself arrested in the one in Dothan."

"Arrested?" I asked. "What'd she do?"

"They accused her of shoplifting a pile a hot sauce packets, but they was trumped-up charges. Downright ridiculous, really. Anybody could a seen the nightgown she was wearin' at the time didn't even have any pockets."

And I thought Winky *was a hick....*

Desperate to change the subject, I blurted out something I'd been saving for the second half of the trip back to St. Pete. I slid into the booth beside Goober.

"Goober, I've been meaning to ask you. I found the note you left me."

"Huh?" Goober asked, his mouth already full of taco.

"The note in the dreamcatcher. The one you duct-taped inside the Skoal tin."

"Oh."

"I figured it out and sent you a letter." *More like a nasty-gram, actually.* "When you get it, you can just toss it. Tear it up, even. It's probably better if you don't read it at all."

Goober eyed me curiously. "What are you talking about?"

"The post office box. Number 3799?"

"That's not my number."

"It's not?"

"No. It's 1113."

"Then what was the note for?"

"Note?" Goober's left eyebrow went up. "What did it say?"

"PObbLE."

"Oh. Yeah. That was the name I was going to suggest for that new puppy of yours."

"What?" I nearly screeched. "That's the stupidest name I've ever heard."

Goober shrugged. "So what'd you end up calling it, anyway?"

My face heated up like a gas stove. "Uh...Sir Albert Snoggles."

"The third," Winky added with a beaming smile.

"Oh really?" Goober said, his left eyebrow forming a sharp right angle. "You're right, Val. That's *so* much better than Pobble."

"She calls him Snogs for short," Winky said.

It was time to change the subject again before I burst into flames of humiliation.

"What do you think about what's happening to Caddy's?" I asked Goober. "Can you believe some idiot developer's going to tear it down and build condos?"

"All good things must come to an end," Goober said. He turned to Winky. "Does that include the donut shop?"

"Pro'lly."

"What will you do then?" Goober asked.

"Thought I might start me a spare parts and handyman business for folks in my neighborhood. You know, I could get me a warehouse built like Betty Jean's Beauty & Feed. Picture this: a big ol' sign over the door that says, Winky's Trailer Fixin's."

"Riveting," Goober said. "But the name makes for an unfortunate acronym."

"A misfortunate what?" Winky asked.

"I wish you every good fortune," Goober said. He shot me a look and changed the subject. "So Val, you said Greg and Norma are missing. What kind of intel have you dug up so far?"

"Me?" I asked, feigning innocence.

"Yes, *you*," Goober said. "Don't forget. I *know* you. There's no way you're just letting this run its course."

"Tom's been filling me in with bits and pieces," I confessed. "I think this developer guy Amsel has something to do with Greg and Norma's disappearance. But Tom's hands are tied when it comes to the guy."

"Why?"

"The mayor doesn't want anything ruining the condo deal. The cops were told to make Amsel a low priority suspect. But like me, Tom feels in his gut that he's involved somehow."

"I feel something else in my gut," Winky said. He patted his belly full of tacos.

"Me, too," Tiny said.

"What do you have on Amsel?" Goober asked, turning back to me.

"Nothing, really. Looks like he's bought Caddy's from Greg. But that in itself I find strange. I would have sworn Greg would never sell Caddy's."

"Amsel must have met his price," Goober said.

"Or had something on him," I said.

"Like what?"

I shrugged. "I have no idea."

"So that's all you've got?" Goober asked. "A bill of sale? If that was evidence for murder, Val, every property owner on the planet would be guilty."

"It's *not* all," I argued. "Last year, another guy Amsel bought property from went missing in Boca Raton."

"Mouth of the rat," Goober said, and crinkled his upper lip. "Never saw the allure in that name."

"Me either. Anyway, they never found the guy. Amsel had worked out the contract so he got total possession of the deed."

"Now *that's* compelling info," Goober said. "Any solid evidence?"

"No. Just footprints in the sand. And the signs of a struggle. Tom said it looked like someone had been dragged away on their heels by two women in size ten Birkenstocks."

"Huh," Goober said. "The old lesbian hat-trick."

"Is that a thing?" I asked.

"I dunno. But it's got a nice ring to it, doesn't it?"

"Goober, I'm trying to be serious here."

"I know. But it's hard when you have an orange taco-grease moustache."

I wiped my lips with a napkin. "Do you want to hear what I know or not?"

"Sure. But wait until we get in the car. I've got an urgent pit stop to make."

I felt my stomach gurgle.

"Me, too," I said.

Thank goodness we're not at my mother's.

Chapter Thirty-Two

"I think Norma did it," Winky said as he turned the hearse onto I-75 southbound.

"But Greg and Norma are *both* missing," I argued. "She could be just as much a victim as Greg. Remember that fake life alert bracelet Norma gave him? The one he always joked around with customers with?"

"Yeah."

"Tom pulled one up out of the Gulf of Mexico on his fishing trip last Sunday."

"Lucky him," Winky said. "Best I ever caught was a rusty tin can."

"Sounds like a pretty suspicious coincidence," Goober said.

"So you think Norma might have gotten rid of Greg?" I asked.

"She's strong enough to," Winky said. "Norma's done beat me at arm wrestlin' more times than I care to admit."

"Okay, yeah. She's tough," I agreed. "But she's also kind-hearted. I remember she was so generous and helpful when Glad passed away. She put on a brave face, but I know she went in the ladies' room and cried after I left."

"Anybody what goes in that Taco Schnell mens' room today's gonna cry, too," Winky said.

"Winky!" I barked, and elbowed him in the ribs. "We're talking about life and death here!"

Winky laughed. "Well, so am I."

"Ugh!" I looked to Goober for support. His silly face wore an amused, contented look.

"So you don't want to think Norma had anything to do with Greg's disappearance," Goober said. "Let me just remind you, the woman's got big feet. When was the last time you saw her?"

"The day Greg disappeared."

"How'd she seem to you?"

I grimaced. "Well, she seemed kind of off."

"Off? How?"

"I don't know. Grumpy. Or jumpy. Something like that."

"What time was it?" Goober asked.

"I dunno. Late morning. Elevenish."

"So when you saw her, no one was aware yet that Greg wasn't going to show up for his three o-clock shift."

"That's true." I was losing confidence in my convictions. "But it could have been that Norma was upset because she knew Caddy's had been sold."

"How would she know that?" Goober asked.

"She's been working with Greg since day one. He tells her everything."

"He trusts her, then?"

"Yes. At least enough to run the cash register and make the bank deposits."

"Good friends, then."

"Sure. Like family, even. I wouldn't be surprised if she was in his will."

Goober's left eyebrow ticked upward. "So, then, the plot thickens. Maybe Norma decided to swipe what was in the cash register and get out of town. Or, maybe by getting rid of Greg, if she *was* in his will, she could keep the whole enchilada."

"Don't say enchilada," Winky said, then belched loud enough to rattle the windows on the hearse.

"Follow the money trail," I said, remembering Finkerman's advice.

"Speaking of money trail," Goober said, "is Tiny still behind us?" He turned and looked back to check on the RV.

"Yep, it's still there," Winky said.

"What's that broken-down RV got to do with money?" I asked.

"Nothing. Except my life savings are stashed in its walls."

"How much you got?" Winky asked.

Goober shrugged. "Just five or six million, tops. Wouldn't fit in the trunk of the Chevette anymore."

Winky whistled. My gut flopped. Either Taco Schnell was launching a second attack or Goober really *was* right when he'd said that people acted funny whenever money was concerned.

"Tell me more about this Amsel guy," Goober said.

"I already told you what I know." I peeled my eyes from the shabby RV tagging along behind us. "He's your typical jerk-wad developer. He doesn't give a rat's about Sunset Beach. He just wants to cash in on the project and leave us with nothing but another beautiful view shot to hell by another lousy building."

"Why do you think he picked Sunset Beach?" Goober asked.

"Because it's my favorite place in the world," I said angrily.

"I doubt *that*. Has he got connections here?"

"Well, yes. He's married to the sister of my writing instructor."

"Angela Langsbury?"

"Yes. You remembered her name."

Goober grinned. "How could I forget *that*?"

"Langsbury says he's a tightwad. He's actually staying with her instead of going to a hotel."

"So we know he's pathologically cheap."

"I didn't say he was pathological."

"Val, he's staying with *relatives* instead of getting a hotel room."

"Okay. He's pathological."

"Has he got any hobbies?"

"Besides destroying the world's natural beauty?"

"Yeah. We need some guise to contact him."

"But Goober," Winky said, "can't we guys do it ourselves?"

"I mean a *reason*, Winky. What's this Amsel guy do for fun?"

"Like I said, he destroys stuff."

"He smokes cigars," Winky offered.

"That's *it*," Goober said.

"What's it?" I asked.

"Our way in. You suspect Amsel's up to no good. We need a way to learn more about him. So we lure him into our trap with the promise of free cigars."

Goober's idea made so much sense it almost shocked me.

"That just might work," I said.

"Cigar aficionados have a language all their own," Goober said, his faraway eyes already deep into his scheme. "They would have to be *exclusive* cigars."

"Oh! I got this one!" Winky hollered. "I got me a whole box a cigars a feller give me. They're hand-rolled from Honduras. We could give 'em to this Amsel feller. No problem."

"You don't want them?" I asked.

Winky shot me a look. "You know what Winnie would do if I lit one up? No thanks. I just finally got used to sleepin' indoors."

"Good," Goober said. "Now all we need is his address, and we can personally deliver them."

"I'm way ahead of you," I said. I reached into my purse and whipped out the envelope with Angela Langsbury's address.

"Well done." Goober grinned like the Cheshire cat. "I do believe, my compadres in arms, that it's time for another stakeout."

"We better make it quick," I said. "We've got the luau tomorrow night, then there's just the weekend before they start tearing Caddy's down on Monday. Why don't you stay with me and Tom tonight? That way we can get an early start."

"Thanks, but I think I'll go stay with the RV."

"To keep an eye on your money?" I asked.

"Huh? No. Jezebel's in there."

"Jezebel? Who's Jezebel?"

"My pet lizard, of course."

Chapter Thirty-Three

"You sure you've got room for Goober at your place?" I asked Winky as he dropped me off in my driveway late Thursday afternoon.

"Yep. Enough for Tiny, too. He can park the RV in the yard and head out tomorrow. See you in the morning, Val."

As I tugged my suitcase up the driveway, I suddenly felt oddly alone after six hours in a hearse with Winky and Goober. But the feeling evaporated when I opened the front door and heard a familiar yip.

"Snogs!"

The tiny pup danced like a crazed dust bunny as I walked over to his cage.

"How are you, sweetie?"

I squatted down to let the dancing doggie out but the doorbell beat me to it. I stood, padded over to the front door and peeked through the hole. Laverne must have missed me, too. She was on my front porch jumping up and down, wringing her hands.

"What's up?" I asked as I opened the door.

"Oh, Val! You're home!"

"Yeah. What's wrong?"

"Randolph's been missing for three days!"

So it's true. I really do *live in a three-ring circus.*

"That's impossible, Laverne. I've only been gone *a day and a half.*"

"Well, Randolph's been missing since Tuesday night," Laverne said, counting the day on a finger. "Yesterday was Wednesday." She counted another finger. "And today's Thursday." The third finger went up. "See? That's three days, Val."

"Okay," I said, giving up on the math lesson. "What happened?"

"Well, after Nancy brought him home Tuesday night, I hosed Randolph down and put him back in his pen. When I got up the next morning, he was gone!"

"You don't think that Nancy took him, do you?"

"No. Like I said, Randolph ran away on his own."

"How do you know?"

Laverne cocked her horsey head at me as if to imply I was missing the obvious.

"Well, Val, he took his goggles with him."

I don't live in a circus. I live in a looney bin!

"Right. Well, I'm sure he'll turn up soon. I'll keep an eye out for him."

"Thanks Val. Remember, he'll be the pig in the brown aviator goggles."

"Got it."

ABOUT AN HOUR AFTER my chat with Laverne, my doorbell rang again. When I answered it, a strange man was standing at my door. A van was parked in the driveway. As I started to unlock the door, a shiver ran down my spine.

Wait a minute. Is this how Greg and Norma got abducted?

"What do you want?" I yelled through the door.

"Delivery," he barked back.

"From who?"

"Receipt here says, 'From Vance with love.'"

I opened the door. "What is it?"

"Follow me."

I kept a wary distance as we walked to the van. But when the guy opened the door, a new kind of fear gripped me.

Posed on a serving platter with an apple in its mouth was a fully dressed-for-roasting young pig. A lei of onion slices and cherry tomatoes was draped around its neck. A tag clipped to its left ear with a pin had one word on it.

Randolph.

Holy crap on a cracker! Could Vance have gotten his wires crossed?

I shot a look toward Laverne's house. Thankfully, she wasn't outside to witness this.

I looked back at the pig. It was the same size and shape as Randolph. But it couldn't be him.

Could it?

Milly was supposed to tell Vance to deliver a roasting pig to Nancy's place for a luau for Randolph, the pig in Laverne's backyard. Could Vance have thought I wanted the pig in Laverne's backyard to be prepared for the luau?

No. It couldn't be Randolph.

"Oh. Here," said the delivery driver. "I think these belong to you." He reached over and handed me a pair of aviator goggles.

Triple crap on a cracker!

"Where do you want it?" he asked.

"The pig?" I asked, still reeling with shock.

"No. The Goodyear blimp."

"Hold on a second."

I ran over to Jake's place and rang the bell.

"Jake, the pig's here."

"Where?"

"In the van."

"Good. "It's about time." He followed me across the lawn.

"There may be a problem, though," I said as we rounded the side of the van toward its open back-end.

"I hope not, Val. I gotta get that pig in the ground before it's too late!"

Jake's words hung in the humid air like a slab of butchered bacon. Laverne was standing on the sidewalk, staring wide-eyed into the back of the van. She turned to face us and saw the goggles in my hand.

A tiny squeak emanated from her open mouth, then she keeled over into the grass.

"Laverne!" I yelled. I dropped the goggles and ran over to her side. I knelt and held her horsey head up, then patted her cheeks, trying to revive her.

"Laverne," I pleaded into her groggy ear, "it's not what you think!"

At least, I hope it isn't!

AFTER GETTING LAVERNE home and set up on the couch with a glass of gin and a promise Randolph was still alive, I left the goggles with her, went home, called J.D., and finally let poor Snogs out for a wee.

I'd already survived my mother, lunch at Taco Schnell, a six-hour trip with Goober and Winky, and possibly being an accomplice to the murder of Laverne's pet pig. I needed a beer. But when I looked in the fridge all I saw was that kombucha crap and a big bowl of broccoli salad Tom must've made for dinner.

"Arrghh!"

After the day I'd just had, no stupid salad was going to cut it.

I was jonesing for some comfort food. What I needed was fried chicken and macaroni 'n' cheese flavored ice cream.

Why hasn't anybody invented that yet?

I slammed the fridge door, then walked into the dining area and pulled the soiled newspapers from Snog's cage.

Perfect way to end this crappy day.

I headed to the garage to put the papers in the bin. When I opened the lid, what caught my eye set my mouth to watering. It was a takeout box from Tasty-Lickin' Fried Chicken.

A flash of jealous rage shot through me. While I was gone, Tom had cheated on me with a juicy, big-breasted hen!

Through the garage door, I heard the familiar sound of Tom's SUV as it pulled up in the driveway. I scrambled back inside, prepared to launch into a full-blown tirade accusing Tom of committing food adultery. But the tired, worried look on Tom's face sealed my lips shut.

From the looks of it, he might have had a day even worse than mine.

"How was work today?" I asked.

"Let's don't talk shop." Tom wrapped his arms around me. "I just want to hold you."

The warmth of his arms felt like a friendly blanket in a blizzard of strangers.

"Fine," I said. "That sounds good to me."

Chapter Thirty-Four

I woke to the sound of grunting.

Randolph!

I shot up in bed. Tom was standing in the doorway, a cappuccino in each hand.

"You snore like a little piglet," he said with a boyish grin.

"I do not!"

"Then who was it doing all that grunting?" He handed me a cup, kissed me on the nose, and slid into bed beside me.

"Probably Randolph. He's on the loose, you know."

Tom sighed. "Yeah. Laverne told me. No one's found him yet?"

"I hope not."

Tom's eyebrow went angular. "Why would you say that?"

I thought about the pig on the platter with the onion lei around its neck.

"I dunno. I guess I just like the idea of Randolph running around, wild and free."

Tom shot me a skeptical look. "Maybe. But settling down has its creature comforts, don't you think?"

I took another sip of cappuccino and sunk into the pillows. "I guess."

Tom grinned and raised his cup to his lips. The tired, worried face he wore yesterday had vanished. I was glad of it.

"You must have had quite a day yesterday," I said.

"I could say the same for you."

"True enough. Are things going okay at work?"

"The same as usual. Why?"

"I dunno. When you got home last night, it looked like you'd had the stuffing knocked out of you. Then you said you didn't want to talk about it."

"Sometimes words aren't what we need." Tom reached across me to put his cup on the nightstand. He stayed on his side and looked into my eyes. "Sometimes what we need goes beyond words, Val. That's when we need each other most."

"Oh."

Tom's words touched me deep inside. Almost too deep inside. My upbringing with Lucille had taught me that intimacy was a terrible, double-edged sword. Being with Tom was slowly reprogramming that lesson, but my initial gut-reaction of fear still lingered inside me, whimpering like a beaten puppy.

It was still painful to let love in.

"I thought something had gone wrong at work," I fumbled. "With the case...."

Tom kissed me. "Yes. I had a bad day yesterday. But mostly because I didn't sleep much the night before."

"Why?"

"Because you weren't here. I missed you, Val. Didn't you miss me?"

"Of course. It's just that I was so busy, and—"

"It's Friday. What say we go out tonight, just the two of us?"

"We can't, Tom. Tonight's the luau. At Nancy's."

Tom's face sagged. "Oh. That's right. Tomorrow, then?"

"Well, we kind of all planned to meet up at Caddy's tomorrow night. To celebrate Goober's return...and Caddy's last night in business. I'd postpone it, but as you know, Caddy's won't be there on Monday."

Tom blew out a breath. "Well, Ms. Popularity, let me know when your social calendar frees up."

"You're not mad are you?"

Tom smiled. "No. Not as long as I'm invited, too."

"You're always welcome, wherever I am."

Tom winked. "Good to know."

"That includes when I go to visit my mother."

Tom laughed. "Darn. I should have known there was a catch in there somewhere."

WITH TOM AWAY AT WORK, it was time to put Operation Cigar Takedown into action. That's the name Winky, Goober and I had come up with for the stakeout we'd planned for today.

Our mission was to find out if that pig-faced Timothy Amsel had something to do with Greg and Norma's disappearance. We only had today to do it, and the plan was sketchy, at best.

I peeked through the front blinds in the living room to make sure no one was looking. Then I realized it didn't matter if someone was or not. They wouldn't know what I was up to.

Stakeouts always made me paranoid.

I grabbed my cellphone and punched speed dial.

"The coast is clear," I said to Goober.

"Ready when you are," he replied. "I've got the cigars if you've got the wheels."

"I'm on my way."

I gave Snogs one last hug, put him in his cage, and stepped out the door. The coast might have been clear, but the sky wasn't. It was shrouded in a thick carpet of light-grey clouds. It looked like one huge, soggy mattress in heaven had lost all its stuffing.

I crept down the driveway and opened the driver's door on Maggie.

"Where you going?" Laverne asked.

My spine straightened like a shot. I turned around to find Laverne on her knees in her front yard. She was kneeling in front of a wash-pan full of apples, placing Randolph's aviator goggles on top of the heap.

"That's rather unusual fall décor," I said.

"It's for Randolph."

Laverne's normally pert strawberry-blonde curls hung limp in the thick air. She brushed a lock from her liver-spotted forehead.

"I'm hoping to lure him back home," she said. "He loves apples, you know. Every time I see him with one in his mouth, it reminds me of—"

"A luau?" I said before I could stop myself.

"A what?"

"Uh...the luau tonight. You still going?"

"Yes. Life goes on, Val."

For some more than others.

"I hope Randolph's okay," I said lamely.

"I *know* he is," Laverne said. "I can just feel it right here, in my gut. Can't you?"

"Sure." *Maybe later. With a slice of pineapple....*

"Well, I better get going," I said. "I'm off to see Goober."

"Oh! That's right! Tell him 'hello and welcome back' from me. I'm so glad you found him, Val. Now we just need Randolph to come home, and the whole gang'll be back together again."

"Right." I shot Laverne the best smile I could muster, given the circumstances. Chances were fairly certain that we'd see Randolph again...when Jake pulled him out of the roasting pit in Nancy's back-yard tonight.

"Okay, I gotta go."

"Oh! Wait a second!" Laverne scrambled off her knobby knees. "I saved my old newspapers for you. Well, for Snogs' cage, I mean."

Laverne toddled over to her garage and came back toting a grocery sack full of newspapers. Her thoughtfulness sent my guilt-o-meter into overdrive.

"Thanks, Laverne." I took the sack of papers. "I hope Randolph comes home real soon."

"Me, too. But what matters most to me is that he finds his forever home."

And that it's not in a barbeque pit.

I really should be taken out and shot....

"I knew he couldn't stay with me forever," Laverne said. "I just want him to be happy."

I smiled at Laverne, and nearly confessed to my role in Randolph's demise. After all, if I hadn't told Milly about Randolph being in Laverne's backyard, then asked for a butchered pig for the luau, this whole miscommunication snafu never would have happened. But I couldn't bring myself to tell poor Laverne I'd been the one who'd put a hit out on her pet pig.

"Me, too." I shot her another fake smile. "Thanks for the newspapers. Have a nice day."

I put the sack of papers in the backseat, plopped my butt onto the red vinyl, and hit the ignition. As I pulled out of the driveway, I hoped the roar of Maggie's glass-pack muffler would overpower my guilty conscience by the time I made it to Pinellas Park.

Chapter Thirty-Five

The yard in front of Winky's doublewide trailer looked like the scene of a vehicular homicide. The Minnie Winnie's guts were strung out all over the place, as if she'd been disemboweled by a serial killer wielding a socket wrench.

Goober was leaning over the hood, a blunt object in his hand. He saw me and straightened to standing. He nodded to greet me, then pointed the pale lamp of a flashlight in my direction.

A second later, Winky's head popped out sideways from behind the hood.

"Val Pal! You here already?"

"Yes," I said, and cut the engine. "How's it going?"

"Oh, it's goin'," Winky said. He looked at Maggie and his lips twitched. "Gee, as much as I love me a stakeout, I can't go. I got to help Tiny finish up here."

"You go on, Winky," Tiny's voice sounded. He stuck his huge head out from behind the hood and grinned at me. "Give me another hour or three, and I think I got this thang up and runnin'."

"You sure?" Winky asked.

"Yep, go on now."

Winky let out a hillbilly yell. "Woo hoo! It's stakeout time!"

Goober rolled his eyes at me, sighed, and said, "Ya hoo."

"WHERE WE HEADED?" GOOBER asked from Maggie's passenger seat. He'd opened Winky's box of Honduran cigars and was fiddling with one, wagging his once-bushy eyebrows at me like a plucked Groucho Marx.

"Put that back!" I'd tried to sound stern, but was betrayed by my own giggling.

"I thought we'd head to Amsel's office first," I said. "It's Friday morning, so most likely he's there. If not, we'll try Langsbury's place."

"Sounds logical," Goober said. Just then, a sheet of newspaper whirled up in the air from the backseat and wrapped around his bald noggin.

"Winky, hold down that sack," I scolded. "That's your job until we get there, okay?"

"I'm on it, chief."

Winky took my words literally. He tucked the bag of old newspapers under his bum and sat down on top of it.

Goober pulled the errant sheet of newspaper from his face and began to read it.

"Looks like they're having a sale at Mega Shoe Universe Emporium," he said. "Don't miss the new Birkenstocks with ultra-grip tread."

"Ultra-grip tread?" I said. "What? Are they afraid you're going to fall of the face of the Earth?"

"Oh, come on, Val," Goober whined like a spoiled child. "Can we go? Pretty please? I've always wanted to see ultra-grip tread in person."

"Ha ha."

"Yeah! Can we go?" Winky chimed in from the backseat.

"It's on the way," Goober said with a raised eyebrow and an evil grin.

"Come on, Val! Pleeeaaasse!" Winky pleaded.

"You two are a pair of lunatics!" I said, shaking my head. But again, my laughter betrayed my attempt to be serious. When we stopped at a traffic light, I snatched the paper from Goober's hands.

"Lemme see that."

"Testy," Goober said.

I rolled my eyes and looked down at the ad. It showed the picture of a sales clerk standing at a cash register, proudly holding a shoe in each hand. One hand displayed the side view of a shoe so ugly it *had* to be comfortable. The other hand held the shoe bottom forward to highlight its new ultra-grip sole. The odd pattern of zig-zags and circles looked eerily familiar.

"This pattern...it looks like the pictures Tom showed me of the footprints they found on the beach at Caddy's. You know, right after Greg disappeared."

I scanned the article. Someone honked behind me. I looked up at the greenlight and hit the gas.

"How long have they been around?" I asked.

"Footprints?" Goober asked. "They're the first clues ever used to investigate a crime. In fact, did you know that the word 'investigate' comes from the Latin word for footprint?"

"No," I said.

"It's true. Footwear impressions are the oldest forensic evidence known to science."

"No," I repeated. "I meant *those* kind of *shoe treads*. How long have they been around? Maybe they haven't sold that many yet. Maybe we could use them somehow to narrow down the possible suspects."

"Oh," Goober said. "There's that, too."

"Yep! There it is!" Winky hollered from the backseat. "Take a right here!"

I looked over and saw the sign for the shoe store. I hooked a wicked right that sent Winky skidding across the backseat.

"Sorry," I said as I pulled into the lot.

"What fur?" Winky asked, pulling himself together. "That sack a papers give me a good slide. Can we do it again?"

"Maybe later," I said, suddenly wondering how my life had come to this. "Come on, you two."

Let the festivities begin.

"YEAH, I SOLD A COUPLE of pairs," the young clerk from the newspaper clipping said as I held up the hideous purple sandals with the new ultra-grip tread.

"Any size ten women's?" I asked.

"Nope," the clerk said. "I'm sold out. Besides, I think you take a seven."

"No," I said. "I meant, have you sold any size tens to other customers?"

"Inquiring minds want to know," Goober said, and waggled his eyebrows. The makeup I'd applied in the parking lot to hide the purple surgery marks on his bald head didn't do a very good job. But, alas, I didn't have a ski cap in the trunk.

"Out-quiring minds want to know, too," Winky joked.

I scrunched my face at them. "Can it, guys."

"Who are you people, anyway?" the clerk asked.

"The *Mod Squad*, okay?"

My answer went over his way-too-young head.

"Look," he said. "When it comes to customer confidentiality, especially women with feet *that* big, we're sworn to—"

"We're private investigators," I said. "We're on the trail of a potential double homicide. Are you going to cooperate or what?"

I flashed him the tin badge Winky had given me for being a Donut Shack VIP. It was amazing how often that stupid thing came in handy.

"You don't look like officers," the clerk balked.

"Of *course* we don't!" I said. "We're *undercover.*"

The clerk looked at Winky. "That's the best disguise I've ever seen."

Winky beamed. "Thanky. I made it myself."

"Okay," the clerk said. "I sold both pairs of size tens on Monday, the first day they came out. A woman bought one of them. The other I sold to somebody I thought was a man, but turned out to be a woman."

"That's weird," I said. "How did you know she was a woman?"

"Well, when I saw her name on the credit card, I almost called the cops. But then she showed me her ID, and man, that dude was a lady."

"You remember her name?"

"Yeah. It was hard to forget. Norma something or other. You know. Like that movie star."

"Norma Jeen?"

"Yeah. That's it."

My heart sunk. "Crap."

"Looks like Norma's our culprit," Goober said.

"Yeah." I sighed and turned to the clerk. "So, what did the other woman look like?"

"I dunno," he shrugged. "Like you, I guess."

"Like me?"

"Yeah. You know, all you middle-aged women look alike to me."

"Thanks," I said through clenched jaws. I handed him my card. "If you remember anything else, call me."

Chapter Thirty-Six

I found a parking spot on First Avenue South and shifted Maggie into it. I set the gear to park and said, "Okay. Time-out is over."

Winky and Goober unfolded their hands from their laps and opened their mouths for the first time since leaving the blasted shoe emporium and its twerp of a clerk.

"Feeling better?" Goober asked.

"Don't push it," I said. "Where's the cigars?"

"I've got 'em right here." Goober reached under his seat and pulled out the box.

"Okay," I said. "This is how it's gonna go down. They already know me, so Goober, you're gonna go up there and pretend to be the City of St. Pete Cigar Club president or some such hooey. Give Amsel the cigars and invite him to Caddy's tomorrow night for a final blow-out party. Then, if you can, try to get a look at Darlene Dimson and ascertain her foot size. Got it?"

"Yes, chief," Goober saluted. "What was the name of their offices again?"

"Gallworth & Haney."

"Got it. Gallworth & Hooey."

I shut my eyes and took a deep breath. When I opened them again, Goober was ambling down the sidewalk wearing jeans, a t-shirt, my floppy pink sun hat, and a blue blazer of Tom's that I'd scrounged from Maggie's trunk. Suddenly, I noticed the peanut-headed ding-dong was still wearing his red Converse tennis shoes. The problem was, they matched his ridiculous outfit perfectly.

I slapped myself on the forehead.

"This is your best idea yet," Winky said, causing what was left of my confidence to drain out of me like water from a cracked flowerpot.

I lay my head on Maggie's steering wheel and resigned myself to my fate.

"I DON'T THINK DIMSON did it," Goober said as he climbed into the passenger seat ten minutes later.

"Why not?" I asked. I glanced around and was relieved to see he wasn't being chased by security guards.

"That shoe clerk guy said she looked like you. But sorry, Val. Darlene Dimson is one lady who's hard to forget."

"Right," I said. "Who could forget that stupid bun of hers? So, how big would you figure her feet were?"

"Her feet? I wasn't looking at *them*."

In the backseat, Winky laughed so hard he farted.

"She's a blonde bombshell," Goober said to Winky as the air cleared. He turned back to me. "And her cute little feet are no size ten, I can tell you that."

"Ugh!" I groaned. "That wasn't Dimson. That was her snotty receptionist, you dimwit! Where's the cigars?"

"I gave them to her, like you said."

I closed my eyes and took a deep breath. "Tell me *exactly* what you said to her."

"I dunno." Goober shrugged. "Something like, 'I'm here to see Mr. Timothy Amsel. I'm from the Cigar Aficionados Club. I want to invite him to join us at Caddy's tomorrow evening to celebrate his new venture with a box of our finest.'"

I opened my scrunched eyes. A pleasantly surprised feeling zipped through me, somewhat on par with not being punched in the face.

"Okay," I said. "You did good, Goober. Thanks."

"Oh, and I gave her one of the cards you put in the blazer pocket."

"What cards?"

"These." Goober pulled out a business card. It was one of Tom's.

Crap on a cracked up cracker!

"You didn't!"

"What? I thought you said you and Tom were working this case as a team."

The punch in the face arrived after all. "Right," I said, and turned the ignition on Maggie. "Where to next? My funeral?"

"Since we're in the neighborhood, could we go check on the Chevy?" Goober asked.

"Sure, why not. I may be in the market to relocate soon myself."

I DROVE MAGGIE SLOWLY down the alley and cut the engine next to Goober's old Chevy. Finkerman's frizzy head popped up.

"What the?" Goober said.

"I guess I should have told you. Ferrol Finkerman's been living in your car."

Goober shrugged. "It was bound to happen."

"Where's Victoria?" I yelled at Finkerman.

"Went back to her husband," Finkerman said as he climbed out of the driver's seat of the rusty, baby-blue Chevette.

"Couldn't take life on the road?" I quipped.

"Actually, we became a clichéd statistic. We fell out over a financial disagreement."

"I can't imagine that," I said. "As far as I can see, you had *nothing* to fight over."

"Har har," Finkerman said. "It was that overdue library book thing. Victoria found out that while I was paying her a buck a name, I was cashing them in for ninety a pop."

"That's like a nine-hundred-percent markup!" I said.

Finkerman scratched his frizzy head. "Huh. That's what *she* said. Anyway, I told Victoria what I told you, Fremden. Everyone works for the terms they negotiate for themselves. As you can see, it didn't go over well."

"Right."

"So, it's been three days. Where's my fifteen bucks?"

"I already gave you a twenty-dollar advance," I said.

"Here. Have another twenty," Goober said.

"Thanks, pal." Finkerman grabbed the money and sneered at me.

"Look," Goober said. "The title's in the glove compartment. Give it to me and I'll sign it over. The Chevy's yours."

Finkerman eyed the rusty Chevette. "Thanks loads."

"What? You don't want it?" Winky asked from Maggie's backseat. "I'll take her!"

"No," Finkerman said. "It's just...well, I gotta get outta here. The neighborhood's gone to the dogs."

"What do you mean?" I asked.

"I'll show you. Come take a look at this pig I found yesterday."

Randolph! "Where?" I practically hollered.

"Follow me."

We climbed out of the car and Finkerman led us down the alley.

"I'm confused," Winky said, tugging on my sleeve. "Has the neighborhood gone to the dogs or the pigs?"

"With any luck," I said, "we're about to find out."

We followed Finkerman about fifty feet to a blind corner in the alley.

"Have a look," he whispered, and put a finger to his lips.

Everyone stopped in their tracks. In the silence that followed, I heard a grunt.

It's Randolph!

I jumped ahead of the guys and stuck my head around the corner. What I saw was pink and fuzzy, but it sure wasn't cute. I whipped my head back around and nearly puked.

Finkerman threw back his head and laughed like a demented piranha.

"What's wrong, Val?" Goober asked. He grabbed me by the shoulders. "What is it?"

"It's Amsel," I said. "He's behind there making whoopee with Darlene Dimson."

Goober peeked around the corner and winced.

"Really?" Winky said. "I always wondered how they made whoopee cushions."

Goober grabbed him by the collar. "It's not *that* kind of whoopee, Winky."

"It ain't?" Winky asked.

Goober whispered something in Winky's ear. A second later, like a chameleon, Winky's face blushed so red his freckles disappeared.

Chapter Thirty-Seven

"What should we do?" Goober asked.

"Turn around and get out of here," I whispered. I blinked my eyes for the millionth time, hoping desperately to un-see what I'd just seen.

"Why?" Goober asked. "Why don't we just confront Amsel right now?"

"I've already seen too much of him for one day," I said. "And if he sees us together now, he'll know you don't belong to any stupid cigar club. Our plans for tomorrow will be ruined."

"Fair enough," Goober said.

I hissed out an order. "Come on, Winky. Finkerman. Let's go." I spun on my heels and started walking as fast as I could back to the car.

"Wait a minute," Finkerman said, catching up to me. "You *know* those two losers?"

"Shhh! Keep your voice down," I whispered. "Yes. That's the guy who's going to tear down Caddy's beach bar."

"I read about that," Finkerman said. "What's his name...Jim Amsel?"

"Tim."

"Kim?" Finkerman asked again.

"Tim," Winky called out behind us in a voice loud enough to wake the dead. "Like Tim the Tool Man."

"More like just Tim the tool," I said to Finkerman, and shot Winky an annoyed schoolmarm look.

"What do I do now?" Finkerman asked.

"What do you mean?"

"Now that Goober's given me the Chevy, my gig guarding it is over. I could use some gainful employment."

"Finkerman, the only thing you're good for is...."

An idea hit me like a rotten tomato in the kisser.

"You know what, Finkerman. I've got the perfect assignment for you."

"WHAT DID YOU SAY TO Finkerman?" Goober asked as we eased down the alley.

"It's a private arrangement," I said, and turned left onto First Avenue North to make a straight shot back toward the beach.

"Well, can I at least ask the terms?"

I looked over at Goober and put a hand on my purse.

"Finkerman could either do what I asked or I was going to rear back and wallop him with my hillbilly hacky-sack, okay?"

Goober picked up my purse. "Sheesh, what have you got in here? Bricks?"

"Rolls of quarters."

Goober looked impressed for a bald Frankenstein. "Ah. Both effective *and* practical."

"That's right," I said smugly. "Not like that stupid Dalmatian purse Dimson had. Did you see it?"

"Like I said once before, that wasn't exactly what I was looking at."

Winky laughed, then chimed in from the backseat. "This Dimson gal. She's got herself a pocketbook made out of a *dog?*"

"No," I answered. "Dalmatian just means it's spotted black and white."

"Oh," Winky said. "Like the one in the picture."

"What picture?" I asked.

"That one for that shoe place."

Goober picked up the newspaper on the floorboard by his feet and studied the picture.

"He's right, Val."

Goober held the paper up where I could see it, and pointed a long, boney finger at the corner of the picture. There, by the cash register, behind the clerk holding up the shoes, was the corner of a black-and-white spotted pocketbook.

"Well, I'll be," I said.

"You think it's the same one?" Goober asked.

My nose crinkled. "Well, like *you* said, I was a little distracted by...you know...too. But it could be."

"That would mean Darlene Dimson bought the other pair of Birkenstocks," Goober said.

"It would, if we could prove it," I said.

"Well, that's what we're working on, ain't it?" Winky asked.

"Indeed," Goober answered. "So, where are we heading now?"

"Well, we know Dimson made one set of those tracks on the beach, and Norma made the other," I said. "They must have been working in cahoots with Amsel to get rid of Greg. I hope that means we're heading toward a solution that puts Amsel behind bars."

"No," Goober said. "I meant, where are we going? If you plan on taking us back to Winky's, you should've turned right and gotten over onto Fifth."

"Oh. Sorry. You're right. It completely slipped my mind."

WHEN WE PULLED UP IN front of Winky's place, I was surprised to see that the old Minnie Winnie's guts were no longer spread out from here to kingdom come.

Tiny was bent over the garden hose, washing his hands. When he saw us, he straightened his enormous girth and waved a huge hand at us.

"Got her runnin'!" he yelled.

"I knew you could!" Winky hollered from the backseat.

"So, we good until tomorrow?" Goober asked me.

"Yeah. I guess so. We've got the footprints solved. I'll tell Tom tonight. Now I think we should do like Finkerman suggested and follow the money trail."

"Hey, Goober!" Tiny hollered.

I looked up to see gigantic Tiny waving a large, red pair of women's pumps.

"Found these on the floorboard," he said in the worst women's falsetto I'd ever heard. "Mind if I borrow 'em? I got a hot date tonight."

"Keep your mitts off those," Goober yelled back. "They're my lucky shoes!"

"Nice one," I said sourly.

Goober shot me a look. "What?" he asked. "Those are orthopedic. A real lifesaver when you're on your feet teasing hair all day."

"Val, you goin' to that luau tonight at Nancy's?" Winky asked.

"Yeah. I don't have much choice. To tell you the truth, I'm not looking forward to sinking my teeth into Laverne's pet pig. You coming?"

"Naw," Winky said. "I couldn't stomach it myself."

Goober laughed and I punched him on the arm.

"I'll see you two at Caddy's tomorrow, then. Hopefully Amsel will show up and bring Dimson with him. If he does, Goober, you've got to pretend to be Tom."

"Why?" Goober climbed out of the car. "No one saw me except the bombshell receptionist."

"Exactly. That means Amsel won't know you're not Tom. That'll come in handy tomorrow night...if all goes to plan."

"What plan?" Goober asked.

"I'll fill you in tomorrow."

"Okay. What time should we meet?"

"My place at six."

I shifted Maggie into reverse.

I ought to be able to come up with a plan by then....

Chapter Thirty-Eight

I peeked through a slit in the living room blinds and shook my head. I could barely make out the hazy, yellow glow of Nancy's front-porch light through the gray wall of rain.

"I think it's a monsoon," I said.

"Nancy sure knows how to put out the *Welkommen* mat," Tom quipped.

I grinned. "I'm going to let her know we're not coming."

"Unless you've got a kayak hidden away in the garage."

"Not even then."

I grabbed my cellphone from the kitchen counter and punched in her number.

"Nancy?"

"Ja."

"I think we're going to have to take a raincheck on the luau."

"Don't joke," she said. "The barbeque pit is a swimming pool. What will I do with all these flowers?"

Like a true Southerner, I felt the need to apologize—even for the weather.

"I'm sorry." Guilt compelled me to add, "We're having a party at Caddy's tomorrow night. It's to celebrate the return of Goober, an old friend. Why don't you come along?"

I waited a beat while Nancy recovered from what sounded like a near-death strangling.

"Really?" she asked.

"Sure. Why not?"

"Okay. I will come," she said stiffly. "Dank...thank you."

"Sure. See you around seven at Caddy's."

I clicked off the phone and sighed with relief. I looked over at Tom. He appeared even more pleased than I was at the sudden freeing-up of our evening's obligations.

"Looks like you're going to get your quiet evening alone with me after all," I said coyly.

He took me in his arms and gently swept the hair from my forehead. As his lips brushed against mine, he whispered, "Who said anything about *quiet?*"

SATURDAY MORNING, IT was still raining. Perfect weather for lying in bed with a hot, steamy...

...cappuccino.

"I wish we could start every day like this," I said to Tom as he slid into bed next to me.

"Me, too. We make a good team, don't you think?"

I nearly choked on my cappuccino.

"Uh...speaking of team, I've got some news I need to share with you."

"What's that?" he asked.

"Hold on. I want to show you something."

Tom grinned seductively at me. "Let me put down my cappuccino first."

"Ha ha. I'm serious. It's about the case you're working on. I'll be right back."

I padded into the kitchen and came back with the ad for the Mega Shoe Universe Emporium.

"Look at this." I handed the ad to Tom.

"Good grief!" Tom said as I crawled back into bed. "Don't you women *ever* stop thinking about shoes?"

I jabbed him with my elbow. "Har har. See the treads on those new Birkenstocks? Do they look familiar?"

Tom squinted at the paper.

"Here, use these." I handed him the pair of pink cheater glasses from my nightstand.

He scowled at them playfully, then popped them onto his nose.

"Whoa! These look like the same shoe impressions as the ones on the beach."

"I thought so, too."

"That's really good, Val."

"Thanks. But that's not all. I know who was wearing them."

"What?" Tom sat up on one elbow and studied me through the pink bifocals. "Who?"

"Norma Jeen and Darlene Dimson."

"How do you know that?"

"I asked the clerk at the store. He told me he'd only gotten in two pairs of size tens, and he remembered who bought them."

"He knew them by name?"

"Yes and no. He said he thought one was a man, but turned out to be a woman. He checked her credit card because he thought it was a guy committing fraud. He remembered her name because it was like a movie star."

"Norma Jeen."

"Yes."

"And the other one?"

"Well, see that corner of a pocketbook on the counter?"

Tom squinted at the newspaper clipping. "Yes."

"Darlene Dimson has one just like it. You know, I hate to think of Norma as capable of this. But she and Dimson are in this together with Amsel. They've gotta be."

"That's unbelievable." Tom shook his head.

"Don't be angry, Tom. I only did all that because you said you couldn't go after Amsel and—"

"I'm not angry," Tom said, cutting me off. "I'm impressed. I think you really might have what it takes to be a detective, Val. Or should I call you Valliant Stranger?"

"Let's just keep it at Val. I'm tired of being a stranger."

Tom smiled. "Okay. But I do have one question. Why didn't you tell me all this earlier?"

"I just found out myself yesterday. I was going to tell you last night, but I didn't want to ruin, you know, the *mood*."

Tom shot me his boyish grin. "I appreciate that. You know, what you've got here is still all circumstantial evidence, but it's good. It gives us something more to go on."

"Are you going to call the office with it?"

"I'd like to confirm everything myself first. Is there anything else you want to tell me? About the case, I mean."

"Only suspicions. Dimson forged my deposition for Langsbury. So I'm thinking, what would stop her from forging the sale papers for Caddy's, too?"

"Good reasoning. I wondered that myself. So, I had Parson's signature on the sales contract compared against samples of his known signature. It checked out, Val."

"Then I don't get it. Why in the world would they get rid of Greg? They wouldn't need to...unless there was some death stipulation in the sale contract. You know, like the one you told me about in Boca Raton."

"Yeah. But I read the contract myself. Parsons wasn't holding the note for Amsel. As far as I know, there weren't any addendums added afterward, either. But there could have been."

"So, why would they have to get rid of Greg?"

"I don't know. Maybe what you said the other day. About Norma being in Greg's will?"

"It was just an idea."

"But your ideas are good, Val. I'm proud of you."

I winced. "Uh...thanks."

Tom eyed me dubiously. "I know that look. What are you not telling me?"

"Uh...just that...well...tonight, at the party? Goober might pretend to be you."

Tom's smile disappeared. "What? Why?"

"We're going to try and get a confession out of Amsel. You see, yesterday, I sort of lent Goober your sport jacket so he could deliver a box of cigars to Amsel and invite him to Caddy's tonight."

"Why would you do that?"

"It was just a spur-of-the-moment idea...part of a plan I hadn't thought through yet. I figured if we could get Amsel to Caddy's tonight, maybe we could find a way to get a confession out of him before it was too late."

"But why did you have Goober tell Amsel he was *me?*"

"I *didn't!* You see...Goober found your business card inside a pocket of your sport coat and...well, it's all a big misunderstanding. I'm sorry, Tom."

"Geez, Val! Were you really going to let me go to Caddy's not knowing about this?"

"I...I'm telling you now. And it's not too late. If you're up for it, tonight we could work on this thing together, as a team."

"This *thing?* Val, I'm a police officer. We have rules to follow."

"I know. But you see, Amsel wasn't in the office yesterday. He never saw Goober. You could take his place as...you know...*yourself.*"

"So let me get this straight. You're saying I could be *me* tonight?"

"Uh...yes."

"Thanks."

"Well...that is, as long as you don't mind also being the president of the St. Pete Cigar Lovers' Club."

"Really Val? I don't know what to say. I'm speechless."

"Then don't say anything. Just come along for the ride and let Goober do the talking."

"That's not what I meant."

"I know. I was trying to be funny."

"We went way past funny a long time ago."

"Okay, Tom. You're right. I get that. But you told me that being a team means we shouldn't hold anything back. I just want you to know that *that's it*. You now know my entire Plan A."

"Good. Wait a minute. Does this mean there's a Plan B?"

"Eeh...yes and no. I thought it might be wise to have a backup strategy."

"Do I want to know about it?"

I gritted my teeth and shook my head. "Probably not, as I haven't got it all worked out yet myself."

I LET TOM STEW IN HIS own juices until lunch time. When he emerged from the bedroom, he looked a little less angry—more like *Robocop* than *The Incredible Hulk*.

"I've had time to process this," he said, walking up to me. "And from now on, we need to hold *nothing* back. If we have a problem, we need to share it, Val. We need to be brutally honest with each other to the bitter end, or you and I are never going to work."

"Is this the bitter end?"

Tom's face registered surprise. "No. Not even close."

My gut relaxed with relief. "Thank you. In that case, I have another confession to make."

Tom winced and closed his eyes. "What?"

"I hate broccoli."

A sea-green eye peeped open.

"You do?"

"I abhor it."

"So do I!"

"Then why on earth did you make a giant batch of broccoli salad for dinner the other night?"

Tom burst into a stupid grin. "So we could eat healthy. I thought that's what you wanted."

"No way. You gotta die of something. Might as well die fat and happy."

"If you hate broccoli as much as I do, then why did you eat it?"

"I didn't want to hurt your feelings."

"See? That's what happens when we keep secrets from each other."

"What?"

"We both end up miserable for no good reason."

"So what do you want to do about lunch?" I asked. "It's still raining cats and dogs. I hate to put a poor takeout delivery guy through this."

"The weather's not supposed to clear up until this afternoon," Tom said. "We *could* defrost the giant bag of Brussels sprouts in the freezer."

"Yuck."

"What have you got against Brussels sprouts?"

"Hopefully anything except my tongue. As far as I'm concerned, sprouts should remain a verb, not a noun."

Tom grinned. "That's funny." He looked down, bit his lip and blew out a breath. "Well, since we're being totally honest with each other...."

"What?"

Tom walked over to the freezer and pulled out the bag of sprouts.

My upper lip met my nose. "I *told* you—"

"Hold on a second." He set the sprouts on the counter and reached into the freezer again. When he pulled his hand out, this time it was holding a pint-sized carton of ice cream.

"You've been holding out on me!" I squealed.

Tom laughed. "My secret hiding place. I knew you wouldn't touch that bag of sprouts. What would you say to just putting on some sweatpants and eating ice cream for lunch?"

"I'd say I never loved you more than this very moment."

Tom grinned. "So, I can take that as a 'yes'?"

"Most definitely. All I ask is one small favor."

"What's that?" Tom's handsome face shone with an adoring expression I hoped one day to live up to.

"When I'm old and gray and big as a whale?" I said.

"Yes?"

"If I lapse into a coma, promise me you won't pull the plug until I'm a size four."

Tom grinned. "I promise."

Chapter Thirty-Nine

"I hope there's a break in the rain soon," I said, and let go of the bedroom blinds. "I'm supposed to meet the guys at Caddy's in an hour...you know, to go over the plan."

"Is that Plan A or Plan B?" Tom quipped.

"Plan A, as far as you know."

"I thought I was part of the team."

"You *are.*" I opened the bedroom closet. "So tell me, detective, which of my outfits would be best for Operation Take Down Amsel?"

"You may want to wear your rubber wading boots."

"You're right. It may never stop raining."

"Rain wasn't exactly what I was implying. You really know how to step in it, Val."

"Ha ha, Tom."

He had a point. I looked in my closet for some rubber-soled shoes that would go with the red sundress I'd pulled out. "Well, I'm going, come hell or high water. It's the last chance the gang has to be together at Caddy's."

"I'm surprised they're still serving food," Tom said.

"They're not. It's alcohol only. And BYOB. As in, bring your own barbeque. Everybody's bringing something."

"We've got the rest of that big broccoli salad...."

"These are our *friends*, Tom. I'd like to keep it that way. Besides, our contribution is the pig. Jake saved it from drowning in the pit yesterday, and was supposed to be roasting it in his oven today."

"Sounds good." Tom's face dropped suddenly. "Oh, geez, Val! What about Laverne? Do you know what Salmonella Sally's bringing? How are we going to switch it out?"

"We don't have to worry about that anymore." I tugged on the sundress. "Zip me?"

"Sure."

"I discovered Laverne's secret ingredient that was giving everyone the squirts. Turns out she was using Krassco in everything."

"Krassco? As in WWII lard?"

"That would be it. Apparently, she'd somehow secured an almost-lifetime supply of it."

"I wonder how many lifetimes she's taken with it."

I smirked at Tom. "Come on, it wasn't that bad."

"Val, in Vietnam, we used to leave tins of that stuff behind to disable our enemies."

"Well, whatever. It's all used up now."

"Wait a minute. I thought you said you'd told me everything."

"We've been together a few years now, Tom. There's bound to be a bit of a backlog I'll need to clear out. You'll have to give me a few mulligans."

Tom grinned. "Okay. As long as they don't contain Krassco."

I laughed and peeked through the blinds again.

"Hey, looks like there's a break in the rain. You ready to go?"

"Sure. But you look much too beautiful for a simple stakeout." Tom slipped his hands around my waist. "Are you sure you don't have anything else planned?"

"I promise. I guess I just wanted to look my best for our last dance at Caddy's."

"Well, my lady, mission accomplished."

JUST AS TOM PULLED into a parking spot at Caddy's, J.D. pulled up beside us in his white Mercedes. I watched as diminutive J.D. scooted around and opened the door for Laverne. Statuesque in her gold high heels, she towered over J.D. like Godzilla over Tokyo.

"Why don't you do that for me?" I asked Tom.

"What? Come up to your waist?"

"Ha ha. No. Open the door for me."

"I thought you didn't like it."

"I never complain when someone's polite."

"Well, aren't you full of surprises today? Sit tight and allow me."

Tom got out and opened my door. I took his hand and emerged from the SUV like a middle-class Marilyn Monroe.

"Hey, Laverne," I waved at the pair. "Hey, J.D."

"Looks like it finally stopped raining," J.D. said.

"Good thing, too," Laverne said. "One raindrop would ruin this whole batch of meringues."

I took a peek at them. "They look delicious, Laverne."

"Congrats on the whole Krassco thing," I heard Tom whisper to J.D. as I admired Laverne's treats.

"I'm a real survivor," J.D. joked with Tom. Then turned to me and said, "Here, Val, these are for you. I figured I owed you them."

I looked down and smiled with delight. "Where did you find these?"

"At the drugstore. It's the first of September. Time for the Halloween candy. You know, right before the Christmas junk arrives."

Tom eyed the bag of chocolate-covered marshmallow ghosts in my hand.

"What's that all about?"

"I claim a mulligan," I said. Tom rolled his eyes.

"Guess what," Laverne said. "Something ate the apples in the wash-tub. It had to be Randolph!"

"It could have been a possum," Tom said.

Laverne shook her head. "Impossible. It was Randolph, all right."

"How can you be so sure?" I asked.

"Easy. The goggles are gone, too!"

I should have known....

I nodded at Laverne and caught a glimpse of the ugly, three-story orange house neighboring Caddy's. "Are you going to miss the place when you move?" I asked J.D.

"I haven't yet, so I probably won't."

"What do you mean?" I asked.

"I moved out on Wednesday. The deal with Amsel closed on Thursday."

"Oh." The finality of his words made everything going on seem real for the first time. A sting of disappointment shot through me.

"J.D.'s been staying with me," Laverne said. "We're officially shacked up...until his place is ready at the Ovation."

"But the lights are on," I said, nodding toward the house. "Who's over there?"

"I don't know and I don't care," J.D. said. "The check's in the bank. Let Amsel do with it what he wants."

We stepped up onto Caddy's open porch. We were the only folks there besides a bartender I recognized from way back, but couldn't remember his name.

"Hi," I said. "We're here for the going-away party. Where is everybody?"

"With Greg and Norma gone, most of the customers quit showing up days ago," he said. "I guess tonight the bad weather's keeping away the rest."

"It's just a little rain," I said.

The bartender sighed. "You know that old saying, fair-weather friends. What can I get you?"

"A Tanqueray and tonic please, twist of lime."

I reached for my wallet, but Tom's hand folded over mine.

"I've got this." He turned to the bartender. "I'll have a beer. Windy tonight, eh?"

"Yeah," he said, and handed us our drinks.

As I took a sip, I glanced over Tom's shoulder and saw Jake come in. He walked up to me and handed me something.

"What's this?"

"It's the tag that was clipped to Randolph's ear. I took it off before I baked him. I thought well, you might want to have it."

"Why on earth would you think that?"

"It might be closure...you know, for Laverne." Jake nodded his head sideways toward the bar. Laverne was leaning over the counter, offering the bartender a meringue.

"Oh." I tucked the tag in my purse. "Maybe I'll show it to her later."

"What's that?" Tom asked.

I winced. "Uh...another mulligan."

Tom shook his head. "Keep this up Val, and you might have to move to Ireland."

Chapter Forty

"Where's the pig?" I asked Jake while Tom was distracted talking to J.D.

"It's in my van. I'm going to need some help carrying it in."

A heavy gust of wind swept through the porch like a whirlwind, bringing enough moisture with it to melt my hair like cotton candy in the rain.

"Should we put it on a picnic table outside?" I asked, swiping at an errant strand of hair.

"Better make it indoors," Jake said. "It looked like it was getting pretty rough on my way over."

I glanced out at the greyish-red sunset fading over the Gulf. "If the weather was gonna get worse, they'd have said something on the news." I nodded over toward the bar. The TV above the bartender was tuned to a tennis match.

"I guess," Jake said. He looked past me in the direction of the parking lot, then quickly said. "If you need me, I'll be drinking in the men's room."

"Huh?" I followed his line of sight and saw Nancy stumble through the door, a squawking parrot on her shoulder. She had Hawaiian leis stacked around her neck up to her chin. "Isn't that ridicu—" I said, turning back to Jake.

But he was already gone.

I WAS MAKING SMALL talk with a parrot when I heard Winky bellow behind me.

"Better watch out, Val!"

I turned to find him standing right next to me, Winnie at his side.

"Hey, you two!"

"Winnie brought you a batch of them awful cookies I told you about."

"Winky!" Winnie shot him a dirty look. "Here, Val." She handed me a sack. "These are for Snoggles. They're *dog* treats."

"Oh," Winky said. "Well that explains it."

I stifled a smirk and strategically changed the subject before those two erupted into another domestic disagreement. "Tell me. When you two get married, are you gonna have kids?"

Winnie opened her mouth to say something, but Winky beat her to it.

"Nope," Winky said. "We got the dogs now. Our Nancy Drew and Hardy Boy. They're enough for anybody."

Winnie opened her mouth again to say something, but this time Milly beat her to it.

"You can never have too many dogs," her voice sounded behind me. I turned around to see my old friend Milly with Vance by her side. "In fact," she said, "we'll be looking for good homes for a new batch of pups in a couple of months."

"It seems Charmine has gone and gotten herself knocked up again," Vance said. "This time by a Chihuahua named Paco."

"So, it appears you two are expecting again," I quipped.

"Really? You, too?" Jorge asked as he and Sherryl walked up. "We can't wait for ours to get here!"

"But Jorge," Milly said, "I thought you didn't want a puppy."

"Puppy?" Jorge's face reddened. "Oh! Is that what you're talking about?"

"Yes," Milly said. "What else?"

"Oops." Jorge cringed and wrapped his arm around his wife, Sherryl. "Well, we don't want to upstage Goober's big day, but we're expecting!"

"Expecting what?" Winky asked.

"A bambino...or bambina," Sherryl said.

Winky clapped his hands together. "All right! I got me some bongos in the truck. Maybe we can start us up a band tonight!"

Jorge glanced around at the rest of us. I couldn't speak for anyone else, because I, for one, was speechless.

Jorge shook his head. "No, Winky. What Sherryl means is that we're expecting a *baby*."

"A gaul-dang baby?" Winky cried out. "Well I'll be! Allow me to correctify myself. Congratulations, you two!"

Tom came over and joined us. "What's going on?"

"Jorge and Sherryl are having a baby!" I said.

Tom eyed me carefully. "You knew already, didn't you?"

I diverted my eyes. "Mulligan."

"This here calls for some champagne!" Winky said to the bartender. He obligingly pulled out a bottle from the cooler behind the bar and uncorked it while everyone congratulated the expectant couple.

I helped Winky pour the champagne into plastic cups, and we passed them around until everyone had one. But when I got to Winnie, she put her hand out to stop me.

"I can't have any," she said. She looked up at Winky. "I'm pregnant, too."

Winky let out the biggest hillbilly yell I ever heard.

"Wooo hooo!" he hollered. He grabbed Winnie, hugged her close and said, "I thought you'd done hard-boiled all your eggs in that hot tub of ours."

"Hardly," she laughed. "Sorry I've been so grumpy lately. I wasn't sure you'd be happy about the news."

"I ain't happy, Winnie. I'm what you call it? Aesthetic."

"Ecstatic?" I asked.

"That's the one!"

"Never a dull moment," Goober said, walking up wearing a ski cap.

"That's a good look for you," I quipped, and handed him a cup of champagne.

He shrugged. "Keeps the stares to a minimum."

I raised my plastic cup. "A toast! To the next generation of our little family!"

"And to the last one," Winky added. "Let's don't forget about Glad."

"Never," I said. "Who could forget her? In fact, let's give her a toast too. You all know what I'm talking about!"

Everyone laughed, raised their glasses and cheered, "Screw you, kiddo!"

THE THOUGHT THAT WINKY and Jorge were both getting another chance to have a family made my heart swell with pride, and my eyes brim with tears of gratitude.

But it didn't last.

Our little family love fest came to a screeching halt when Amsel showed up carrying his shoes in his hands and Dimson on his arm.

I shot a glance at Goober. He nodded. I looked over at Tom. He cocked his head and looked at me sideways.

One out of two wasn't that bad. I nodded back at Goober.

Operation Take-Down Amsel was officially in play.

AMSEL STEPPED UP TO the bar next to me, slipped his expensive Gucci loafers back on, and bellowed into the crowd, "Where's the idiot who gave me that box of cigars?"

I glanced over Tom, then Goober, wondering which one would step up to the bat. Goober beat Tom to the punch—in more ways than one.

"*I* did," Goober said, adjusting his ski cap. "I'd like to officially welcome—"

That was as far as Goober got before Amsel punched him right in the schnozz.

"I put those rotten cigars in my humidor," he screeched as Goober stumbled backward into Tom's arms. "Now my entire collection is infested with weevils!"

Couldn't have happened to a nicer guy.

Goober took a step toward Amsel, but the pig-faced coward ran out the door. Tom held Goober in a bear hold. I heard him say, "Let him go, buddy. Amsel's not worth it."

"Story of my life," Darlene Dimson mumble under her breath as she watched Amsel disappear out the door. She walked over to the bar and ordered a vodka on the rocks, laid a ten-dollar bill on the bar, and headed for the ladies' room.

I took a step to follow her, but was stopped in my tracks by a vision even uglier than Amsel. Hobbling up onto the porch was either the ugliest woman in the world, or it was Finkerman...*in drag.*

Chapter Forty-One

"Dear god. Is that you, Finkerman?" I asked the frizzy-haired hag.

"It's me. But tonight I'm Sharon. As in share-n-share alike. Get it?"

"Classy."

Finkerman waggled his drawn-on eyebrows. "I thought you'd like it."

"I told you to dress sexy, Finkerman. Not *hexy*. You look like a witch in that."

"I thought a little black dress was *always* in vogue."

"Yeah. If you're a *woman*."

"Whatever. Listen, I just saw Amsel run over to that ugly orange house across the beach."

"Yeah, I know."

"How am I supposed to do my thing now?"

"Plan A is in the crapper." My own words lit a lightbulb in my head. "Hold on. Dimson just went to the ladies' room."

"That alley skank?"

"Yeah. I'm gonna go in there. Maybe I can figure out something else while I'm in there. Wait here."

Finkerman glanced around. "Where else would I go?"

I TOOK A SEAT IN THE other stall next to Dimson and, for lack of any other ideas, flushed the toilet.

"Is that you, Karen?" she asked.

"Uh...yes," I answered.

"You showed this time. Good. Listen, the plan's changed. But it's actually better. That jerk Amsel's gone and gotten himself in trouble again running his big mouth. What a surprise. Anyway, he's ditched me and run over to that house he owns next door. He's right where I want him for our original plan. You understand?"

I waited in the silence for a beat and said, "Yes."

"You've got the recorder ready?"

"Yes."

"Okay. I'm going to slam down a very necessary glass of vodka, then I'm going to meet Amsel at his place for a quickie. I'll leave the blinds open. Don't mess it up this time. I'm not doing that alley stint again, you hear me?"

"Yes."

"Get us doing the deed on tape, then tap three times on the window when you've got what you need. Do it right and you've earned yourself ten percent of a hundred grand. Are we clear on this?"

"Yes."

"Wait ten minutes, then head for the ugly orange house on the right. No. Wait. Knowing Amsel, better make it just five minutes."

"Got it."

"Okay. See you over there. Remember, if you don't get a picture of us getting laid, you don't get paid."

"Got it."

"Good. Because I honestly don't think I can do this another time. Not for just a hundred grand."

I heard Dimson's heels click across the floor. They stopped. I held my breath. Finally, she said, "Nice shoes."

The door closed behind her.

MARGARET LASHLEY

Great. Now what?

I waited until I figured Dimson had downed her vodka and left the bar, then I slunk out of the restroom.

Tom was busy helping Goober staunch his bloody nose. And, just my luck, Finkerman was over in a corner talking to Nancy.

"Sorry," I said, barging in between them. "I need to borrow him...I mean *her* for a minute."

I snatched Finkerman's arm and tugged him out of earshot of Nancy.

"Listen, you brought your recording equipment like I asked, right?"

"Of course." Finkerman patted his fake boob. "It's in my bra."

Too much information. Again.

"Okay. We're going with the same basic plan...but a new location and new...uh...subject matter. Instead of recording Amsel's confession, I want you to record his...uh...*indiscretion*. Can you handle that?"

Finkerman rolled his eyes at me. "This ain't my first rodeo, Fremden."

"No. But you do look like you've been ridden hard and put away wet."

Finkerman scowled. "You want me to do this or not?"

"Sorry. That was too good to pass up. Okay, so just get over to that house you saw Amsel run into. Dimson will be there, you know, uh, ready and waiting."

"Geez! Amsel and *Dimson* again? I should be getting hazardous duty pay."

"I promise when this is all over, I'll figure out a way to make it worth your while."

"Okay. I'm going."

"Wait. There's one more thing we need to do first."

"What?"

"We're going to have to trade shoes."

"Huh?"

"Don't ask," I said, yanking off my shoes. I handed them to him. "Just put these on and go."

Finkerman crammed his feet into my sandals, winced, and minced his way out the door. As I slid my feet into his floppy pumps, something clicked into place in my brain like a missing jigsaw piece.

Shoes. Trading shoes....

"That's it!" I said aloud.

"What's it?" Tom asked.

"*Shoes*. I think I figured it out, Tom! Norma was always complaining about her feet. She bought those new Birkenstocks on Monday, but when I saw her on Wednesday, those weren't the shoes she was wearing. Maybe she tried to break them in, but they hurt her feet too much."

"So?" Tom asked. "Where are you going with this?"

"Well, let's say Norma took off her *new* shoes, put the *old ones* back on, and stowed the *new* ones somewhere in the back of the restaurant. Then later, someone took her new shoes and wore them to disguise themselves...or so they wouldn't get their *own* shoes dirty. Did you notice Amsel when he came in? He was carrying his expensive loafers."

"You think he was the one who wore the other pair of Birkenstocks...along with Dimson?"

"Exactly. A man wearing Norma's shoes. Like Goober wearing those red pumps. And Finkerman wearing mine."

"What?"

I bit my lip. "Mulligan."

Tom closed his eyes and took a deep breath.

"Okay, Val. So, you're pretty sure Amsel's behind Greg and Norma's disappearance."

"Yes. But I think Amsel's too stupid to pull off anything that elaborate all by himself. Dimson's got to be the brains behind this, Tom. She's setting Amsel up to take the fall for everything. Finkerman's here working with me. He's getting it all on tape as we speak."

"Finkerman? What do you mean? Taping what?"

"Mulligan."

"Val, you can't say mulligan every time you—"

Just then, a gust of wind blew my dress up over my head. As I yanked it down, the scabbed-on roof above my head made a horrible cracking noise. A second later, it blew off and disappeared into the dark, wind-swept night.

Chapter Forty-Two

I felt my feet lifting out of Finkerman's shoes. Suddenly, warm hands gripped my waist and pulled me back down to earth.

"Val!" Tom's voice said. "Are you okay?"

I pulled my dress back down, away from my face, and thanked my Southern upbringing for making sure I'd wore nice panties tonight.

"Yeah, I'm okay."

"Tell me what's going on."

"I don't know. But that was one huge gust of wind!"

"I didn't mean the weather," Tom said. "But you're right. I don't think the plastic window flaps are going to help with this storm."

"Let's go check the TV weather report."

Tom and I went up to the bar, where everyone else was already glued to the screen of the old TV mounted on the wall.

A local Tampa Bay news weatherman was talking. He waved his hands around a swirling backdrop that looked eerily like a rendition of Picasso's starry night.

"...surprise cluster of cyclonic activity reminiscent of the 'No-Name Storm' that blew through in March of 1993," he said.

The screen shifted to two reporters sitting at a news desk. The woman said, "If I recall, it blew ashore in the middle of the night, Chet."

"Yes," said the newsman on her left. "Like this one, the No-Name Storm spawned nearly a dozen tornadoes."

Tornadoes!

"If I remember correctly," the news woman said, "it brought with it a storm surge of over seven feet in some parts of Pinellas County."

"That's right, Mindy," Chet said. "It packed winds of over a hundred miles an hour. The damage was horrendous. Thousands of homes were destroyed, and nearly fifty folks lost their lives in that storm. I believe that was more than Hugo and Andrew combined."

Mindy mugged a concerned look for the camera. "You folks inland, thank your lucky stars. You along the coast, batten down the hatches. This may turn out to be another 'No-Name' Storm!"

"Should we make a run for it?" I asked Tom.

"I think we should all stay here," he said. "It's too dangerous to leave. Tornadoes can pop up anywhere."

"Oh, great," Jake said. "Now no one will help me get that pig out of my van."

"What pig?" Winky asked.

"Rand—," Jake began.

"Dee," I said, cutting him off. "Randy."

Laverne eyed me suspiciously. I knew the jig was up. I pulled the tag out of my purse and handed it to Laverne.

"I was going to save this for later, but...."

Laverne read the tag and smiled brightly. "You found Randolph!" She hugged me, then Jake. "Oh, thank you so much!"

I bit my lip. "Laverne, I've got to tell you something. You see...err. It's not what you—"

Suddenly, the lights went out. We were plunged into pitch-black darkness.

"Are there any candles?" I heard Tom call out.

Somehow, in the dark, the bartender found a flashlight. He switched it on. In the dim halo of light it provided, I saw him and Tom rifling through the bar shelves. Meanwhile, the wind picked up and Caddy's creaked like an old ship caught in a Nor'easter.

"Do you think she'll hold?" I asked Tom as he found me again. I was huddled together with the rest of the gang under a table wedged into a corner.

"This place is tough," Tom said. "It's been here forever. We've got as good a chance here as any."

Just then, the side door blew open. Tom ran over to close it, but I caught a glimpse of something moving in the dark.

"Wait, Tom! Someone's out there!"

"Where?"

I ran over to him and pointed. "Over there! Oh, no! Watch out!"

Tom and I watched in disbelief as the roof came off J.D.'s house.

"Holy smokes!" Tom called out against the gale.

A few seconds later, a scrawny, weather-beaten woman wearing a black dress and my shoes came tumbling halfway through the door.

"You guys, the tide's rising!" Finkerman said as we pulled him inside.

As we pushed against the door trying to shut it, the entire third floor of J.D.'s house went airborne. Suddenly, in the dim starlight, I made out a fat, pig-like figure running toward us.

Amsel!

Debris circled around Tim Amsel like Frosty in a snow-globe. What looked to be a large board beaned him on the head. Amsel tripped, grabbed onto the board, and skidded toward us across the sand. He stopped a few yards from the door.

Winky shone a flashlight on him. It was Amsel, all right. He looked like a wet lab rat in his ragged t-shirt and underpants. Through the howling rain, I saw that the plank he'd ridden over on was actually the surfboard-shaped sign from Winnie & Winky's donut shack.

"Well, that's somethin' you don't see every day," Winky said.

As we watched, Amsel stumbled to his knees, then to his feet. He took a step toward us. Something flew out of the whirlwind hit him square in his fat gut. He collapsed like he'd just caught a football made of lead.

Or, more accurately, of pigskin.

"Randolph!" Laverne cried out.

"Shore is," Winky said. "And looky there. He had the good sense to wear his goggles."

"I think Amsel got the wind knocked out of him," I said. "Looks like he's gasping for breath."

"Somebody should resuscitate him," Tom said. "Besides, Randolph, I mean."

I shook my head in disbelief. "Nothing in the world could possibly top this."

Then, as if on cue, something orange came crashing through what was left of Caddy's porch and proved me wrong, yet again.

Chapter Forty-Three

Pushed up on the rising tide, an orange kayak surfed a huge wave and crash-landed onto what was left of Caddy's porch. Two bedraggled, weather-worn men tumbled out of it.

I noticed one of the men had boobs.

"Norma!" I screeched. "It's Norma and Greg!"

Tom and Goober dropped the jabbering, hysterical Amsel in a corner, leaving him to the tender care of the Knick Knack Nazi. Nancy promptly slapped Amsel on an already red cheek and said, "Snap out of it, pansy boy!"

Laverne and J.D. entertained an enthusiastic Randolph with a plate of meringues, while the rest of us helped the waterlogged pair out of the battered kayak.

"What the heck is going on here?" Tom asked.

"First, I need a beer," Greg said.

"Me, too," Norma said.

"Me, three," Tom said. "Welcome back. We've been looking for you for a week."

"WE WERE CAMPING OUT at Fort DeSoto," Greg explained, after a long slug of beer. He looked over at Norma, who was huddled in a towel. "After all that rain today, we decided to take advantage of the break in the weather and go kayaking this evening. But then this huge storm came up outta nowhere. I've never seen anything like it in all my days here. We couldn't get back to the campsite. It was all we could do to try to stay upright. The winds pushed us all the way here. Right to Caddy's doorstep."

"It's a sign," Norma said, shaking her head. "We shouldn't have sold it."

"You're right," Greg said. "But it's too late, now."

"Why would you just up and disappear?" I asked. "We've all been worried sick about you two."

"I didn't know we *had*," Greg said. "I just wanted to get away. I turned off my phone. I couldn't bear the calls from customers anymore. Or the sight of this place, knowing it was going to be demolished."

"Well, it looks like Mother Nature's doing the job for you," Tom said.

"My punishment for being a traitor," Greg said. "I'm sorry I let you folks down."

"We thought you'd been murdered," I said. "Tom found one of those life-alert bracelets you used to wear."

Greg shook his wrist. The silver bracelet on it jangled. "As you can see, I've still got mine. It's my good luck charm. Besides you, I mean." He looked over at Norma. They shared a sad smile.

"You can still have this bloody dump, too, if you want it," Amsel said, marching up in his underpants, red palm prints covering his face. "I've *had* it with this crazy Florida weather. You're all *nuts* to live here! Where's Dimson?"

"Someone brought dim sum?" Goober asked.

A bedraggled woman stumbled in out of the rain, but it wasn't Dimson.

"Uh...What's going on here?" she asked.

"Are you Karen?" I said.

"Karen?" Tom asked.

I grimaced. "Mulligan."

"Yes. I'm Karen. Where's Dimson?"

"That's what I want to know," Goober said.

"It's *Dimson*, not dim sum," I said to Goober. I grabbed Karen by the arm. "Come with me." I looked over at Tom. "You, too."

I took a step toward the door, then turned back and said, "Oh. And Finkerman, I'm gonna need my shoes back."

WE FOUND DIMSON COWERING in a corner of the soggy living room in what was left of the ugly orange house Amsel had bought from J.D. two days prior.

"There she is," I said to Tom.

Dimson looked Tom, Karen and me up and down. When she got to our feet, she realized it was *me* and not Karen who was wearing the shoes from the ladies' room. Her face went from "smug" to "oh crap" in one-point-five seconds.

"Tom," I said, "Dimson hired Karen here to videotape her having sex with Amsel. She was going to blackmail Amsel for a hundred grand."

"That's preposterous," Dimson said as she crawled to her feet.

"I've got it all on tape." I patted a square recorder on my chest. "Ladies'-room confession."

"Arghh!" Dimson growled. "I can't believe you blew it again, Karen! I had sex with that disgusting pig for nothing. *Again!*"

"Not for nothing," Tom said. "I think you'll get something out of the deal."

Dimson looked at him, a glimmer of hope in her eyes. "What?"

Tom shrugged. "Probably around five years."

He reached behind him and pulled out his cuffs. As he slapped them on Dimson's wrists, Tom said, "You know, Val, I wouldn't mind having you as a partner."

I smirked. "I thought we already were."

Chapter Forty-Four

When the storm cleared that next morning, Caddy's was a bit worse for wear. But, like the rest of us, it was still standing.

As daylight broke, the side door popped open and old lady Langsbury came stumbling in. I'd alerted her to Amsel's presence last night. She must've lit out for the beach at the crack of dawn. She spotted me in the huddled crowd of damp, hungover folks and shot me a quick nod. Then she headed straight for Amsel, who was curled up in a corner in his tidy whities, sucking his thumb.

The storm had delayed the second half of Plan B. But as it turned out, Langsbury's timing couldn't have been better. She gave the folks waking up around me a one-of-a-kind morning show.

"Get up, you lousy ingrate," Langsbury hissed. She reared back and kicked Amsel on his ample butt.

He rolled over. "What do you want, you old hag?"

"I want my property back."

"What are you talking about?"

"The quit-claim deed you forged. I want you to sign a new one, or else."

"Or else what?"

Langsbury reached in her purse and pulled out an industrial-sized can of Aquanet. "Or else I'm gonna make it rain."

"And I'm going to start an investigation," Tom said, rising to his feet.

"Okay, already," Amsel said. "I'll get one to you next week."

I nodded at J.D. He got up and dusted off the knees on his Armani pants. "Why wait?" he asked. "I've got the forms right here. All we need is your signature."

"Fine," Amsel hissed. "I hate Florida."

"Then you wouldn't mind signing another document," J.D. said.

"What for?" Amsel asked, grabbing a pen to sign Langsbury's quit-claim deed.

"For Caddy's. Cancelling the deal." J.D. shot a glance toward Greg. "Does that work for you, Mr. Parsons?"

Greg's groggy face switched to startled surprise. "Sure, if Amsel's game, I am."

"I'm game," Amsel said. "I never want to see another one of you lousy people again for as long as I live."

"Well then," J.D. said, "I think we have come to a meeting of the minds."

TWO WEEKS HAD PASSED since tropical storm Randy had blown through St. Pete Beach and taken out the hideous orange house J.D. had sold to Amsel. The storm was officially named "Randy" because it had put the kibosh on Randy Towers, once and for all.

With a few repairs, Caddy's was back in business with Greg and Norma as co-owners. After re-hanging the sign, Winnie & Winkie's Bait and Donut Shop was none the worse for wear, either. Turns out it's hard to hurt a concrete block box.

That human leg bone in the Gulf turned out to belong to a pig. But, thankfully, it was nobody we knew personally.

Faced with Finkerman's sex tape, the audio recording I got on her in the ladies' room, and the corroborating testimony of her unreliable accomplice, Karen, Darlene Dimson had faked her last legal document and performed her last hanky-panky for profit. She'd done the deed with Amsel twice, hoping for ninety grand. I wouldn't have done it once for ninety million.

Not wanting to ever set foot in Florida again, Timothy Amsel dropped the charges against Dimson and left town, promising never to return. As an act of good faith, and to avoid further criminal investigation, Amsel donated the lot where J.D.'s house stood to the city, to be designated as a park.

Regarding Finkerman, I guess no one is all good or all bad. After all the sand had settled, Winky and Greg offered Finkerman a job cleaning up the grounds around their properties, just like my real dad Tony used to do.

Jorge and Sherryl are expecting twins next March, Winny and Winky a son next April, and Milly and Vance six pups this October. Our little family continues to expand.

With Laverne's blessing, last week Goober took Randolph for a ride in the RV to visit that friend of Jake's who had that petting zoo place near Ocala. We haven't heard from either one of them since.

Meanwhile, J.D. moved into the Ovation downtown. It's still a toss-up which place they're going to live in when Laverne and J.D. get back from their honeymoon...but that's another story altogether.

As far as Tom and I go, well, like he promised, Tom took some time off after the case was closed. We headed down to Sarasota to see Cold Cuts, Bill and Freddie at their Sunset Sail-Away Resort. They were so happy to see us that Bill even let the two of us borrow his boat for an overnight sail.

When we woke up the next morning adrift at sea, Tom and I climbed up on the deck to take in the sunrise.

"Look, Tom. It's as if the whole horizon is on fire."

Tom wrapped his arms around me from behind. The wind whispered along with Tom as he said, "Red sky at dawning, sailor take warning."

"That's rather ominous," I quipped.

"It's just an old fisherman's saying."

"Are you an old fisherman?"

Tom laughed. "I've been known to be nautical."

"Have you *ever!*"

Tom spun me around. "Permission to kiss the captain?"

"Wait. Are you saying *I'm* the captain?"

Tom shot me a boyish grin. "Everyone's the captain of their own ship, Val."

A warm, comforting feeling seeped into my heart, swamping the fear that had reigned there for so long. It felt awkward and strange, but I pushed past it and said, "Well, in that case, permission granted."

As Tom held me in his arms, the sound of his voice and the touch of his hand soothed the niggling restlessness that had plagued me my entire life.

I realized that my lungs took in the salt air a little easier when I was in his embrace. A calmness...a *lightness* lifted me. I felt as if I weighed no more than a feather.

I was still *me* when I was with Tom...but I was also *something more.*

Something intangible.

Something transcendent.

As the sun rose and the breeze tickled my face, I finally realized that there were no mysterious answers to life waiting outside of me, hiding somewhere in the mist waiting for me to discover them. There were no "wrong" or "right" ways to go, either.

There were only experiences waiting to unfold.

And my future was totally up to me.

Looking back on it all now, it had been some kind of miracle that Tom and I had gotten together in the first place.

I turned and looked into Tom's smiling, sea-green eyes.

An iridescent dragonfly with rainbow wings landed on his shoulder.

My heart smiled.

I was home.

DEAR READER,

Thanks so much for reading Cloud Nine, and the entire Val Fremden Mystery Series. I had so much fun writing it, I hate to see it end.

Many of you have asked why I chose the name Val Fremden for my heroine.

Well, for many reasons, actually.

For one, her first name, Val, is short for Valiant. Perseverance and endurance are traits we all need to get through this life. And Fremden? It means "strangers" in German, and was the last name of her German ex-husband. (Fremder, the singular word for stranger, seemed too, pardon the pun, "strange" to pronounce, so I used the plural form.)

I thought Fremden was the perfect name, because, like many of us, Val sought to find herself in relationships. But after three failed marriages, she realized no one else could do the work for her. At age 45, Val found herself in a fierce battle for belonging. But this time she knew she would never feel at home as long as she remained a stranger to herself.

It's a tough journey. One all of us must take—though many of us never finish. Not even in middle age. Not even in old age. Maybe not even in death.

Allowing ourselves the permission to explore our true feelings and desires is rarely given easily. And it's mostly an internal battle. If we're wise, we eventually understand that the people who come into our lives are actually our teachers—if we'll sit up and pay attention to their lessons.

Relationships come in as many forms as there are couples on earth. There is no wrong or right way to love. Our goal is to simply find a way that works.

For us.

And whether we end up with a partner or not, we are never alone if we've taken the time to make a friend of ourselves.

In a way, Val got lucky. She found out she wasn't actually genetically related to her family. *Wink.* But then again, Val and her adoptive mom were just as connected as any flesh and blood could have ever bound them.

So family is something we can't escape. But it's also something we can add to, and improve upon. Throughout Val's journey, she was the glue that held a group of strangers together. They formed their own makeshift, oddball family. Granted, some were odder than others. But they were all accepted, just the same.

So I invite you to accept yourself now, just as you are. Make a friend of yourself. A lifelong friend.

Because deep inside you lives your own Valiant Stranger.

And she is spectacular.

Until next time, all my best.

Sincerely,

Margaret Lashley

What's Next for Us?

As Winky would say, "It ain't over till it's over!"

As a special thanks for reading and loving the entire series, I'm offering you one final chance to hang with the gang.

Get set for *Two Weddings and a Free-For-All*. It's my exclusive gift for die-hard fans like you!

While you're there, if you care to, you can also sign up to my newsletter. It's totally optional! If you do, every month you'll get insider info on what I'm working on next. And what's up in St. Petersburg! So join me on Sunset Beach one final time and read about the day Winnie and Winky got hitched. Just click the link and I'll see you there!

https://dl.bookfunnel.com/6qq2y6z108

WANT TO KEEP THE LAUGHS coming?

Your wish is my command! In fact, I've got two options for you!

First, get set for a brand new adventure starring loveable, laughable Doreen Diller. They say life begins at 40. Well, when Doreen takes an acting gig in St. Pete, Florida, she inherits a role she didn't see coming, and a family she didn't bargain for.

The Golden Girls meets *Married to the Mob* in this hilarious new series featuring an actress who just can't catch a break.

Check out Doreen Diller, ***Almost a Serial Killer*** here:

https://www.amazon.com/dp/B09XFDFV98

Second, if you want to follow the hilarious exploits of Goober, and meet a few new friends along the way, check out Moth Busters, the first book in my Freaky Florida Mystery Adventures Series. It's a fun-filled, raucous spoof of The X-Files, with Goober at the helm! Enter a whole new world of fun that could only happen in Florida. What could possibly go wrong?

Check out Moth Busters and Freaky Florida Mystery Adventures here:

https://www.amazon.com/dp/B07RC7HVD2

ONCE AGAIN, THANK YOU so much for reading my Val Fremden Midlife Mystery books. If you'd like to leave a review for Cloud Nine, here's a convenient link to the Amazon page:

https://www.amazon.com/dp/B07HDTXZZ2

If you'd like to stay in touch, you can reach me here:

Website: https://www.margaretlashley.com

Email: contact@margaretlashley.com

Facebook: https://www.facebook.com/valandpalspage/

If you want to be the first to find out whenever I add a new book to a series, follow me on Amazon and/or BookBub and you'll be notified of every new release. Again, thanks so much for being a fan!

Follow me on Amazon:

https://www.amazon.com/-/e/B06XKJ3YD8

Follow me on BookBub:

https://www.bookbub.com/search/authors?search=Margaret%20Lashley

Bye for now!

About the Author

Like the characters in my novels, I haven't led a life of wealth or luxury. In fact, as it stands now, I'm set to inherit a half-eaten jar of Cheez Whiz...if my siblings don't beat me to it.

During my illustrious career, I've been a roller-skating waitress, an actuarial assistant, an advertising copywriter, a real estate agent, a house flipper, an organic farmer, and a traveling vagabond/truth seeker. But no matter where I've gone or what I've done, I've always felt like a weirdo.

I've learned a heck of a lot in my life. But getting to know myself has been my greatest journey. Today, I know I'm smart. I'm direct. I'm jaded. I'm hopeful. I'm funny. I'm fierce. I'm a pushover. And I have a laugh that makes strangers come up and want to join in the fun. In other words, I'm a jumble of opposing talents and flaws and emotions. And it's all good.

In some ways, I'm a lot like Val Fremden. My books featuring Val are not autobiographical, but what comes out of her mouth was first formed in my mind, and sometimes the parallels are undeniable. I drink TNTs. I had a car like Shabby Maggie. And I've started my life over four times, driving away with whatever earthly possessions fit in my car. And, perhaps most importantly, I've learned that friends come from unexpected places.